CAST THE FIRST STONE

Cast the First Stone

Rebbie MacIntyre

FIVE STAR

A part of Gale, Cengage Learning

GALE
CENGAGE Learning™

Detroit • New York • San Francisco • New Haven, Conn • Waterville, Maine • London

GALE
CENGAGE Learning

Set in 11 pt. Plantin.
Printed on permanent paper.

LIBRARY OF CONGRESS CATALOGING-IN-PUBLICATION DATA

Macintyre, Rebbie.
   Cast the first stone / Rebbie Macintyre. — 1st ed.
     p. cm.
   ISBN-13: 978-1-59414-746-3 (hardcover : alk. paper)
   ISBN-10: 1-59414-746-9 (hardcover : alk. paper)
     1. Mexican American women—Fiction. 2. Dowsing—Fiction.
3. Brothers and sisters—Fiction. 4. Missing persons—Fiction. 5.
Colorado—Fiction. I. Title.
PS3613.A272543C37 2009
813'.6—dc22
                                                  2008049394

First Edition. First Printing: March 2009.
Published in 2009 in conjunction with Tekno Books and Ed Gorman.

For Dan, who never doubted.

CHAPTER ONE

A knock rattled her screen door, demanding and impatient, and she gritted her teeth in irritation. She wanted to be left alone, to bake her bread in peace. She could ignore the summons, tiptoe back to her bedroom and wait for the intruder to leave, but again the fist on the door frame; a fist, she was certain, that would keep pounding.

Trini Bates wiped her floured hands on a tea towel, crossed the kitchen and pulled open the heavy oak door. Through the black mesh of the screen, she surveyed the trio on her porch: the sheriff, his deputy and her brother Parnell, his mouth rabbit-twitching like it always did when he'd been caught.

This was trouble.

"Morning, Mrs. Bates," Sheriff George Mallis said. He touched the brim of his hat with a finger. "I'm sure you've heard about Merle Woodson's disappearance."

She nodded.

"I'm taking your brother into the office for questioning. He wanted to talk to you first, and just to show that I'm being fair, I agreed."

She slumped against the doorjamb, crossed her arms and studied her raggedy brother. "What now?" she asked.

"I ain't seen him, Trini. Not since before he left." Parn Shannon bounced as he spoke, and shifted his gaze to the sheriff. "I told you that last week."

"Well, you can tell me again, only this time at the office,"

Mallis said. "I've got my own theory about Woodson's disappearance."

"Trini," the deputy said, "we're following every lead we can think of. And I've been thinking." He flicked his eyes to the sheriff. "You could dowse for us. Dowse to find Woodson."

Aiming into the flowerbed tangled with the shriveled leaves of bachelor buttons left after the first frost, Mallis leaned over the porch railing, snorted and spat.

Hinges squealed when she pushed open the screen door, and Trini stepped into the cold morning air. Her brother stood before her, twitching with nervous energy. She resisted the urge to soothe the new scrape on his forehead; he was no longer her motherless little brother but a twenty-five-year-old man who'd immersed himself into man-sized trouble.

"When was the last time you saw Woodson?" she asked.

"I swear, Trini," Parn said. "I haven't seen him for three weeks. Maybe more."

A laugh shot from Mallis. "I don't believe that. They're bootlegging partners. And according to Woodson's daughter, your brother was the last person to see him before he left for Denver."

He pushed his hat back on his head, and Trini suppressed a shudder: Even though the sheriff had the posture and bearing of a man who'd barely crossed into his forties, deep creases smothered every inch of his face, as if his skin had once been tightly wadded like a piece of parchment then applied over his bones.

"Parn," Trini said, "you're bootlegging again? You promised me you wouldn't. Months ago."

"We didn't mean for it to get that big," Parn said. His jiggling stilled, and he scuffed a toe of his boot on the floorboards. "I was just going to make enough money to get out to Oregon. And I would have, too, if Woodson hadn't gone away."

Mallis jabbed Parn's arm. "Well, too bad for you that he did 'go away,' as you put it." He turned to Trini. "Fact is, ten days ago Merle Woodson disappeared. He told his daughter he was heading to Denver with your brother and he'd be back that night. He never showed up, never called. I've had bulletins out all over the state, to the police up in Denver and even Montana. He's gone."

"I told him, Trini." Parn gnawed on a ragged cuticle. "Merle never told me he was going to Denver."

Mallis continued, "And another thing: Everyone in town saw him and your brother fighting at the Plainsman Café several weeks ago. As far as I'm concerned, that makes Parn Shannon a suspicious person."

"A suspicious person for what?" she asked.

"A suspicious person I want to question." Black eyes stayed flat under the folds of eyelids.

Trini took a moment to catch her breath and let her gaze drift across the prairie and to the distant Rocky Mountains jutting into a crystalline sky. The November wind bit her face and tugged a dark curl from its place. She tucked it behind her ear then turned her face to keep it there. "Sheriff, doesn't it seem likely that Merle Woodson doesn't want to be found?"

"Not according to the daughter. She says he'd never done anything like this before. And he left things undone, things he promised his daughter he'd do the next day when he came home. She thinks he's dead." Mallis crossed his arms. "And if Woodson's dead, and Parn here was the last one to see him alive, well then, that makes him a suspect, doesn't it?"

Suspect. Her stomach knotted. She didn't trust George Mallis. He was an interim sheriff who had the reputation of being corrupt. His arrogant stance, plus the brittle face, gave him the appearance of nonchalant cruelty; someone who'd kick a dog aside to make room on the sidewalk. "Sheriff, I don't think you should jump to any conclusions. Woodson's car could have gone over a cliff. Or he could have decided to drive up to Canada or down to Mexico or anywhere in between. I'm sure with a little thought and thorough investigation—"

"Don't tell me how to do my job, missy. I reckon I know more about investigation than you ever would."

Trini examined his expression, trying to read him, but failed. Impossible to make sense of the rocklike visage. And the black eyes buried deep in the sockets; she'd have to quarry to read those eyes. She glanced at his deputy. She wondered what Roy Eastman thought of his boss, but his Stetson sat low on his brow, shading the nuances of his expression. He stood with arms crossed over his chest, studying Mallis. How could he tolerate the sheriff? She answered her own question in an instant: It was 1932. The country was in the middle of a Depression. Most people did whatever was necessary to hold a job. But surely Roy didn't think Parn could be connected to Woodson's disappearance; Roy and her late husband had been friends. Although . . . come to think of it, she hadn't seen Roy since the funeral eight months ago. She briefly wondered why. In these last dark months, it would have been nice to have a friend of Jim's to talk to.

Roy tipped his hat up with a finger and looked at her with frank gray eyes. "As I said, I've been thinking." He glanced at Mallis then back to her. "I've seen you dowse for water, and Jim told me you could find about anything you put your mind to. Do you think you could dowse for Woodson? Give us an idea of where to look?"

Parn sputtered and lurched forward. "You could do it, Trin. I've seen you dowse for lost stuff all the time. That lost kitten when we were little, and Mom's necklace, right after she died. I seen you do it on the map when—"

"I don't believe that," Mallis said. He darted his eyes to his deputy, and the chaw of tobacco shifted from one cheek to the other. "I know folks claim you can find water, but finding bodies is different." He turned and spat again.

She looked at the brown glob, then back to the eyes. Mallis's attitude didn't surprise her. Many people refused to acknowledge her dowser's talent, even when they saw water drawn from the exact place she'd indicated—and at the depth she'd said it would be. And she'd found people before, as well as lost valuables, but only for her immediate family. She had no use for skeptics, and right now she'd like to turn around, go back into her kitchen and plunge her hands into the bread dough. She'd like to brew herself a cup of tea. She'd like to be left alone.

"Trini," Roy said, "if you could find Woodson or his body, pinpoint a location, we could contact the authorities and go from there. If he's alive, then we can all go home. If he's dead, well, we'd start an investigation."

He was right. And if Woodson was dead, he more than likely was lying in a remote mountain pass in his wrecked car. Or at the bottom of the Denver sewer, a gangster's bullet in his head. Wherever he was, after she dowsed, the entire ugly event would be over for Parn.

She examined her brother who wiggled in front of her, his eyes darting like a trapped hare, his cuticle torn and bleeding, and made her decision. "I'll come to your office. I assume you have local maps?"

Roy nodded.

"I'll drive myself and meet you there."

Mallis stared at his deputy a moment, but kept silent. They turned and clattered down the wooden stoop, Parn stumbling across the grass as the sheriff led him by his elbow. She closed her eyes for a moment and shook her head. A small headache pressed into her temples.

Untying her apron strings at the small of her back, she

entered the kitchen, pulled the apron over her head and hung it on the hook by the stove. The bread would be cool by the time she got home, ready to take to the Plainsman Café for sale. After that, maybe she could still salvage some of the day. She walked through the parlor to her bedroom, the same bedroom she'd shared with her husband for twelve years.

She opened the drawer to her bureau and reached inside, feeling under socks and chemises, then removed a length of cotton twine wound around a quartz rock about two inches long and as thick as her little finger. Her mother's dowsing crystal. The piece rested in her palm for a moment, and she savored its comfort, its history. She walked back to the kitchen, grabbed her coat from the rack and pushed her arms through the sleeves. The crystal she placed in her pocket. Closing the door behind her, she headed to her truck. She hoped she'd be back in a few hours, her wayward brother in tow.

CHAPTER TWO

Her house stood at the edge of town on a three-acre lot surrounded by open plains and a big sky on the north and west. Trini pulled from the gravel drive, and the 1929 Model A truck bounced over the dusty road leading from her house to the highway. Surveying the vast desolation of the prairie around her, she found, as usual, her jumbled thoughts ordered themselves. Perspective.

Of course she loved her brother. He was all she had left of her family. But he needed to take responsibility for himself. It would serve him right to have to wiggle his way out of this noose without her help, and if the situation wasn't so serious, she'd let him suffer the consequences. But the thought of leaving him to learn a lesson at the end of Mallis's tether sent a squiggle of fear up her spine. No, she had to help him, at least this time.

She turned onto the blacktop where the Baptist, Methodist, and Lutheran churches shared the crossroads. Attached stores and businesses lined the highway. Most were two stories, shops with living quarters above and with flat, square fronts left over from the town's founding in 1876. Dust coated the whitewash of the wooden structures, and black shutters punctuated the brick buildings. Trini drove past the Plainsmen Café, where she sold most of her baked goods, and the mercantile, owned by her friend, Jefferson LeClair. She stopped at one of the two traffic lights in town and scanned the sidewalks for familiar faces.

None today, which was unusual. She'd been born, married and widowed in Ludlin, lived here all the thirty years of her life, except for ten months in Kansas City. Ten months fourteen years ago, but she wouldn't think about that now.

The sheriff's office sat in the middle of the row of shops on the south side of the highway, and Trini pulled into an empty parking spot in front. The door with an inset of plate glass bore the sign, "Sheriff's Office, Coyote County, Colorado," printed in shiny black ink. It rattled when she pushed it open.

A waist-high wooden railing with a swing gate in the center divided the entryway from the main room. She waited there and took a moment to survey the office. Two desks stood to her right. Les Taggert, Mallis's other deputy, sat at the one farthest away, his buck-toothed mouth gaping. Roy must use the other one because to her left, a lone desk bore a wooden name plate: "George Mallis, Sheriff" stamped in black. A row of oak file cabinets lined the back wall. Beside the cabinets, a narrow hallway led to the rear of the building and ended at the back door. She shifted to get a better view of the hall. The closed door must lead to the jail cells.

The back door opened and Mallis, Parn and Deputy Roy Eastman walked in. The clatter of men's boots moving across plank floors filled the room.

Taggert scraped back his chair and stood. "So she really gonna do it?" he asked. His eyes bulged with stupid wonder.

"Les, get all the maps out of the file cabinet." Mallis stayed on the other side of the wooden railing but turned to Trini and growled, "What maps do you need?"

"I'll start close to home, with Coyote County. If I don't find him, I'll go to the state map. And I'll need something of Merle Woodson's. A shirt or something."

Mallis shook his head and laughed, a yelp that said idiots surrounded him. "Damn it to hell." He looked at Taggert. "Hold off on the maps. Drive out to Woodson's house and pick up one of Merle's old shirts."

The deputy's eyes widened in indignation. "Send Eastman over," he said.

Mallis thundered, "Goddamn it. Just do it."

Taggert muttered under his breath as he jammed his hat on his head and strode down the back hall. He slammed the door as he left.

Mallis glanced at Roy. "Eastman, get those maps she needs." He grasped Parn by the arm. "I was going to keep you out here, but I changed my mind. I think I'll put you in the cage until we're ready."

The sheriff darted a look to Trini, and she wondered if he had the right to keep her brother behind bars. Just as she was about ready to protest, he spoke, "I can keep him in the pen without charging him with a crime. So long as it's only for a few hours." A man who shored up his defenses before attack.

Parn pulled away, but stopped short of jerking his arm out of Mallis's grip. He pleaded in desperation, "Sheriff, let me stay here. Please."

"I'll come get you when she starts her mumbo jumbo, but it'll be a while before Taggert's back. Meanwhile, you can get out of my hair. Come on."

A pleading look and a stumble were her good-bye as Mallis led Parn down the hall. Using a key on a large circle key ring, the sheriff unlocked the door, pushed Parn through the threshold and followed him inside. The door slammed closed.

She wondered about her brother's relationship with Mallis; the sheriff's harsh treatment indicated a rocky history between them. It was rumored that Mallis took a cut of all the bootlegged liquor that passed through the county, as well as a piece of the profits from regular poker games and the house of "gentlemen's recreation" in Digstown. Had Parn and Woodson withheld the

15

sheriff's cut of the bootlegging profits? Was that why he so obviously disliked Parn?

Anger rumbled inside her. She hated this whole business, hated the way Parn lived his life. Hated this horrible bootlegging. Roosevelt's election two weeks ago and his promise of ending Prohibition couldn't come soon enough for her. But the change in the law wouldn't be for several more months, maybe even a year, until all the states had ratified the repeal amendment. Meanwhile, Parn had dipped once again into bootlegging, apparently over his head. After today, as soon as they'd settled this situation with the missing Woodson, she was going to take a strong hand with him, make sure he started in a new direction. No more of her brother living on his own, aimless or chasing foolish dreams.

Trini became aware of her clenched fists and drew a deep breath to calm herself. She turned to see Deputy Eastman shift his eyes away from her. He'd come into the entry area and was hanging his tan Stetson on the hat tree beside the door. Her face usually mirrored her emotions, and she was certain that this moment was no exception. A flush crept up her neck and settled into her cheeks; he'd witnessed her silent turmoil.

"You know . . ." she said.

He smiled a little and ran his hand through silver hair. It ruffled then dropped back into place like thick fur. She briefly wondered if premature gray ran in his family. If she remembered correctly, he was Jim's age, forty-two.

". . . I haven't seen you since Jim's funeral."

"Yeah, I know." He ambled toward her, not exactly a swagger, Trini thought, but more like a limber comfort in his masculine skin. "I wanted to let a little time go past before I came by."

His smile showed even, white teeth and a dimple in his left cheek. She examined the gray eyes and found warmth and something else. Tentative feelers? Her stomach did a flip and surprise and flattery flushed through her, then confusion. She didn't know what to say. Roy Eastman was too . . . she couldn't name it. He was lean and broad shouldered, only an inch or two taller than Trini, but his presence filled the room. Something stirred inside of her, something she hadn't experienced in a long time. Flustered, she stepped back and tried to sound casual.

"Do you think Merle is dead?" Her voice shook. She didn't mean that to happen, and she cleared her throat a little.

"I assume so," he said. "From what Katherine Woodson said, he wouldn't just abandon her and her brother. If he was alive, she would know where he was."

"Well, I hope I can help." She smiled. "Thanks for suggesting that I dowse. For Parn's sake, I appreciate it."

He shrugged. "We're up against a brick wall. Mallis is grabbing at anything right now, trying to figure out something to do to make it look like we've got some leads."

"He sounded like he believes Parn had something to do with Woodson's disappearance."

"I think he's just pawing the ground, mad and frustrated. Try not to let him buffalo you. Mallis makes a lot of noise, especially when he doesn't have anything to go on. He's just hoping something will come his way."

"Hmm. Well, he sure doesn't like Parn."

" 'Fraid you're right about that." Roy looked around the room and fingered his silver-filigreed belt buckle. A nervous gesture, Trini thought.

"I wondered if it had something to do with the bootlegging. I was just thinking that. About Mallis's interest in the bootlegging."

His mouth pressed into silence, and he turned away from her to adjust his hat on the hat rack. Roy had to know about Mallis's greedy fingers, but she didn't think he was a part of it. Jim

17

had thought the world of Roy, said he was one of the most honest men he'd ever known, and Trini had trusted Jim's judgment of people. Roy probably kept silent in order to keep his job. She wanted to tell him she didn't blame him, that everyone accepted things now that they wouldn't have before the Depression. She reached out to touch his arm, then drew back. She didn't know him that well. And she didn't want to encourage any complications in her life.

Mallis sauntered into the room and fell into his chair, the springs creaking as he leaned back and propped his boots on the desk. "Eastman," he said, "you found them maps she needs?" He shook his head and his mouth split in what Trini supposed passed for a smile. "This is just the goddamnest thing I ever seen. Bunch of . . ." His words trailed off as he lifted a folder from the desk, opened it across his legs and began reading.

Roy stared at Mallis a moment, his hands jammed into his pants pocket. Trini watched the edge of his jaw quiver, but he opened the small gate, entered the desk area and walked to the file cabinets. Trini sat in one of the chairs in the entry. The only sounds in the room were Roy's paper shuffling and the tick of a round wall clock behind Mallis's chair.

When the front door rattled open, Taggert entered accompanied by a sunken-faced girl with darting eyes, hugging a faded blue work shirt to her chest. Bright red spots capped her pale cheeks, and blond tufts protruded from her scalp. When she looked at Trini, she smiled slightly, but the eyes remained skittish below the mound of flesh where eyebrows should have grown. Trini tried to keep her face composed to hide her shock, although she doubted her success. She hadn't seen Merle Woodson's daughter in the eight months since Jim's funeral, either, which was odd, now that she thought of it, not to have seen the girl occasionally in the mercantile or post office. The reason for her isolation was apparent; Katherine Woodson was losing every hair on her head.

God help her, the child must be deathly ill. But Trini hadn't heard about it, and that seemed odd. In Ludlin, most people knew what their neighbors carried in their back pockets. And with such a drastic condition as baldness, surely Merle had consulted Doc Cockrell, who would have characteristically informed the townspeople of Katherine's illness.

Trini stood from her seat and held out her hand. "Katherine."

The girl looked at Trini briefly, then lowered her doe-like eyes as they turned liquid. "Trini," she whispered. "Deputy Taggert says you maybe can find Pa. I . . . I just don't know about anything anymore."

Katherine bent her head into her hands and cried, her body shuddering. Maybe she wasn't sick. Maybe worry and misery had caused her to lose her hair. Without a mother, fifteen-year-old Katherine undoubtedly bore most of the responsibility for the home and her brother, a boy of twelve who had the mental age of five. Merle was known to disappear from time to time, although he was reliable enough to hold a job in the Coyote county land claims office. Katherine must have a difficult life.

Trini put an arm around her shoulders. "Katherine. Come on now. Let's see what we can do."

"Let's see what we can do?" said Mallis. He came out from behind his desk, walked to the wooden railing and leaned on the top with both hands. He crossed one ankle over the other and his weight shifted to one leg, casual and dismissive. "Can you find him or not? I don't know why we're wasting our time if you can't do this."

A smirk lifted the chalk-line lips to one side, and while the black eyes looked at her, he stood to his full height. He dug into his shirt pocket, retrieved his tobacco pouch and opened it.

After withdrawing a clump of stingy leaves, he used his stained fingers to stuff it into the back of his cheek. He refolded the bag and shoved it into his pocket.

Trini forced herself to examine his wizened face. She allowed the ever-growing contempt for George Mallis to shade her voice. "It would seem to me, Sheriff, you'd want to do just about anything to find some answers."

He flicked his eyes to Roy who was standing beside his desk, spreading a map over its surface. "I can't hardly put any credence into some wetback finding a missing person using a map. Seems like a waste of time to me."

The casual slur insulted her, but she didn't stoop to address it. "But time is all you have right now, isn't it?" Trini asked. "Unless you have other leads that you need to attend to?"

Coal eyes bored in on her. "No leads, missy. Just a missing low-life conniver and a kid who I'd like to—" He clamped his mouth closed, swaggered down the hall and with an aggressive shove against the door, disappeared through the threshold that led to the jail cells.

What did Mallis stop himself from saying? He'd like to do what? She tried to swallow, but her throat had turned solid. A cold knot began to form in Trini's stomach. Why did the sheriff hate her brother? Was it the bootlegging? Had Parn and Woodson stolen the illegal profits from Mallis? Her anger flared against Parn. Prohibition had done nothing but enrich the outlaws, and her own brother was one of them. Maybe he deserved the wrath of the law. Maybe she should leave him to lie in his bed. Their parents would have been appalled at their son's behavior. She was half tempted to walk out this minute, just get in her truck and leave, drive into the prairie—

Katherine placed a translucent hand on Trini's arm. "I hope you can help us," she said.

Trini patted Katherine's hand. "I do, too," she said. "I do, too."

Yes, maybe she could at least help, if she could concentrate enough to dowse. Mallis's obvious spite toward her brother had left her shaken.

The cell door slammed, and Parn stumbled as Mallis pushed him into the room. When he saw Katherine, he ran to the railing. He leaned over it, desperate for her to listen to him. "Katherine, I ain't seen Merle since before he left. I never even knew he went to Denver. I swear it."

"Keep your mouth shut, Parn Shannon," Mallis said. He yanked Parn's arm. "I don't want you talking to her."

"Here, Trini," Katherine held out Merle's blue work shirt, crumpled and sweat-stained around the collar, and Trini took it. They opened the small gate and walked to Roy's desk.

Trini faced the map, and the others surrounded the desk in front of her. She reached in her coat pocket and took out the dowsing instrument, then shrugged off her coat and laid it across the back of Roy's chair. He adjusted it to stop its slip to the floor, but avoided her eyes.

Trini folded Merle Woodson's shirt once over, then gathered it together and clutched it in her left hand. Between her thumb and index finger of her right hand, she pinched the end of the twine and dangled the crystal a fraction of an inch above the map over the town of Ludlin. "I'm ready," she said.

The afternoon sun slanted through the window beside them, casting a ray of light across the map and bouncing off the crystal. Its reflection flickered on the far wall above the file cabinet. Roy stood closest to her, on her left, and she caught a whiff of him, a tinge of the piney outdoors.

"Where is the man?" she whispered. She glanced up to catch Roy's intent stare. "Show me the man. Where is he?" she said.

"Is it supposed to move or something?" asked Taggert.

"Shh," from Katherine.

"Show me the man," murmured Trini. "Where is he?"

The crystal remained motionless. Parn cursed under his breath.

"This ain't going to work," said Mallis.

"Wait, Sheriff, please," said Parn. "Just wait a minute."

Setting her shoulders square, Trini took a deep breath. She didn't like Mallis's skeptical stare. Just ignore him, she told herself. This is for Parn. She refocused her attention on her fingertips, relaxed the muscles around her eyes and slackened her jaw. She hadn't realized she'd been clenching her teeth.

The crystal swiveled at the end of the twine like a child's toy spin-top in motion. "Where is the man?" Trini said.

"She's just making that rock turn like that," Mallis said.

A tickle on the ends of her fingers signaled the talent was awakening. She moved the crystal an inch west so that it hovered above the town of Jackson. The instrument became a tiny pendulum swaying above the map, an infinitesimal movement that she wondered if she felt more than saw. Not yet. Not yet.

"Come on," Mallis said. "I'm not wasting any more time doing this. Eastman, this was one hare-brained idea." He grasped Parn's arm and took a step toward the jail cell.

"We'll wait it out." Roy stated an evident fact, as if remarking on the pleasant weather as he walked outside into a sunny day.

Whatever Roy did or said to impact Mallis worked, because Mallis held his gaze, and after giving a snort of derision, dropped Parn's arm from his grip.

Roy looked at Trini and nodded, his expression neutral except for a slight tic at the edge of his jaw. "Go on," he said.

She moved the crystal again, an inch to the north, over the hamlet of Walsh's Hole. Just keep open. Keep loose. It's coming now. It's coming. "Show me the man," she repeated.

The energy surged into her hands, and the crystal increased

its sway. The whorls on Trini's fingertips swelled and throbbed, her hands flamed crimson and the skin appeared to stretch near bursting. At the end of her motionless fingers, the string and the crystal turned in a perfect circle the size of a silver dollar. Her veins jutted like mountain ranges winding their way up her forearms into her biceps, and she felt pinpricks along the tops of her arms.

Katherine Woodson gasped, "Trini! Your hands."

As the crystal turned, the sensation deepened; the pinpricks became deep talons that dug into her flesh. Heat, then burning ice, seared her arms, her shoulders and chest, and the muscles in her neck. She didn't know how much more she could take. In the back of her mind, she registered surprise; the dowsing had never hurt like this. She must be more nervous than she thought.

One final surge of energy to her reddened fingertips and she knew she'd found her target. She withdrew the crystal, set it on the desk and massaged her bloated hands.

"Holy God," whispered Taggert.

Trini glanced at Mallis who regarded her through squinting eyes. His granite face remained solid and inscrutable.

"Trini, are you all right?" asked Roy.

His voice soothed her, and she felt her shoulders drop and the tendons at the back of her neck relax. She was glad he was here. "Yes, I'm all right. And I think you'll find Merle Woodson right here."

She rested her swollen finger on Dawson's Gully, a large stretch of land owned by Lodge Dawson, land that ran through a section east of Walsh's Hole.

"There ain't nothin' out there," Taggert said.

Mallis craned his head to look at the map.

"I think we should take a look, Sheriff." Roy spoke with calm logic. "We searched there a few days ago, but that area is pretty thick brush. We don't have anything to lose by looking again."

Mallis shrugged. "I guess."

Why was he so reluctant to search? Even if he didn't believe the accuracy of her dowsing, what did he have to lose by trying? Was this entire ordeal simply too much trouble for him?

"You know, Sheriff," Trini said, "I'm seriously beginning to wonder . . ." She was about to say that she wondered if he really wanted to solve the mystery of Woodson's whereabouts, but an instinct of caution stopped her. She needed to be careful with him, and he'd surely take her statement as an insult.

"What are you wondering, missy?" he asked. "About how your brother could have gotten up to his neck in a mess like this? I think there's a lot you don't know about him, even if he is your own brother."

A cold trill wiggled up her spine. That wasn't what she was thinking, but God help her, he was right.

Mallis studied her a moment, then glanced at Roy. "All right," he said. "Let's go take a look."

Trini slumped back into Roy's chair as the group scrambled around her: Mallis to retrieve his keys, Roy to gather his hat and holster from the coatrack, Taggert to return Parn to the cell. Katherine, pale and shaking, leaned over Roy's desk and watched her.

Trini rolled her head to stretch her tired neck. It had worked, thank God. It usually did, but there'd been a time, years ago, when it hadn't. A lost child had suffered in a snowstorm, his feet damaged forever, because even though she could bring the crystal to life, it was inaccurate in its direction. A few weeks after the incident, she had learned she was pregnant. She figured when the chemistry of her body altered, it had affected her ability to dowse.

She squeezed her eyes closed to shut out the memory. No. She didn't want to think about being pregnant, about the decisions she'd had to make, the irrevocable decisions that she questioned to this day. She wanted to think about her mother, and her dowsing legacy from her mother, and her mother before her and as far back as she knew, clear through Mexico to the island of Trinidad, her namesake. And today the gift had worked for her. Worked for Parn.

They'd find Merle Woodson, she was sure, his car wrecked off one of the dangerous highway curves near Dawson's Gully. And Parn would go home with her tonight. She'd talk with him, reason with him. Maybe this close call would finally impress him with how irresponsibility had almost cost him dearly. She'd help him get a job . . . somewhere. Maybe in one of the new work programs Roosevelt promised. Then she could go back to her life, be by herself to think and be quiet. They'd figure it out. Just a few more hours to wait.

CHAPTER THREE

Trini rose from Roy's chair and once again rolled her head and stretched her arms. Should she go with the men to Dawson's Gully? She didn't want to. She didn't want to see Merle Woodson's limp and bloody body. And she didn't want to be around Mallis anymore. She wanted to go home.

But when Parn turned away from her as Taggert led him to jail, Trini saw the back of his matted and tangled hair where he'd rested his head on the cot in the cell, and a memory flashed through her mind. After their mother had died, every morning for several weeks, Trini's little brother would dash out the front door on his way to school with uncombed hair and dirty teeth. She'd chase him down, and when he finally allowed her to catch him, he'd squeal with giggles as she wrestled him back into the house and helped him with the scrubbing and brushing. The game was their way of forging a new bond, one that would not include their mother. Now, as he walked away from her and she saw his mussed hair, Trini felt as if the little schoolboy still needed her, and the desire to protect and care for him surged through her again.

No, she didn't want to go to Dawson's Gully, but she would for Parn. She'd take her own truck, though. The last thing she wanted was to ride in the same car with George Mallis. Trini pushed her arms through the sleeves of her coat and grabbed her purse that she'd left on a chair. She placed her hand on the latch, ready to open the door. Katherine Woodson's voice stopped her.

"Could I ride with you, Trini?"

She smiled at her. "Sure," she said, "let's go." She caught Roy's eye. "We'll meet you out there."

He nodded.

The office door rattled closed behind them. Trini squinted in the brilliant sunlight, and a sudden raw wind whipped her coat and housedress around her calves. They hurried to the truck and, after pulling out of the parking place, headed toward the clear peaks poised on the horizon, north toward Dawson's Gully. As Trini drove, the truck's seat jostled and bounced causing the little crests of hair that dotted Katherine's head to dance with the truck's movement.

"Thank you for letting me ride with you," Katherine said. "I was afraid Sheriff Mallis would make me go with him, and I just don't like him very much."

You're not the only one, Trini wanted to say, but she didn't. Better to keep her negative thoughts to herself. Merle Woodson was most likely dead, and Katherine would be left with the responsibility for her childlike brother, a responsibility far weightier than most fifteen-year-old girls had to bear. The girl already had enough on her mind without Trini's pointed remarks.

The brisk air swirled into the truck cab when she cracked her window, the plain gave way to the gentle rolls of the land and the fall sky provided a brilliant blue canopy. She sighed with regret and thought of working in her garden, baking bread with the door open, letting the cool air spread through her yeasty kitchen.

Katherine gazed out the passenger window, and when Trini glanced at her, she startled again at the sight of the girl's tender white scalp. She'd almost forgotten about Katherine's appearance. Trini felt her face heat with an embarrassed flush and mentally hunched with shame. Here she was longing for time alone when sitting next to her was a newly orphaned girl whose life would never be the same. And this in addition to whatever had caused her hair loss. She didn't want to make Katherine withdraw from her, but maybe she could gently probe her about her condition. If she was ill, Trini could offer help until relatives arrived.

"I haven't seen you for a while. Did you go back to school in September?"

The sprouts of hair jiggled as Katherine shook her head. "No. I have to take care of Jake."

"That's too bad. I mean that you can't go back to school."

Silence.

"Didn't you have someone to help you, last year? Didn't Mrs. Darby take care of Jake during school hours?"

"She can't do it anymore."

Most teenagers were reticent. She decided to keep trying.

"Maybe you could study from home. I know little Debbie King did that last year when she had whooping cough. She was very sick with it for months, remember? You know her, don't you?"

Katherine stared at Trini with defiance in the set of her jaw and the narrowing of her eyes. "I guess if I was sick they might do that, but I doubt they would go to all that trouble just because I have to take care of my little brother."

"Oh." Trini couldn't think of what else to say. Katherine's spit of anger had caught her off guard. The balding head turned away from her.

At least she discovered two things: Katherine wasn't ill, or at least she wasn't going to confess it to Trini, and she was angry. Trini wondered, had Katherine been traumatized? Had Merle addressed the issue? Trini decided enough for now. This was not the time to ask painful questions.

She turned off the blacktop onto a dirt and gravel road, and the truck rocked and rumbled over the ruts. Trini slowed to a crawl, then stopped. A moment later, the sheriff's car pulled in behind them. Car doors slammed, and Trini and Katherine followed Roy and Mallis. They walked to the edge of the dusty roadway and overlooked a broad gully stretching below them.

Tangled brush, as dense as a rock wall, lined the bottom of the ravine. Boulders punctuated the area like someone had stood on the mountain behind them and tossed a giant fistful of rock that scattered when it hit the earth. Dust from the heartland's once fertile fields overlaid everything: the brush, the boulders, the hidden target of Trini's crystal. A dust blizzard, worse than a cyclone, had blown through the area two months ago, in September. People tied kerchiefs over their faces, turned their headlights on in the daytime, and stuffed wet sheets around windows and doors to stop the assault. Ted Ransom found jackrabbits dead in his fields, suffocated from the billowing powder, and small birds as well. The dust storm carried the land from Kansas, many said. The sight of Dawson's Gully reminded Trini of that terrible day and the black cloud from hell.

"Can't see nothing in here," Mallis said. He stood with his hands resting on his hips, elbows jutting outward, marking his space. Trying to look authoritative, Trini decided, like he knew what to do.

"No. We're going to have to go in," Roy said.

Mallis shifted his weight in impatience. "I don't see no need to go traipsing through this mess based on what some woman says she can find with some rock on a string."

Trini started to rail at him, had the word, "You" almost out of her mouth, when Katherine spoke.

"What's that?" She pointed toward a stack of boulders, larger than the rest, surrounded by a particularly dense thicket.

"I don't see anything," Mallis said. The cords on his neck flexed and quivered as he strained to look.

"Where, Katherine?" Roy asked.

She walked several yards from them, stepped onto a protruding rock platform and pointed again. "There's something shiny. Right there at the edge of the brush. See? Right between that big boulder and the brush."

Roy joined her on the platform, holding his hands at the brim of his hat for additional shade. They stood in silence for a minute.

"I see it," he said. "Let's go."

Mallis and Roy plunged into the stickers; their canvas pants and the long sleeves of their uniforms would protect them from the worst of it. Trini drew her coat under her chin against the cold wind and waited with Katherine in the sparse weeds surrounding the thicket. Clouds raced above them, and their shadows changed the gully from gray to brown and then back to dusty white. The men trudged to the far side of the rock formation. Behind the boulders, invisible from the roadway, a band of brush the width of a car lay broken and flat. At the end of the trail, the back end of a black Ford sedan protruded. The corner of its bumper gleamed in the sun.

Mallis and Roy clawed their way to the car; brush snapped and crunched under their boots. Roy reached the vehicle first, and Mallis stood a few feet away while Roy tugged on the driver's door until he finally forced it open. His head and shoulders disappeared for a moment as he bent into the car. He stood up, looked back at Trini and nodded.

Trini draped her arm across Katherine's shoulders. "Oh, Katherine," she said, "I'm so sorry."

The girl bent her face to her hands and sobbed.

An accident, Trini thought, just as she had suspected. She was sorry for Katherine, but now Parn could come home with her. She blew out a deep breath, and the knot in her stomach loosened.

For several minutes, she watched Roy tramp through the brush, circumnavigating the car while Mallis crossed to the passenger side. The sheriff stopped in thick weeds up to his thighs, and cupped his hand around his chin as if he was deep in thought. He bent over to peer into the car's interior then stood and surveyed the area around the scene. He must see something. Maybe clues as to how the car had plunged off the roadway and ended up jammed into the tangled gully. He stepped high and long, pushing his way through the weeds around the front of the car to the driver's side. He bent over and looked into the car. In a few seconds, he straightened and with a determined stride waded around to the back. Again he rubbed his chin as he examined the vehicle, nodded and went back to the passenger side to join Roy. They spoke there for a few moments, Mallis gesturing with a sweep of his arm, a fist punching the air and a pointed finger to the roadway. Roy answered occasionally, and gave a reluctant nod.

They climbed the hill, panting with exertion, then stopped beside Trini and Katherine. Despite the coolness of the air, sweat glowed across Roy's upper lip, and a rivulet of water that started at Mallis's temple swerved through the creases on his cheek and lost itself in the bracket beside his mouth. Trini looked at the sheriff carefully. Was it her imagination, or did an expression of smug satisfaction seem to settle in his eyes? Dread shot through her. Why should she be afraid? Merle Woodson had died in a car accident. Her brother would be released. But her stomach quivered.

Roy rested his hand on Katherine's shoulder. "I'm sorry, Katherine," he said.

She lifted her ravaged face, her pain as naked as her pale scalp and brow. "Did he . . . ? I want . . ." She lowered her face once more to her hands, and Roy helped her to sink onto the boulder behind her. Her shoulders shook with sobs.

Roy took Trini's arm and motioned with his head for her to come with him to join Mallis who stood several feet away, out of Katherine's earshot. Trini felt the hair on the back of her neck stiffen when she got close to the sheriff. She stood between the two men, shifting her weight to be nearer to Roy.

Roy spoke low, "Trini, it doesn't look good."

A feeling of dread again bloomed within her. She shifted her gaze to Mallis. His hat shaded his face, but still she saw the glint from the ebony eyes: a man relishing the moment.

Mallis spoke, "Merle's head is bashed in. From the back. That couldn't have happened in the accident."

"Of course it could have," she said. "He had to have been flung all over that car, hit his head all over."

"That's true, Trini," Roy said. "And he does have injuries to the front of his head. But his skull is . . . he's had massive injuries to the back of his head. It doesn't look like it happened in an accident."

"So what are you saying?" she asked.

Mallis's face remained a frozen, wrinkled mask as he spoke, "What we're saying, missy, is that Merle Woodson was killed somewhere else and put here. Someone pushed his car off the road up there."

Disbelief crowded her thoughts. The man's logic, or lack of it, was appalling. "That's a fairly quick conclusion after a fairly quick examination, Sheriff." She studied the wrinkled lips pursed together like a fist. Smug and arrogant. Her gut told her the truth: Mallis was after Parn. "And if that's what happened, I'm sorry, for Katherine's sake, but that hardly has anything to do with Parn. And don't try to twist things around so it does."

Mallis took a step toward her. He lowered his head, a bull ready for the charge. "Nothing's changed here, except now we know Merle was murdered. And my suspect is still a suspect."

"This is unbelievable." She glanced at Roy, who was staring at the ground, then turned back to Mallis. "You don't know for sure he was murdered. That's the point. You're drawing ridiculous conclusions."

"Missy," Mallis whispered, taking another step toward her, "don't you ever, ever call me ridiculous again. I can make your life—" He caught himself and his throat bobbed as he gulped his words.

Roy held out his hands, palms down, calming the storm around him. "What we'll do," he said, "is get Doc Cockrell out here. He needs to look at the scene and look at Merle."

Trini looked back and forth from Roy's steady gaze to Mallis's complacent smirk. "Fine. And meanwhile Parn can come home with me."

Mallis snorted. "That kid isn't going home with you or anyone else. I'm holding him in jail until Doc gets through looking at Merle."

"On what charge?" Trini asked.

"Suspicion of murder."

She flared. "But you have no reason to be suspicious of Parn."

"I had my reasons before we found Merle and I've still got them." He clamped his mouth closed; the lips disappeared into a slit.

"What reasons? That he had an argument with Merle two weeks ago at the café? That they had a falling out over that wretched bootleg liquor?" She paused for a moment, crossed her arms and nodded. "That's something you'd know plenty about, isn't it, Sheriff? What happened? Did Merle and Parn cut you out of the split?" She knew she was dangling bait in front of a coiled snake, but she couldn't seem to help it.

Mallis took another step toward her and started to speak, but Roy held a restraining arm across his chest. The deputy looked at Trini, and his voice was low and reasonable when he spoke. "I think we have a lot more to do here before we can say anything for sure. After Doc has a look at Merle, we can get a better handle on the situation. Don't worry about Parn in the jail cell, he'll be . . ."

She flared. "Oh that's just fine for you, Deputy Roy Eastman. Just fine. And wouldn't Jim be happy to hear that you're a part of this, keeping his kid brother-in-law in jail for a bunch of trumped-up charges from a trumped-up sheriff?"

Another derisive snort from Mallis. Trini examined the creased face. Something emanated from him. Evil? Anger? Hatred? She felt a corner of her courage curl in on itself. Dangerous, Trini thought. A dangerous man.

"Please," Roy said. "Let's just wait. We'll get Doc out here and then we can get answers instead of speculating."

Trini glared at him, wanting him to feel her anger, be shocked by it. She soaked venom into her words. "You just do that, Roy Eastman."

Trini turned on her heels, strode over to Katherine, put her arm around her and led her to the truck. She settled the girl and then climbed in the driver's seat. After slamming her door closed, she turned the ignition and stomped on the gas flinging a cloud of dust into the air.

So, they'd found Merle's body. Thanks to her. And they wanted to hold her brother on suspicion of murder. Fine. She'd go see an attorney. What was Sara Stansbury's husband's name? Carl? Good Lord, she couldn't even think straight. Yes, Carl. She'd go by his office on the way home. No, too late for that today. She'd call him at home then go first thing in the morning. Somehow she'd find someone to intervene for her and her brother. A state representative. The governor.

The truck lurched off the dirt road and rolled onto the blacktop, and Trini pulled to the side. Leaning her head back on the window behind her, she closed her eyes and took several deep breaths. Her heart slowed to normal, and the nausea that had threatened to overwhelm her subsided. She glanced at Katherine and saw that the girl held the back of her hand to her mouth, her elbow resting on the windowsill, snuffling.

What a mess. And she'd blown up at Roy, and now she deeply regretted it. Shame pushed down on her shoulders; she hated to lose her temper. How could she have let anger get the best of her? She knew enough of Roy to know he was steady and fair. She would say something to him. Apologize.

She pulled back onto the blacktop. As Trini drove toward the Woodsons', dusk drifted over the eternal and empty plains. The only sound was Katherine's occasional sniffle and the steady hum of the engine. She'd take Katherine home, telephone Dottie Kerr, Merle's coworker and friend. She'd see if Dottie could stay with Katherine and Jake a few days, until relatives descended. A wave of hopeless exhaustion, a familiar feeling since Jim died, settled behind her eyes, and Trini sighed. Crawl in a hole, that's what she wanted to do. Or run away.

But then, of course, there was Parn. She needed to go home, try to think things through, soothe the panic in her soul, then go to the jail tomorrow and talk to him. A picture came to her mind of Parn curled on a bare cot, the moon shadows of jail bars slanting across him. Who stayed there at night with a prisoner? If it was Roy, fine. But if it was Mallis, or even Taggert—her stomach twisted again. After she dropped Katherine at home and made arrangements with Dottie to stay there, she'd go by the sheriff's office. She'd insist that Roy stay there, or she'd stay herself, sleep huddled in a corner if she had to.

Anger at Parn welled once again to the surface. She was furious with him for putting them into this predicament. She had to talk to Parn. She must discover the source of Mallis's hatred. Maybe then she could tackle this thing. She only hoped he'd be able to tell her something that could shed light into this black abyss.

CHAPTER FOUR

Early the next morning, Trini pulled to a stop in front of the sheriff's office, turned off the ignition and stared at the rivulets of water drizzling down her windshield. A fuzzy haze clung to her swollen eyes, and she rubbed them with her gloved fingers. She imagined the rain washing the dust from the boulders and sage thickets in Dawson's Gully, seeping into the cold interior of Merle Woodson's car through the fractured windshield, cleansing his blood from the seat back where his head had lain. A grayness as heavy as the clouds settled on her.

Last evening, after getting Katherine and Jake Woodson settled at their home under the care of Merle's friend, Dottie Kerr, she'd driven back to the sheriff's office and talked with Roy. She apologized for her outburst. He gracefully dismissed the incident and assured her he'd stay the night in the office. She didn't see her brother.

After that, she'd telephoned the lawyer, Carl Stansbury, but his wife said he and his son, the only two members of Ludlin's law community, were in Denver for the week. Although she sympathized with Trini, all she could promise was that her husband would meet with her when he returned on Monday. Five days was too long to wait. She would get to the bottom of this today. She wouldn't tolerate Mallis's manipulations. She vowed that when she walked out of this office, her brother would be with her, a free man.

Trini climbed from the truck cab and hurried up the steps to take cover under the awning. She smoothed the front of her dress and adjusted the belt buckle in the center. The mid-November morning chilled her, but she'd chosen not to be seen in her frayed winter coat. Instead, she'd dressed in one of her best dresses, a pale blue wool with a row of black buttons down the front. The dress was minus lace and flowers; she wanted the appearance of a stern schoolmarm who would tolerate no nonsense. She hated to wear hats, so she didn't, but she tied back her mass of dark curls with a black ribbon. Wearing her silk stockings, her only pair of pumps and white gloves, she hoped she looked like she meant business. Taking a deep breath, she climbed the steps to the office and grasped the door handle. The plate glass rattled as she pushed against the door and entered, then rattled again as she closed it behind her.

Mallis sat at his desk writing, and on the other side of the room, Roy leaned back in his chair, a sheaf of papers in front of his face. Taggert wasn't in sight. The door to the cells where Parn was jailed stood closed and final. Lowering the papers to his desk, Roy regarded her with his gray stare.

Trini opened the small gate and entered the office area. Mallis came from behind his desk and lumbered toward her. If he'd stuck his thumbs in his belt, he would have been an aw-shucks cowpoke, casual and at ease, except for that face. Its jagged stone matched his heart.

"Morning, Sheriff." She was determined to be polite and calm. She turned toward Roy. "Morning, Roy."

Roy nodded as he stood.

"Sheriff, I have to talk to you. I want—"

"Now hold on one minute, missy," Mallis said. "We're in no hurry here."

"But, Sheriff, I have to—"

He held up a hand to stop her then lifted a brown paper bag that had been sitting on a chair. He stood before her holding the bag by its crumpled top. "I said just to wait a minute here. We're not in any hurry. Not anymore."

She didn't like the expression around his mouth. She didn't like the condescension in his voice. And she didn't like the sense of sick foreboding swelling inside her.

Roy rested a hand on her shoulder. "Trini, Parn's been charged with Merle's murder."

She struggled to find air. "What?"

"After I saw you here," Roy said, "Taggert stayed with Parn for a couple of hours while we drove Foster's hearse out to Dawson's Gully and brought Merle back to town to the funeral home. Then we drove out to Parn's cabin."

The bag rattled as Mallis opened it. "That's right, missy. And we found this." He reached inside and withdrew a hammer. Using his thumb and forefinger to grip the tip of the wooden handle, he held it up for her inspection. A dark substance, dried and thick, coated the iron head, and a few strands of hair stuck out like errant feathers. On the handle, three clear fingerprints stood in relief against the blood.

"Yessir," Mallis said, "Roy here was right with me. This here hammer was tucked under the woodpile behind your brother's cabin. Hidden like."

Pictures flashed through her mind: her father, hammering planks together for a workbench in their shed; Parn, building a coop for an orphaned raccoon he'd found down by the creek; her father again, repairing a trellis shattered by the tornado the summer she turned eight—all with the hammer Mallis dangled in front of her.

The room swirled before her, and she felt Roy's grip on her upper arm. Through a fog, she heard him murmur something about a chair. She collapsed into it, still staring at the tool.

"This is impossible," she whispered.

Mallis's mouth tilted up higher on one side, as if he took

satisfaction from his cornered prey.

"Trini," said Roy, "is this Parn's?"

The rain chose that time to let loose, and water pounded on the plate-glass windows. The roar took her by surprise, and evidently the men, too, because they all looked toward the clamor. A curtain of water obscured the view. The room shrank into itself, its own universe, outside the realm of laws or nature and away from God's gentle hand.

A delayed emotion punched her in the stomach: Fear—sharp and dizzying. For the first time since yesterday when she'd heard the knock on her screen door, Trini didn't know if she could manage this thing that had mushroomed before her.

"Is it?" said Mallis. He thrust the hammer at her.

She nodded. Of course it was. Even after all these years, her father's initials, ES for Edwin Shannon, showed deep and clear in the carved handle. Her thoughts whirled in confusion and when she spoke her words sounded far away. "But this is insane. There must be some mistake."

Roy stood beside her chair, his hand on her shoulder, his forehead creased in concern.

She shifted her gaze to Mallis. He preened in superiority with a half sneer and hooded eyes. "There isn't any mistake. And you led us right to the body," he said.

She looked back to Roy. "You were with him? Mallis? When he found the hammer?"

He nodded.

Nausea surged, and she closed her eyes then bent her head to her lap to keep it from spinning. There was something about the hammer . . . She struggled to dig through the shock for the memory, but it eluded her.

Only one certainty floated to the top of her emotional mud: Mallis had framed Parn. Had he done more than that? Had he murdered Merle Woodson, stolen Parn's hammer, doctored it to look like a murder weapon and then, sometime while Roy wasn't watching, buried it in the woodpile? It would be a perfect plan, and Parn would be hanged for murder. George Mallis would be the sheriff and a rich bootlegger.

Anger roared to the shore of her consciousness and flooded all reason. She bolted to her feet. "I'll be calling Denver. I want to talk to a United States marshal."

Mallis leaned back against the railing and crossed his arms over his chest. A smirk played around the corners of his mouth. "I already telephoned Denver. Taggert will take the hammer up there and get it analyzed at that new Bureau of Investigation lab. Doc Cockrell got caught up last night with business in Pueblo, but he'll be back in a couple of days. As soon as he confirms the murder, we'll wait for Judge Slaton to get here and make the arraignment. Everything should be wrapped up in a few days." His voice was nonchalant, unhurried, confident; everything in due time.

How did things go this far? Mallis was dangerous, more dangerous than anything she'd faced before; a monster snake, a giant diamond-back rattler, and his fangs were exposed and ready to strike at her heart.

She swallowed to wet her throat. "I'd like to speak to Parn," she whispered.

Mallis turned and ambled back to his chair. He sank down, rested his hands across his stomach and brought his fingers together to make a steeple.

"Well now. Visiting hours aren't until later in the day. Sorry."

"When?"

An offhand shrug moved his shoulder. "Maybe two, three o'clock."

Trini looked at Roy. He stared at Mallis, an unreadable expression on his face, the muscles in his jaw flicking. Why didn't he say anything? Was he that cowed by the sheriff? Afraid for his job? Maybe he was just a coward at heart. A worthless coward. He met her gaze, but she turned her eyes back to the viper's stare.

Yes, she felt certain, Mallis was a murderer, and if she wasn't careful, her own brother could die next. He could easily shoot Parn, right here in the jail, then claim that it was the only way to stop an escaping criminal. Trini wouldn't make the mistake of underestimating him again.

"Well," she said. "You certainly got what you wanted, didn't you, Sheriff? This will all benefit you very nicely, won't it?"

"Trini," Roy's voice bore a note of caution, but she focused on Mallis and kept going.

"You get to keep your hand in the steady flow of liquor from Denver. With Merle and Parn both gone, southern Colorado is yours for the taking, isn't it?"

Mallis tossed a look at her, like swatting an annoying fly. "Don't get carried away with your mouth, missy."

Trini lifted her chin a notch. "Sheriff Mallis, my name is Trinidad Bates."

With a glance at Roy, she turned and walked out the door.

She huddled against the office door, her back pressed against the large pane of glass to keep out of the rain that pelted the awning above her. Roy and Mallis could see her back, but she didn't care. Leaning her head back against the glass, she gulped down tears. No. She would not succumb to weeping numbness.

She took several cold, deep breaths to clear her thinking. This entire situation didn't feel right. There had to be something else going on, some history here, something she wasn't aware of that was acting as a catalyst to the sheriff's steel-eyed determination. She needed to find out. How could she? Where would she start? She opened her eyes, looked through the rain and caught sight of a movement inside the mercantile.

Of course. Jefferson LeClair. If anyone knew the sheriff's

personal history or could discover it, Jefferson could. As the owner of the Ludlin Mercantile, not only did he handle people's everyday needs, but he handled the special items: copper tubing for a still, breath mints to mask tobacco, and tonics for bodily functions. And he was Trini's friend. After Jim had died, before the life insurance settlement, money had been tight, and Jefferson had extended one kindness after another. Gradually their friendship had deepened. Trini found his sophisticated observations about life humorous and comforting. Holding her pocketbook over her head, she trotted down the steps and dashed across the shiny blacktop.

With a jangle of doorbells, Trini entered the cavernous store. The pressed-tin ceiling colored the interior darker than the gloomy day, but she could see that the room was vacant. Three stocked aisles led to the back of the store, and to her right, boxes and jars of candy jammed the shelves behind the counter that held the cash register. Beside it stood a poster advertising the upcoming Fall Festival, resting on top of a display of canned peaches. In the center of the room, a small fire glowed behind the grate of a pot-bellied stove. Jefferson must be in the back storeroom, or in his office. She started down the canned goods aisle.

"Don't give me that rot," a woman shouted. "I want Stephanie with me every day after school. She's better off at home." Camille LeClair, Jefferson's wife.

Trini stopped. Either Camille hadn't heard the bells when Trini came in, or she didn't care. Jefferson said something, but Trini couldn't make it out.

Camille shouted again. "No you can't. You can't offer her one thing better than I can, and you know it."

"She wants to come here with me," Jefferson shouted.

"That's because you give her anything she wants, and she doesn't have to do a damn thing for it."

Past the last aisle on her left was Jefferson's office, and Camille backed out of the doorway, her stiff arms ending in tight balls. She jerked to a halt as she caught sight of Trini, and her lips compressed into a thin red line. Red hair, as fiery as her temper, swirled around her face. Trini had always thought of Camille LeClair as pushy and aggressive. At this moment, her behavior was reinforcing that opinion. She marched toward Trini, her shoulders swaggering with her gait.

She brushed Trini's shoulder as she passed. "Get an earful?" she asked.

The door frame shook and the bells slapped as she opened the door and stomped out.

"Well, Trinidad. You obviously did get an earful," said Jefferson. He came toward her tying a starched and gleaming full apron at his waist. As he stopped in front of her, he reached to his throat and adjusted a black bow tie. "But the question is, did hearing it make you deathly ill?"

"Jefferson, I'm sorry. I obviously interrupted something."

"No more than Camille's usual rant at me for hurting her. Hurting Stephanie. Hurting the dog. I'm surely the worst of beasts. I do nothing but inflict pain on the universe."

"Oh, Jefferson." Trini laid a hand on his arm.

"Ever since I've moved out, she's taken to coming by the store every day. And now she doesn't want Stephanie here after school anymore. I've incited a veritable war, Trinidad." They walked to the front counter. "Well. It can't be helped now, and I'm not sorry," he said. "But, enough about me and my woeful life. What about you? I heard they jailed Parn, but he's released now, isn't he? Since they've discovered the accident?"

Trini perched on the counter stool as Jefferson, his elegant hands resting flat on the countertop, waited with serious brown eyes. She examined his thick dark hair and mustache, both oiled, combed and neatly trimmed. His nose, eyes and mouth were all perfect in size; nothing overdone or too full or narrow or uncomfortable to look at. Ordered was the word for Jefferson.

The LeClairs had arrived in Ludlin three years ago, right after the stock market collapse in October of 1929. Before that black day, they'd lived an affluent life in Philadelphia, riding the wave of prosperity like so many did in the booming decade of the 20s. During that time, Jefferson had purchased a half dozen general stores across the country. One slow afternoon after he'd known Trini for several months, he confessed with a self-deprecating smile that he had wanted to be the next retail magnate, establish the new Woolworths, he'd said. When the market crashed, the only business he'd been able to salvage was the Ludlin Mercantile. He'd packed up his worldly possessions and his family and headed west to live a quiet life in a quiet town. Despite his travails, Trini was glad he was here.

He leaned over the counter and placed a hand on her shoulder. "Trinidad, what is it? What's happened? I'd heard they'd found Woodson. I also heard you dowsed for him. I'd have liked to seen their faces when they found him right where you said he'd be." He smiled a little under the perfect mustache.

"Yes, I led George Mallis right to Merle's body. And now he can use it to convict Parn of murder."

"Murder? But I heard Woodson died in an accident. In Dawson's Gully."

"That's where they found him. But evidently Merle had injuries to the back of his head. He'd been beaten, and they've named Parn the killer." She stammered her way through the story of how Mallis and Roy found the gory hammer with carved initials in Parn's woodpile.

He shook his head in disbelief. "Good God. Merle Woodson murdered. You know, a lot of people didn't like him. He had the reputation of a man of no honor. He'd do anything for money, evidently. Camille hated him. She maintained he'd sell his own children if there was a market. But why would the sheriff blame Parn for Woodson's demise? It was an unlikely alliance, but Parn and Woodson have been friends and bootlegging partners on and off for years."

"I don't know why. Jefferson, I'm afraid. I'm afraid of Mallis. I think Mallis wants the bootlegging route and he'll do anything to get it."

"But he already has a piece of it. Everyone knows that."

"I know. And at first I thought Parn and Woodson had kept Mallis's piece of the pie and he was out to get back at them. But I think Mallis wants it all. I had no idea how deeply Parn had gotten himself involved in running liquor. They were supplying all of southern Colorado."

"Good Lord, Trinidad."

"They evidently work out of Denver. I don't know all the details."

"Damn George Mallis to hell. Pardon me, Trinidad, but he has his greedy claws into this entire county. And now Parn is in jail, and with Merle Woodson dead—well, that does rather free up all that whiskey for the taking."

He paused for a moment and shook his head. "Southern Colorado. The sheer size of the operation is a daunting thought. And I suppose now with Roosevelt's election, all the bootleggers are trying to make their fortunes before the repeal of the Volstead Act. I've heard they truck the liquor down from Canada through Montana into Denver, then through the state. Where would Parn and Woodson store it?"

Trini shrugged. "I remember Parn saying something about using the abandoned mine on Woodson's land. That was a few years ago, when they first started bootlegging, but I suppose they'd still be using it. I've heard some bootleggers cut the liquor with poisons, iodine or even embalming fluid. But I'm sure Parn isn't involved in doing that." She put her hand to her chest to quiet the nibble of doubt in her heart.

Jefferson regarded her with silent sympathy.

A wave of hopelessness overwhelmed her again, and she had to fight the temptation to run out the door, run anywhere, away from all this. But she could not. She needed to help Parn. He was depending on her, and there was no one else.

"Jefferson, what do you know about Mallis? I mean, he's been sheriff for what, two years? Have you heard anything about him? I know he's a widower from Denver. Do you know anything more?"

"No. Just that when Bud Carevich died, Mallis used some very influential friends to get the temporary sheriff's appointment from the governor. He'll have a tough time winning a legitimate election, I think. But that's not until next year."

Trini nodded. "I know. But I just wonder, Jefferson. I have a suspicion, that Mallis—" She stopped. She was ready to say she had a suspicion Mallis murdered Woodson himself, but even with Jefferson, she needed to be wary of her words. Instinct told her that if she started accusing Mallis of Merle Woodson's murder, the sheriff would find out about it.

Jefferson waited, his eyebrows lifted in anticipation.

"I'm just afraid," she said. "I'm afraid for Parn."

"I know." He squeezed her shoulder. "I know."

She hesitated for a moment, then plunged ahead. "Jefferson, you know Gilbert Hardy fairly well. Would you ask him about Mallis? See if he knows anything from his past?"

Even though Gilbert Hardy was Ludlin's only banker, he had business interests across the state. It was rumored his state-wide influence was as massive as his greed. Trini personally knew one farmer who was one week late on a twenty-dollar payment for his mortgaged farm; it was now a part of Hardy's holdings. However, she figured if anyone in Ludlin would know about

George Mallis, or had the connections to find out, it would be Hardy.

"Well I, rather, that is, I'm not certain when I'll be talking to Mr. Hardy."

"Mr. Hardy? I thought you might be on a first-name basis with him. I know he's a good customer, and Margie Snowfeather said the two of you have dinner at the café a couple of times a week. I assumed you were friends."

"We are. Of course, we are. I was referring to how you'd address him."

"Oh. So would you? Ask him about George Mallis?"

He lowered his eyes, took a cloth from under the counter and began moving it in small circles over the immaculate surface. He kept his eyes on his cleaning, cleared his throat then spoke, "It's just that I don't like imposing on Mr. Hardy's—Gilbert's friendship. He's a powerful man in the state, and I don't want to bother him with every little thing."

Trini gaped at him. "Every little thing?" she whispered.

"Well, of course I didn't mean that." He stopped wiping the counter and heaved a sigh as he leaned forward. "It's not that I don't want to help, Trinidad, I do. I really do. I just, you understand, have to be rather careful. Well, I don't mean careful, but mindful of what I talk to Gilbert about. He's an exceptionally busy man. You know he has contacts all over the state."

"I think we've established that, Jefferson."

"Yes. Well."

What was the matter with him? Obviously she'd misjudged the situation. She should have handled this herself. She stood to leave. "That's all right. Don't worry about it. I'll ask him myself."

Jefferson's eyes widened, and he reached out to clutch her arm. "No!" He stepped back and shrugged his shoulders a little.

"No. I'll do it. I'm . . . I'm sorry, Trinidad. I want to assist you. I'll ask him."

"But you're uncomfortable doing so, I can tell. I don't want that. I shouldn't have asked the favor."

"No, please. I'll ask him. Let me ask him." The sincerity in his voice wove through his words.

She relaxed back onto the stool. "All right, and thank you."

"I'm desperately sorry for hesitating. It has nothing to do with you. It's just something between Gilbert and me."

"Oh." She was almost ready to add that she understood, but in fact she didn't.

She examined his eyes for a moment and saw pain. Of course. With his separation from Camille, he was confused and upset about everything. She should have been sensitive to his turmoil.

"You have a lot on your mind," she said. "If this only involved me, I wouldn't ask. But with Parn in such deep trouble, well, thank you again. I would appreciate anything you could find out about Mallis."

He smiled and bent in a mock bow, his face relaxed and open, back to their easy camaraderie. "It's my pleasure to help a damsel in distress."

He seemed fine now, back to his easy humor.

"I'm going home for a few hours, then back to the sheriff's," Trini said. "Mallis is playing games. He wouldn't let me see Parn just now, you know."

"What reason did he give?"

"No reason. He said visiting hours weren't until two or three o'clock. If he wants to play that way, I'll force his hand. I'm going to be at that office at two o'clock sharp."

He grew serious. "Be careful, Trinidad. The man is unpredictable. Just don't push him too hard."

Trini shut the door behind her as she left, and stood on the sidewalk in front of the mercantile. The rain had stopped, but the clouds settled on top of the roofs, heavy and ominous. Through the sheriff's window, she could see Mallis, his black leather boots propped on his desk, crossed at the ankles. Roy wasn't in sight and Taggert was evidently still gone. She'd come back at two and, God help her, she'd get past George Mallis and see her brother.

She pulled from the parking place and headed south on the county highway. The mist lingered, making the blacktop slick and shiny, and as she turned onto her own soggy roadway, an image came to her, unbidden and shocking: Parn, holding the hammer above his head, then driving it into Merle Woodson's skull. Where had that come from? It didn't happen. It didn't. Parn wouldn't kill Merle. He didn't have the capacity for it.

She turned into her drive and pulled to a stop just as the doubter whispered in her ear. What about Parn's wild dreams of moving to Oregon? And his greed? Maybe Merle's death wasn't purposeful, but caused by Parn nonetheless, an accident Parn tried to hide. No, she scolded herself.

She had to talk to Parn. She had to look in his eyes. She had to reaffirm that he was still the brother she'd always known.

CHAPTER FIVE

With the rattle of the plate glass, Trini pushed open the sheriff's office door. Two o'clock, Mallis's announced visiting hours. Roy Eastman looked up from the papers on his desk. His welcoming expression, accompanied by a smile, lit his face for a moment, but then he turned somber. Trini nodded to him and scanned the empty room. He stood and greeted her, then ambled around from behind his desk, his hands thrust into his pants pockets. She opened the small gate, entered the main room and stopped in front of him.

"I came to see Parn," she said.

"Mallis isn't here right now. He had to go over to Colleton. He said he'd be back by four." A thick hand came out of his pocket and ruffled his silver mane. Gray eyes stayed steady on her face.

"So?" she said.

"Trini, I can't help you. I'm sorry, I—"

"Sorry?"

"Yeah, I'm sorry. Mallis left orders that you couldn't see Parn unless he was here. He said he'd be back by four or so. Sorry."

She narrowed her eyes, studying him for a moment. So Roy was Mallis's lackey? Had he no sense of right or wrong?

"You're sorry? My brother is being framed for murder by a corrupt sheriff and you're sorry?" Disgust shook her voice. "How can you be a part of this? I always thought you were a decent man, like Jim. And now you tell me you're *sorry*?" Her tirade increased her outrage, and she felt her lips and cheeks tighten, sharp and belligerent.

The gray eyes narrowed. "Look. First of all, you don't know that Mallis is framing anyone. That's for a judge to determine, and he will as soon as he gets here. Second, as far as you visiting Parn, there's nothing I can do about that. Mallis runs this office like he runs the county—tight and closed."

"Well that's just fine. But Mallis wouldn't know if I visited Parn because he isn't here right now, is he?" She flinched at the brazenness of her words. She asked too much. She should leave and come back later. But her feet stayed still, and she waited for his response.

Roy shifted his weight and ran a hand through his hair again. He crossed his arms over his chest. The narrowed eyes glared at her. "Who do you think you are? You know what you're asking me to do? If Mallis comes back and finds out I let you back there," he waved a hand toward the cell door, "I'll lose my job. I'll get fired. There are plenty of men who'd do anything to keep a job, including doing what their boss expects them to do."

His words sent a jolt through her. That was a good question. Who did she think she was? She was asking him to jeopardize his job. What was she thinking? A chair caught her as she collapsed into it. "Sorry, Roy. Sorry."

"Look. I'd like to help, but I don't have the authority to let you in there."

"I know. I know. It's all right. I don't blame you."

How could she blame him? He was only doing what was expected of him. Her audacious request appalled her, and she sank into herself. How did everything all of a sudden get so big? And so hard? Hopelessness pressed on her shoulders like a mammoth ox yoke, complete with iron rings and chains for pulling a load.

Her gloved finger traced the buckle on her purse, and she listened to herself speak. "I'm just so scared, Roy. You know, just so incredibly scared. Seems like since Jim died, all I am is scared."

She looked up at him from her place. The arms were still crossed, but he didn't seem stiff with anger, only still, intent and slightly stunned.

"I'm sorry," she said again. "I don't want to sound like I pity myself. I don't mean that. It's just that the world all of a sudden got so different. I mean, everything changed. I know everyone has bad things in their lives, especially now with the Depression and all, and there's no reason why I shouldn't have them, too. Compared to many, I'm lucky."

"Trini—"

She ignored him. She hadn't meant to let this out where he could see it, but the words kept coming. "I don't know anymore. It seems like every single day I have to reach down inside of me really deep, and it scares me because I don't know how deep it goes down there. And now this thing with Parn. I know he's not much, but he's all I have." She shifted her eyes as she thought of the ten months, fourteen years ago in Kansas City. "He's really all I have now." She stood and smoothed her dress. "Well." She walked toward the door. "I'm sorry. You've got your own problems. Everyone has their own problems. I mean it. I don't blame you. I'm sorry. Sorry for doing this."

"Let's go." He walked to Mallis's desk, opened the top drawer and withdrew a ring of keys.

"What?"

"Let's go. You wanted to talk to Parn, didn't you?"

"But . . . are you sure you want to do this?"

He laughed. "Not if you keep stalling me about it. It's a little after two now, and like I said, Mallis said he'd be back by four.

But you never know about him. If we're going to do this, let's go."

What had she asked him to do? Worry churned in her stomach, then she snapped herself back. She wanted to see Parn. She had to see him. "Thank you, Roy. Thank you."

Guilt pressed on her chest. He was putting his job on the line. As a favor to her. Her second favor today. She watched the sway of his broad back as he led her through the office and down the hall.

Parn was there. Just behind the door.

Using the key on the iron ring Mallis had used yesterday, Roy opened the hall door. He led her into a visiting area just large enough for two people to stand. A dim bulb and shade hung from the ceiling and gave the brick-walled room a sinister feeling, as if malicious beings with unharnessed passions lurked in the shadows. Only one thin horizontal window set high in the outside wall showed the sky's leaden clouds. Trini's shoulders shook with a cold shudder. Two cells defined by dense iron bars were in front of her. One cell was empty. Parn was in the other.

He lunged from the cot and gripped the bars. His eyes filled with tears. A three-legged wooden stool sat in the far corner. Roy placed it behind her, and Trini sank down, suddenly exhausted. Parn knelt in front of her.

"I'm not going to open the cell door," said Roy. "You can talk through the bars."

Trini nodded and watched him leave.

She smoothed her fingertip over one of Parn's battered knuckles, and his face blurred through her tears. "How'd that happen?"

"Oh, wasn't much." He choked through his words. "Trini, I didn't kill Merle. I hope you believe that."

She clutched his words for assurance, holding them close to her like lost children finally found. "I know . . . I know you wouldn't lie to me."

He nodded then settled himself on the cement floor in front of her. "I've been worried about you."

"Me?"

"Yeah. I'm sorry, Trin. Sorry for causing you all this heartache. If it weren't for me, you could be baking your bread or working your garden."

Here she'd been doubting his innocence, and he was only concerned for her welfare. Embarrassment flushed her face. "Oh, Parn. We'll get out of this somehow, I swear."

"How come Mallis let you back here? He told me to not count on seeing you."

She cast an eye toward the door, knowing Roy was on the other side, probably tossing his keys from one hand to the other. "Roy did it."

"Roy's a good man. Jim always said so."

She nodded.

"What's everyone say?"

"I don't know about everyone. All I know is Mallis. Why is he doing this? Is it for the bootlegging?"

"I guess. I'm scared, Trin." His eyes clouded with tears again. "I'm scared of Mallis. He might arrange it so's I die of some accident here in the cell. Maybe a getaway attempt or something. He's got it all thought out, I know it. Yessir. All figured out."

She cringed at his words. He'd voiced the unspoken fear she'd carried with her since yesterday. "But why? Why would Mallis be doing this? Would he be greedy enough to kill Woodson and frame you for the murder, just to get at the bootlegging? Is that what he's after?"

He shifted his eyes and stood. She looked up at him. "What is it?"

"It's a long story. And it goes back a ways."

"Back a ways?"

His eyes shifted again and his mouth twitched. After a moment, he stopped the nervous gesture, and his face opened and relaxed, as if he'd just recognized a fact of life and made up his mind to quit fighting it. He heaved a sigh. "You remember several years back, maybe five or six years ago, when Merle and me started running whiskey, I went with him up to Denver?"

"Yes." She'd remembered all right. He'd been gone for a week, and Merle had left Katherine and Jake for the entire time. "Jim was furious. He figured that's when you and Merle started bootlegging."

"It was. And that's the first time I met Mallis, too. He was working for this man, Mr. Colletti, who ran all the routes in Colorado."

"Mallis was a bootlegger?"

Parn nodded.

"That's unbelievable. So what happened?"

Parn licked his lips and darted his eyes around the dim room, as if one of the lurking shadows might overhear. He leaned closer to the bars. "Mallis was married with two little boys and working his way up in Colletti's organization. But Mr. Colletti got suspicious of how Mallis was running things. You know. He figured Mallis was doing some funny stuff, stealing from him. So that week when we went up to Denver, Colletti told Merle and me to—"

Trini heard the front door slam and rattle. She bolted to her feet, toppling the stool to its side.

"What the hell!" Mallis bawled. She heard Roy's muffled response then Mallis's roar again. "Her truck's out front! You let her back there. I knew it, Eastman, I knew it. Pack up your goddamn gear." His bellows ricocheted through the building.

Roy's voice rose to match it. "Damn it, Mallis. You've got some damned quarrel with them that has nothing to do with—"

"I don't need direction from you, Deputy. In case you forgot,

I'm the one wearing this star."

Trini envisioned Mallis thumping himself on the chest. Her eyes darted around the cell block, instinctively looking for a way out, but she was as caged as Parn. She covered her brother's hand with her own.

Boots clomped in the hallway and the door shot open. The bull loomed in the threshold. The crevasses in his face looked like they were gouged from granite, and his eyes blazed inside their narrow slits.

"Out!" He jerked his head over his shoulder indicating the way.

Her mind was numb, but her feet obeyed his command. Trini gave one final glance to Parn, turned her shoulder to pass Mallis and walked down the hall.

Roy sat in his chair, the top desk drawer open in front of him. He reached in and added to the growing pile of paper, ink wells, and pens on the top of his desk blotter. He kept his eyes to his sorting.

Mallis growled behind her. "I said out, and I mean out." She turned to face him.

"Sheriff, I told you before. I'm calling Denver. I want a marshal brought in."

He showed her his teeth. "You just go right ahead and make all the calls you want to, missy. It won't make no difference. I got the body, I got the suspect, and I got the evidence. All the marshals in the state won't change that."

Defeat, as heavy as a boulder, dropped inside her. He was right. God help her, he was right. A marshal would take one look at the hammer, talk to Doc Cockrell who would confirm the cause of death, and stand back to let Mallis's plan plow into action. There was nothing she could say that would prove Mallis framed Parn, much less that he'd murdered Woodson.

Trini glanced again at Roy, but he kept his eyes down. He'd

obviously been fired, and it was all her fault. Guilty tears burned her eyes; she wanted to tell him how sorry she was, to please forgive her. She watched him a moment, hoping he'd look up, but he didn't. Mallis stood his ground and Trini felt his hate boring into her. Suddenly, she couldn't stand being in the same room with him another instant. She flung the door open and stomped out.

A cold rain shrouded the shops. Across the street, lights burned in the mercantile, and she saw Jefferson through the window at the counter with a customer, ringing a sale. Someone walked out of the bank, and holding a newspaper over his head, ran a few feet to his car. Life in Ludlin went on. It all looked so normal. Trini walked down the steps to her own truck, opened the door and got in.

The sheriff's door opened and Roy stepped from it, holding a bulging paper bag, his deputy star absent from his chest. She cranked down her window and leaned out.

"Roy," she called.

He looked at her, then turned and walked away. She wanted to call to him again, to dash from the truck, run to catch up with him and clutch his shirtsleeve begging him to forgive her. But she sat, staring at his retreating back in numb disbelief, while the rain stained his tan uniform shirt with brown splotches.

CHAPTER SIX

When Trini entered her kitchen, her muddled thoughts refused to order themselves, and her first impulse was to run to her bedroom and fling herself across the bed in a torrent of tears. Instead, she found herself walking past the sink stacked with dirty dishes and the oak table still littered with her morning toast crumbs. She stopped at the attic door and turned the iron knob. The hinges squealed in protest as she opened the plank door, and the walls of the stairwell brushed her shoulders as she climbed to the top. She felt her way to her father's old pine desk and tugged the lamp chain; the yellow light illuminated the gouges on the desktop, his slat-back oak chair and the slanted ceiling close above her head. On the opposite wall stood the old dresser, its hinged mirror peeling with age. In the corner of the cramped space a camelback trunk punctuated with tarnished brass brads stored, among other things, her mother's wedding dress.

She tugged open the top drawer of the desk, lifted out a map and smoothed it by brushing her hand over the frayed creases of the United States. She removed the crystal from her pocket and dangled it by the string above the center of the country: Kansas City.

"Where is she? Show me where."

The crystal spun to life like a miniature top on a cord. Probably from memory, she thought. She'd done this so many times.

"Show her to me."

She moved her hand north, and the dowsing instrument continued to spin until it hovered over the small town of St. Joseph, Missouri. Her blood swelled the vessels in her arm and rushed into her fingertips, and the rock began to sway. Trini pulled back the crystal and cupped it in her tender hand.

Still there. Her little daughter. Her Lucinda.

She hadn't seen her child except as an infant a few hours old, but she imagined a dark-eyed, dark-haired thirteen-year-old girl who had oversized, competent hands like her own. In her mind, she'd named the baby Lucinda. What was she doing right now? Maybe she'd be helping her adopted mother bake a cake or tend to chickens. Maybe her daughter would be like herself as a girl: always outdoors, cloud-gazing or strolling through the gentle hills, skimming her palms along the tops of the prairie grass as the nettles brushed her legs. No matter what she was doing, her child would be safe and normal and loved. She'd have a family.

She leaned back in the chair and sighed. The old questions rose like recurring ghosts. Had she made the right decision all those years ago? Should she have scoured the continent in search of Ethan Daniels? If she'd found him, they could have been married, and Lucinda would have been theirs. And if she'd not found him, should she have kept her child, despite the stigma of illegitimacy?

When she was sixteen and in love, she had learned she was pregnant. Ethan Daniels, the boy who she figured would be her husband until she died, had urged her to elope with him, but the strength of will to defy her father refused to rise to the surface. When she'd told her father about her child, he'd sent her lover packing. The eighteen-year-old Ethan, immature and impressionable, had been no match for the gravel-voiced black Irishman, Edwin Shannon. He left, and then her father sent Trini away, too. For the sake of the town gossips, he invented a dying aunt who needed care in Kansas City. Alone, grieving for Ethan and broken by her father's will, Trini took the train to Kansas City and lived for seven months in the Florence Crittendon home for Unwed Mothers. There she gave birth to her child. And there, she'd given her away. Three months later, she'd returned to Ludlin.

She should have defied her father. She should have insisted on keeping her baby, *Ethan's* baby. She should have found him, and if she couldn't, she should have run away with her daughter, maybe to Mexico, to the village where her mother's mother had lived as a child, worked in a bakery or sold her dowsing to support her little family.

But she didn't. And years later, in the exhaustion of a day or when Jim had gazed at her with a worshipful stare, she'd think of caring for the illegitimate child and find herself glad she'd given up the baby for adoption. Glad . . . and ashamed. She must have prairie dust for a heart: glad for her comforts and her husband's adoration rather than her own flesh and blood. Those were the times she hated her father. And herself.

And God had exacted payment for her sin: For all the years of praying, she and Jim were never blessed with a child. After her Lucinda, she was barren.

Why, every few months, did she climb the attic steps and dowse for her daughter? Why do this to herself? The event did nothing but heighten the fantasy of seeing the child. Now she'd have a week of restless dreams, her traitorous subconscious planning the details of a new life: how she'd go to her daughter, Lucinda's cries of joy at finding her real mother, running into her arms. Trini slammed her palm onto the map. Stupid. She was stupid to do this.

Quit wasting time, she scolded herself. She wanted to call the marshal's office in Denver, and she figured it would take a while to wend her way to the correct person. She needed to get started. She refolded the map and opened the drawer, ready to put it away, when two short rings and one long sounded from the telephone hanging on the wall in the kitchen. That was her line.

Trini switched off the light and dashed down the staircase. Maybe Roy was calling. Where did that ridiculous idea come from? She doubted she'd ever see him again, except by accident. The sudden burn of tears surprised her, but she blinked them away. She lifted the receiver from its cradle. Katherine Woodson's small, breathy voice sounded in her ear.

"Trini, I'm afraid. Could you come over here? Just for a little bit?"

"Katherine, are you all right?"

"Please, Trini." The line went dead.

A twenty-minute drive south of Ludlin, the Woodsons' house hid in the middle of ten acres of jagged rocks and scraggly trees. Trini knew that on weekday mornings, Merle Woodson had driven Katherine in for school and Jake to the Darby house to be cared for. It must have been an inconvenience for the motherless family to live out here, remote from help, but an abandoned gold mine occupied a hillside about a half mile from the house, and this is where, according to Parn, Merle Woodson had stashed their bootlegged liquor. A selfish man, thought Trini, putting the children through the hardship of isolation to satisfy his own greed.

When she pulled into the driveway. Katherine ran down the steps, her tufts of hair bouncing above a pale face drenched with tears. She flung her thin arms around Trini's neck, and her small white head bobbed with her sobs.

"Oh, Trini. I'm so glad you're here."

"Katherine, what is it? What's happened?"

The girl shook her head, mute, staring at Trini with red-rimmed eyes.

"Where's Dottie?" Trini said. "I thought she was staying with you until your aunt and uncle arrived."

"Dottie had to go home last night. Jake and I spent the night here alone, but I just can't do it anymore."

"Now calm down. It's all right." Trini put her arm around Katherine's tiny waist and led her into the house. "Dottie had to go home? Why?"

A small choke and a shake of her head was all Katherine could manage.

Dottie Kerr, a widow and Merle's coworker in the Coyote County land claims office, was known to be reliable, fond of both children and a good friend to Merle Woodson. The town gossips figured Merle and Dottie as lovers who would one day be married. When Trini had telephoned Dottie yesterday and asked if she could stay with Katherine and Jake, she'd accepted with quick delight, answering she'd stay for as long as the children needed her.

Maybe an emergency had demanded Dottie's return, or, heaven forbid, she'd taken ill. But if that had happened, why wouldn't Dottie have telephoned Trini and asked her to make other arrangements? Why would she leave the children un-tended?

"Katherine, didn't Dottie telephone anyone else to come stay with you?"

The girl shook her head again.

"Did she get sick or say why she had to leave?"

Again Katherine shook her head. It was bizarre that Dottie didn't call her or Mrs. Darby—someone—to come over before she left. Granted, at fifteen and without a mother, Katherine could do a woman's work while caring for Jake. But to leave Katherine here at this time . . . Trini was tempted to get back in her truck, drive to the Kerr's and give the thoughtless Dottie a piece of her mind.

"All right," Trini said. "I'm here. I won't leave."

When they entered the Woodson kitchen, Trini saw evidence of Katherine's hard work. Clean pans hung from the rack above the stove, the counters gleamed, and the smell of soap clung to the air. In the center of the room, a round oak table surrounded by four chairs held an array of food: a layer cake with white icing, a plate of oatmeal cookies, and two loaves of bread.

Trini put her arm across Katherine's bony shoulders. "You didn't make all this yourself, did you?"

"No. People started coming by last week, when Dad was missing. And Mrs. Burns brought by the cake this morning."

No doubt as the news of Merle's death circulated through town, the table would fairly collapse with the weight of the food that the ladies of Ludlin, Colorado, would prepare to fortify the process of mourning.

Trini followed Katherine into the parlor. Clean and ordered tables stood next to the chairs and sofa, and the wood floors gleamed with polish. The open drapes on the front window let in the dull light from an overcast sky, but despite the gloom, the room appeared homey and cheerful. Twelve-year-old Jake, dressed in denim overalls, and thick-knitted socks, sat cross-legged on the floor in front of the radio. Trini heard the faint melody of the organ music theme from *Little Orphan Annie*.

"The house looks good, Katherine. You've done a nice job."

"Thanks." She wiped her eyes and blew her nose with a handkerchief.

Trini walked over to Jake, patted him on the shoulder, and smiled into vacant blue eyes. Even though he was seated, Trini could tell he had the beginning bulk of a man: muscled shoulders and the edge of a jawline. She hadn't seen him often enough that, with his five-year-old memory, he would recall her.

"Hi, Jake. I'm Trini."

He blinked at her once then turned back to the radio in time to listen to Orphan Annie capture a crook. Katherine again blew her nose into her handkerchief as she settled on the sofa. Trini sat next to her and covered Katherine's translucent hand with her own.

"Were you afraid of being alone?" she asked.

Katherine twisted the handkerchief into a tight spiral. "I guess."

Trini watched her a moment then decided to ask the question that was foremost in her mind. "Are you feeling all right? Are you sick, Katherine?"

"No, I'm not sick." Her voice was strong, anger around the edges. "I just got afraid."

Trini knew there had to be more and wanted to press for an answer, but she needed to be as gentle as she could. She withdrew her hand. "I want to help you, I really do. And I'm glad you called. But you have to tell me the truth."

Katherine pinched her bottom lip and stretched it, then moved her fingers and pulled again. Trying to get the words out? "Someone broke in last week, one night in the middle of the night."

"You mean while your dad was missing?"

She nodded.

"Did you call the sheriff?"

Katherine shook her head. "I don't like him."

"But Roy could have come. You could have told Mallis to send Roy." Guilt pinched the back of her mind. Thanks to her, that was no longer an option.

"I don't like even talking to the sheriff."

"I don't blame you for that," Trini said.

"Pa talked about him, about the sheriff, and something about it being too late to get him out of his pants pockets."

"I wonder what he meant by that."

Katherine shrugged.

Just as she suspected. George Mallis had been trying to stick his greedy fists into the bootlegging profits, extort money from Woodson to allow the bootlegging to operate in peace. She'd like for Roy to hear this. And a marshal.

"So . . . about this break-in," Trini said. "Did you hear anything?"

"No. Jake and I slept through the whole thing. But the next morning I saw the window in the kitchen was busted and Pa's papers in his desk over there," she nodded to the rolltop desk, "were scattered all over, like someone had been searching for something. And they stole my ten dollars."

"It was your money?"

"Dad always left ten dollars in the drawer for me, you know, in case I ever needed it when he was gone." She reddened from her chin to the top of her bare scalp and lowered her eyes, obviously embarrassed and ashamed of her far-traveling, bootlegging father.

Trini patted her arm. "You've carried a big load on your small back, Katherine, being the woman of the house, taking care of Jake. My mother died when I was ten, so I know how you feel. It's hard."

Katherine smiled and seemed to relax a little, but she still fingered her lip.

Trini didn't add that unlike Merle Woodson, her own father hadn't bootlegged whiskey, traveling for hundreds of miles and days at a time to buy and sell his illegal product. It's a wonder Merle wasn't fired from the county land claims office. How did he get by with his long absences? She fumed with silent anger. She shouldn't think ill of the dead, but Merle Woodson had done no favors for his children.

"I'm just glad you and Jake are all right," Trini said.

"We are, but I got scared last night thinking about the burglar.

Did you hear all that rain? It was so loud."

Using her index finger, Katherine flapped her lower lip; it made little popping noises as she released it several times. It dawned on Trini that Katherine had no one to talk to—no schoolmates or neighbor girlfriends. She was isolated out here away from town with a retarded brother and a criminal father. Isolated and alone.

Trini had to step in. She'd known that when she'd heard Katherine's panicked voice over the telephone. All she'd wanted to do since Jim had died was to be alone, and instead here she was about to volunteer to take care of two kids.

She heaved a sigh and straightened her back. "I don't blame you for being afraid. If Dottie can't stay with the two of you, I will. At least for tonight. Maybe you and Jake could stay with the Darbys after that."

The smile that had been about to light the delicate face faded away with disappointment.

Ashamed and embarrassed, Trini reached across for Katherine's hand. "I'm sorry. What I mean to say is I'll stay of course, if you'd like, for as long as you need."

The smile came then, showing small, even teeth and crinkling Katherine's eyes in genuine pleasure.

A glow ignited inside Trini's chest; she'd done the right thing.

"Thanks, Trini. Aunt Phyllis and Uncle Jay will be here in three days. They have to come from Nova Scotia."

"I didn't realize you had relatives in Canada."

She nodded. "I guess Jake and I will go there to live."

Trini squeezed her arm. "Don't worry about that now. When your aunt and uncle get here, you'll all decide together what to do. I'm just sorry about the break-in."

"Yeah. It was scary. And everything was an awful mess. Want to see?"

Katherine led her to the rolltop and lifted the lid. Crumpled papers, pens, clips, and a paperweight crammed the small interior. Evidently, Katherine had shoved everything back inside without regard to order. Trini lifted a few documents and examined them: receipts for bills, a ledger book, and scrap paper containing calculations, circles and arrows designating numbers and connections. Katherine opened the top drawer to reveal papers covered in Merle Woodson's spindly, exact script.

Trini reached in and thumbed through the stack. "Looks like these are just household items. Bills from the gas company. Here's a statement from the mercantile. Nothing particularly valuable."

"Not in here. He has another desk in his room."

"Was it searched, too?"

"No. I don't know why. Maybe the person was too afraid to look anymore. Or maybe they just took the money and left."

"Ten dollars is a lot of money to most people, but not enough to warrant breaking into a house, risk getting caught. Although, I would assume the person knew that your dad was gone, and that you two kids were alone."

"I know. And that's why I'm kind of scared." Katherine opened the bottom drawer on the left. "He always kept the ten dollars in this drawer. But it's gone."

The two of them kneeled down beside the open drawer and Trini flipped through papers. Under the stack was a small key. Trini picked it up.

"Is this to your post box?"

"No. Pa keeps that in the top drawer. I don't know what that's to."

"Maybe a safe deposit box. Did your dad have a safe deposit box at the bank?"

Katherine shrugged. "I don't know."

"Well, when your aunt and uncle get here they can sort that out."

She replaced the key and her fingers brushed the edge of a thick envelope imprinted with *First National Cattlemen's Bank* in bold script. Trini lifted it from the drawer. If Merle kept money in here, why wouldn't the burglar take it?

"Is there money in this bank envelope?"

"No. He kept my money in a little coin purse, and whoever it was took that along with the ten dollars. I don't know what that is. Open it."

"You sure?"

She nodded, her tufts bouncing. Trini lifted the unsealed flap, withdrew a sheaf of papers and scanned the contents. Her breath caught in her throat.

"What is it?" Katherine asked.

She didn't want to alarm Katherine, but on the other hand, she'd find out soon enough. "Did you know your house and land were mortgaged?"

"You mean like Pa owes money for it?"

"Yes."

"But he doesn't. He always bragged about how we owned the house free and clear. He even talked about how one of these days soon we'd buy some land near Bear Lake, build a cabin there so we could go up and fish. We own this house."

Trini grimaced with pity for the children. They would be given no adjustment for extenuating circumstances. The signature at the bottom of the papers read "Gilbert Hardy" in an aggressive black script. The note was due January 31, 1933, only a couple of months from now. No matter what the needs of the orphans, Hardy would demand his due from the estate. Another scheme of Merle Woodson's, this one gone awry?

"I'm sorry, Katherine. But according to these papers, and this is dated, let's see, about six months ago, your house is mortgaged. Wait a minute. It's more than just the house, evidently. I don't understand all these terms, something about unsecured loans." She read in silence for a minute, then raised her eyes to Katherine's. "I hate to tell you this, but it looks like your dad owes the bank about twenty thousand dollars."

Katherine dropped into the nearest chair. "But that's impossible." She looked at Trini and swollen tear drops traced a path on her pale cheeks.

"Oh, Katherine. I'm so sorry. Listen, as soon as your aunt and uncle get here, we'll sort this out. I'm sure it's not as bad as it sounds." Trini didn't like lying to her; she had every reason to suspect things would be even worse than they sounded. But saying that to Katherine wouldn't help anything.

Frown lines appeared on Katherine's forehead and she shifted her eyes to the window behind Trini. She rose from the chair, parted the curtain on the front window and squinted through the pane. "I saw something moving outside. What's—who is that?"

"Where?"

"Out there. Under the elm."

Trini joined her at the window and followed Katherine's line of sight to the front yard. A man stood resting his hand on the back of a small burro that was tethered to the giant tree trunk. Trini dropped the papers onto the desk and ran to the back door. Whoever it was better understand he would not prey on helpless children—not while she was here.

She pushed open the screen door and marched down the length of the porch. Katherine's footsteps echoed on the floor behind her. "Who is it?" Trini called.

Leaving the burro in its place, he stepped out of the shadows. The dim light of the late afternoon showed his scraggly features. What in the world was Lyle Butcher doing here?

He reminded Trini of a grizzly bear wearing stained buckskins, the fringe swaying as he walked toward her. His battered boots creased so that the toes pointed straight up. He clutched a leather hat in his hands, and Trini recoiled as he stopped in front of the porch; the stench of his body permeated the few feet between them. Stringy hair clung to his head, and his gray beard was tangled and streaked with tobacco juice. Even standing on a step, Trini had to look up to him.

She'd never talked to Lyle Butcher, but she'd seen him around town, on and off, since she could remember. He'd never caused trouble. As far as she knew, he kept to himself, but now she wondered if he was dangerous. He lived something like an old-time mountain man, complete with his burro. During the warm months, he was a common enough sight in town and the surrounding countryside, then he'd disappear, no doubt to a mountain den, for the winter. It was odd that he was here now, in the late fall, and just when the Woodson children had been left alone.

Trini felt the flint in her tone before she spoke. "What do you want, Mr. Butcher?"

"I need to talk to the girl about her pa," he rumbled. "He owed me." As he spoke, Trini glimpsed the black gaps between his teeth.

Katherine's voice shook as she spoke. "I don't know what you're talking about."

"Your pa owed me."

"Katherine just told you she doesn't know anything about it," Trini said. "We can't help you, Mr. Butcher."

He held his hat by its brim and his thick fingers, the nails outlined in black grime, molded and pressed the cracked leather. "Me and him, we had some business. And I knowed he kept records. I need to see them." His beard split in a crooked smile. "Yes, I can read."

"You're not going to see any records," Trini said. "And now you need to leave. Katherine doesn't know anything about her father's business. When her relatives arrive, they'll sort through all of the financial dealings. Meanwhile, the children will not be here alone."

"I just need to see them records. It won't hurt none for me to look."

"Mr. Butcher, I've half a mind to telephone the sheriff. Someone broke into the house in the middle of the night last week and searched through Merle's papers."

The caterpillar eyebrows shot upward. "You blamin' me for that?"

"I'm not sure, but right now I want you to get off the Woodson property. And please don't come back."

A hundred years ago he'd have been taken for a gold miner or fur trapper. Now, he looked, and smelled, like a madman, or at the very least, a dangerous misfit. Not even the hobos crossing the country in the railcars looking for work would want to claim him as one of their own.

He eyed her with a pair of shiny slits peering from their hairy lair. "You knowed who I am. You seen me around all your life, so don't act like I'm some kind of maniac roaming the countryside." Trini blushed that he'd guessed her characterization of him. "And I knowed you're Lucinda Fernandez's daughter."

She hadn't heard her mother's maiden name in decades. It took her a moment, in fact, to understand who he was talking about, and she fumbled through her thoughts.

The old bear nodded, his snarled beard bobbing against his chest. "You're surprised I knew your ma. Well, I did. Most beautiful woman in Colorado. You could match her, and that's sayin' somethin'. And she married Edwin Shannon." He shook his head in disbelief and sorrow. "I knowed he was your pa, but he weren't good enough for Lucinda. Your brother reminds me of him years ago, wild and stupid."

It was odd, to hear her parents discussed like this. Since they were both dead, she tended to hold their memory a bit more ideal than real. But how could a man like this have known her elegant mother?

Her confusion must have shown on her face because Butcher held up his hands in surrender and backed away. "All right. All right. I can see I upset you and the girl. Now listen. My business was with Merle Woodson. I ain't going to do no harm to no one, but when that estate's settled, I want my due."

"My mother's been dead for twenty years," Trini said. "When was the last time you saw her?"

A half smile showed through the tangled nest of his beard. His voice was soft when he spoke. "I ain't seen Lucinda since a long time 'fore she died. I just remember her like it was yesterday. But don't go worrying about that. I come here about the money Woodson owed me."

Her intuition told her as distasteful as he was, he was telling the truth. Trini almost laughed with the absurdity of Merle Woodson's manipulations. He'd been like the Al Capone of the Rockies: bootlegging, twenty thousand dollars in debt, and now a business connection with Lyle Butcher, of all people. Like Parn, Merle had lived a secret life. Trini still wanted to know about her mother and Butcher, but for now, she decided to get him away from the house as quickly as possible.

"I've told you, you'll have to take that up with Katherine's guardians," Trini said. "Nothing can be done now. You'd better leave."

He stared at her a minute. "I heard all this business about your brother murdering Woodson."

She felt like the breath had been squeezed out of her.

Butcher spoke again. "I don't believe it. He's stupid, but he ain't a killer."

Despite herself, she felt her resolve to make him leave soften. "What makes you say that? Do you know anything about

Merle's death?" She glanced at Katherine. She hated talking about Merle Woodson in front of his own daughter.

"I know more than you might give me credit for, but I don't know anything that'd help clear Lucinda's son, if that's what you're askin'. If I did, I'd say something. For her sake."

A cold wind pushed at them, and Trini wrapped her arms around herself. She needed her coat; it felt like snow.

"I'll just keep an eye out for them relatives," he said. "I'll come back after the funeral."

The buckskin fringes swayed as he turned and walked across the yard toward the elm, untied the burro's rein from the tree trunk and headed down the driveway. His sour odor clung to the air. Trini put her arm around Katherine's shoulders and turned back toward the house.

Butcher had denied entering the house, and Trini tended to believe him. He was intent on seeing Merle's records, but now that she'd talked to him, she didn't believe he was the kind of man to sneak through broken windows. His style would be to march up to the front door and bull through.

But then who did the break-in? Was it an itinerant traveler, a hobo who'd jumped from a boxcar as the Santa Fe train roared through town? Trini didn't think so. The invasion was too convenient in its timing and too ordered in the search; a vagrant would do more than shuffle through papers and take ten dollars in a coin purse. No.

There was only one man who would have reason to break in, and it wouldn't be to steal ten dollars. Sheriff George Mallis would have every reason in the world to want to search Woodson's papers. Maybe Merle knew his life was in danger from Mallis. Maybe as he begged for his life, he told Mallis he'd never get away with murder because he'd kept records of the extortion attempts. Mallis could have killed Woodson, then come to the house to search for the incriminating evidence.

Trini led Katherine back into the kitchen. She could call Denver, try to get through to the marshal's office to request someone be sent to Ludlin to listen to her case against Mallis, such that it was. But she needed more.

Could she prove he'd murdered Woodson? For right now, all she could allege was that Parn, Woodson and Mallis had all been bootleggers with some vague tie between them, and that Mallis had been in a mad rush to throw Parn in jail. Not much in the way of incriminating evidence. And it was four o'clock, probably too late in the day to talk to anyone with authority in the marshal's office. She'd wait until tomorrow morning to call.

Katherine removed an iron skillet from the rack above the stove to prepare dinner, and Trini, her chin in her hand, sat at the oak table piled with the food gifts and thought. Merle worked with Dottie Kerr at the land claims office. Because they were close, at least rumored to be close, maybe Merle had confided his financial situation to her. Dottie might know something about Merle's massive debt or Butcher's wild claims. Also, she wanted to talk to Dottie and find out why she'd left the Woodson children alone. She visualized her plans for the evening falling into order.

"Katherine, don't start dinner. I'm going to take you and Jake into town with me and drop you by the café to eat. I don't want the two of you here alone, and Margie Snowfeather would love to have you there. I want to go to my house and get a few things I'll need while I stay here, and I have some other things to do. I'll pick you up at the café later, and then we'll come back here for the night. How does that sound?"

Katherine nodded and smiled, already heading toward the parlor to fetch Jake. They returned to the kitchen, and Trini gathered her coat and purse while Katherine readied Jake to leave. While his sister buttoned him up, he picked up a stuffed bear from the table, hugged it to his chest and laughed.

"He's laughing because he loves to go places," Katherine said. "Don't you, Jake? We'll have fun." She turned her back to him, pulled her coat on one arm and twisted her other arm behind to find the coat sleeve.

Jake's arm shot out and he shoved her forward. Katherine stumbled and fell across the kitchen table, clattering the sugar bowl onto the floor and thrusting the layer cake precariously close to the edge. Jake screamed with delight.

Trini righted the cake and grabbed his arm. "Jake!" she shouted. "Don't do that."

He lowered his gaze to the floor. Katherine stood, brushing sugar from her knees and hands and adjusting her clothes. "He doesn't mean it, Trini. He thinks he's playing."

"He's too big to play like that anymore. He needs to stop." Trini glared at Jake, but his eyes darted away in confusion.

Katherine retrieved the sugar bowl and swept up the crystals with her hand. "I know. I know. I've been working on it with him. And Pa didn't help. They'd get to wrestling."

She set the bowl on the table. Taking his arm from Trini's grasp, Katherine turned him to face her, and pointed a finger in his face. "No."

His impish grin turned down, and the bottom of his eyes reddened.

"Understand, Jake? Don't push."

He lowered his head and stared at his shoes.

"See, this always happens," Katherine said. "He just doesn't know how to take it."

Jake peered at them both below the bill of his plaid hat. The earflaps jutted outward above his ears. Clutching the teddy bear against his chest, he turned back and forth to rock it.

"Side," he muttered.

"What does that mean?" Trini asked.

"He wants to go outside." Katherine turned to him and

adjusted his collar. "Okay, Jakey. We'll go outside."

He beamed at his sister, then cast his smile of well-being on Trini.

He was mentally only about five, Trini reminded herself, and he appeared to be a sweet boy. But Good Lord, Jake had the strength of a full-grown man. Trini didn't know how the aunt and uncle would deal with a boy like that. She hoped he wouldn't wind up in some sort of asylum.

Trini ushered the children out the door and closed it tight behind her. Katherine locked it. They climbed in the truck sitting Jake in the middle. Trini pulled away from the house scanning the yard for any sign of Butcher, but he was gone.

She had two stops to make after she dropped off the children at the café. The first would be to Dottie Kerr's house.

And the second would be to Roy's.

She at least had to try to apologize to him. She hoped he'd forgive her, because she also knew she needed his help to get a marshal here quickly. It would take her a day to work through the layers of bureaucracy; Roy would at least be able to use his title—rather his former title, as deputy—to make that first call for her. And she wanted to tell him what Katherine had said about Merle feeling like Mallis was in his pants pocket. And much as she dreaded seeing him, she was also aware of the excited tumble of her stomach.

The truck rolled and lurched down the half mile of the Woodsons' dirt driveway that led to the blacktop. Steep curves took it through several stands of pine and birch and forked around a huge oak. Trini glanced at a small rocky meadow to her left, now brown and sleeping for winter, that in spring must burst with wildflowers. When they reached the blacktop, she turned right and headed toward Ludlin.

She tightened her grip on the steering wheel and pushed the accelerator to the floor. Glancing at the children next to her, she let up quickly. Her surge of aggression harnessed, she examined her feelings. Since Parn had been arrested, she'd felt victimized by Mallis, but power and strength coursed through her now. Mallis had somehow inserted himself into Merle Woodson's life, probably to gain control of the rich bootlegging territory. She didn't know the particulars, but she intended to find out. George Mallis had just met his match.

CHAPTER SEVEN

After leaving the children at the café in town, Trini drove the few blocks to the Kerrs' manicured property. She stopped in front and examined the bare elms and a towering walnut tree guarding the walk that led to the white clapboard house. A hedge of thick evergreens bordered the front porch. Several yards to the side of the house stood a three-sided shed that housed their black Buick sedan, a table power saw, rakes and hoes, a wheelbarrow and a pegboard hung with tools. She climbed the porch steps and knocked with the bronze horseshoe. The door opened, and a towering man with hard muscles forged from manual labor stood before her.

"Hi, Daryl. I was hoping to see Dottie. Is she here?"

Dottie's son stared at her through two summer-blue eyes set wide apart above well-defined cheekbones. Trini noted the shadow of a dark beard. A lock of blue-black curly hair rested on his forehead, and his full lips frowned. He shook his head as if to make sense of it all. Evidently, she thought, I'm the last person he expected to see at his door.

"Yeah, sure," he said. "Sure. Come on in."

Trini cringed at the soprano scratch of his voice, like a pre-pubescent boy with a case of laryngitis. His voice had been permanently damaged by his abusive father who, on Daryl's tenth birthday, had slammed a baseball bat into his throat, then disappeared forever. She'd gone to school with Daryl, they were the same age, and she'd always more or less pitied him. But since adulthood, she seldom had occasion to talk to him; the strained croak-like voice startled her.

He held the door open, and Trini scooted past his mountain-like chest. Once inside, the odor of fried onions and cabbage burrowed into her nose.

"I'll get Mom. Just a second," he said.

The floorboards creaked under the weight of his bare footfalls, and she watched the pack of muscles move under his T-shirt as he walked away.

Someone had turned on one of the table lamps, but much of the room was left in shadow. A soft fire burned in the fireplace, lending the room a cozy, homey appearance, but as Trini surveyed the area, she realized the hominess blurred into squalor. Newspapers littered the floor and tabletops. A stack of dirty dishes, the top one smeared with the leftovers of a berry pie, balanced precariously on the coffee table. Daryl's work boots, though clean and newly polished, lay in front of a rocking chair, and he'd tossed a wadded ball of dirty socks under the side table.

She walked to the fireplace and stood with her back to the warmth. Dottie, wiping her hands on a dish towel, bustled through the kitchen doorway. She wore a cherry-patterned apron over a faded housedress and blue house slippers that made a soft flipping sound as she moved. A few wiry wisps surrounded her drawn face in a gray semi-halo, and she met Trini with a frazzled smile.

"Oh, Trini. I imagine you're here about the Woodson kids."

"Yes, I did want to talk to you about them," Trini said. "How are you, Dottie?"

"Oh, I'm tolerable, I suppose. Land sakes, I've been busy at the land claims office, though, what with Merle gone. He'll leave a big hole. Sakes alive, he will." She choked a little on the last word and occupied herself with folding the dish towel.

Daryl sat in a frayed brown rocker, crossed his long, knobby feet at the ankles and dangled large, loose hands over the ends of the chair arms. His whisper-squeak broke the silence. "What brings you out this afternoon, Trini?"

"I had something I wanted to ask Dottie about."

Trini smiled and turned her attention to the woman next to her. Dottie gave a nervous twitter as she glanced at Daryl. "I know it's about those children. But you see, Trini," she paused and cleared her throat, "well I had to get back here all of a sudden last night, you know, and I didn't have time really to call anyone. And I knew the children would be all right by themselves because you know, Merle left them alone before . . ." she twittered again, ". . . many times. Before he was . . . he died."

Trini surveyed Dottie's face. She certainly didn't look sick, and Daryl looked strong and healthy. "I hoped it wasn't an emergency. I mean the reason you had to get home quickly. I hope everything was all right."

Dottie blinked, and the movement gave her large eyes, the same blue as her son's, the appearance of startled confusion like an animal caught in headlights. Silence stood between them.

Surely she could expect more from Dottie than this mute wall. Her nervousness was disquieting. Maybe Dottie felt Trini was bullying her. "I didn't come here to scold you, Dottie," Trini said. "And the children are fine. I'll be staying there now until the aunt and uncle get here. But I was a little worried about you. I know you wouldn't have left them unless you felt like you really had to."

Dottie nodded and the gray wisps floated with her head. "Yes, yes, of course. I just had to get back here. But I knew the children would be fine." She glanced around the room as if wondering what to do with her guest.

Evidently, Dottie was not about to disclose her reason for

leaving the children. But why was she so upset? Did talking about Merle cause her pain? Dottie had always been high-strung. Maybe if Trini helped her to feel more comfortable, she'd relax and open up.

"Could we just sit down a minute?" Trini asked.

Dottie gestured to the faded floral sofa. "Oh, of course, dear. Over here."

The spring on Daryl's chair squeaked as he swiveled to follow their movements. They settled, Dottie grasping the dish towel on her lap.

Trini kept her voice tone even. She didn't want to come across as desperate for information or too serious. For some reason, Dottie was already skittish. "I wanted to ask you, Dottie. Did Merle say anything to you about his bootlegging? Did he mention it?"

Daryl snorted. "Everyone knows he and your brother been runnin' liquor for years."

Trini's first instinct was to defend Parn, but she kept silent. She wanted to get answers to her questions, then leave. Making excuses for Parn's behavior would not help her do that.

"I'm not trying to pry," Trini said, "so please don't think I mean anything bad against Merle. I'm concerned with Sheriff Mallis. Did Merle ever say anything to you, Dottie, about Mallis pressuring him about the bootlegging or," the thought occurred to her, "having to borrow money to get Mallis off his back?"

Dottie clamped her teeth on her lower lip and threw a glance at Daryl. "You know, Trini." Dottie stopped and cleared her throat. "You know, he didn't talk to me about that."

"Mallis?" snapped Daryl. "What're you asking about him for?"

Trini shifted her eyes to him. She wished she'd waited to talk to Dottie at her work, away from Daryl. Dottie might be nervous talking about her reputed lover in front of her son. Too late now, and Daryl was obviously intent on being a part of the conversation. Trini sharpened her voice the slightest bit when she spoke to him. "I asked about Mallis because of a few things Katherine said, Daryl."

She debated with herself for a moment. Should she say more to the Kerrs? She didn't want to spread her suspicions about Mallis too widely. She'd already alienated the sheriff; it wouldn't help if he heard that she was going around town asking questions about him. On the other hand, Dottie and Merle Woodson had been coworkers as well as close friends, maybe more; if anyone would be privy to Merle's business dealings, it would be Dottie. And Trini wanted information more than she feared retribution from Mallis. She decided to state her suspicions, at least part of them. "I have a feeling Mallis was forcing Merle to pay him a lot of money, possibly to allow the bootlegging to continue."

Daryl nodded as if she'd confirmed his own suspicions. "Wouldn't surprise me one bit," he rasped. "You think it's tied in with Merle's death?"

The knot in her stomach tightened. She didn't want to go so far as to reveal her suspicions that Mallis murdered Woodson and was trying to pin it on Parn. Her innate caution told her to stick to the subject of bootlegging. She focused on Dottie. "I just wanted to know if Merle said anything to you about the bootlegging or feeling pressure from Mallis."

"You didn't answer my question," Daryl said. He smiled at her, but not with his eyes. "You wouldn't give a hoot about what Mallis had been doing to Woodson if you didn't think it was tied in to his death, would you? 'Cause if all that could be tied into Woodson being killed, then you're thinkin' that might be just the thing to get Parn off the hook. By the way, I'd heard you found Woodson by dowsing. What'd ole George Mallis think of that?"

Trini took a deep breath as unobtrusively as possible and let it out. So much for trying to get the information she wanted. She had to either drop the entire thing and leave now, or answer Daryl. Dottie sat silent, twisting the dish towel. Daryl, serene and smiling, waited. Trini decided to dive in.

"I think Mallis was surprised when I found Woodson, but to answer your question, yes, I do think that Woodson's death and Mallis's involvement with the bootlegging are connected. I just don't know how deep that involvement went, or what form it took. But I intend to find out. Because you're right, that information may be the key to free my brother. I just . . . I just don't think it's a good idea for me to be waving my theories in Mallis's face."

She held back from telling Daryl to keep this conversation to themselves. She didn't need Mallis knowing about her speculations, but it would be rude to come right out and tell Daryl to keep his mouth shut. He obviously didn't like Mallis anyway, so she doubted he'd say anything about her visit. She was heartened to see him smile and nod.

He looked at his mother. "So, Ma, answer the lady's question. Woodson ever talk to you about Mallis being involved with that bootlegging business?"

Dottie gave him one of her wide-eyed blinks.

"What's the matter, Ma?" he asked. "Cat got your tongue?" He grinned and winked at Trini.

He's laughing at her, thought Trini, at Dottie's expense. And, Trini guessed, this happened quite frequently. Dottie's fluttering and wringing of the towel had increased to uncomfortable proportions.

"Well," Dottie said. "I . . ." she glanced at Daryl. "No. Merle never said nothing to me." Dottie jumped up from her seat. "I really need to get dinner started, dear. I don't mean to rush you, but I've got the onions done and my roast will be black if I don't get to it. I'm terribly sorry, but I really can't help you."

Dottie had to know something. She just had to. "But I figured since you and Merle worked together, I mean you were together for so many years, that he'd at least mention something to you." The desperation in her voice was evident, even to herself, but she didn't care. She needed information if she had any hope at all of helping her brother.

Dottie straightened her back, reaffirming her position. "I'm sorry. I can't help you."

Awkward silence hung in the air, thick as the odor of fried onions from the kitchen. Trini's buoyant mood that she'd worn when she arrived shriveled with disappointment.

"Trini might want to stay for dinner." Daryl tilted his head and smiled at Trini, the quintessential Western host.

"No, no thanks," she said. "I have to go. It's getting late."

Suddenly the thought of being here one more minute, one more second, was beyond her. She had to get away from Dottie, her jittery hands and darting eyes. Why Dottie was so upset and nervous, she had no idea. Maybe because she felt guilty about leaving the Woodson children. Maybe because she didn't like talking about Merle in front of Daryl. Or maybe because her son intimidated her, made her feel silly. Whatever the case, this would not be the end of it. She'd talk to Dottie again tomorrow at work. Away from Daryl.

She stood and crossed to the front door, and Daryl stood up from the rocker and followed her. She stopped at a table in a dark corner near the doorway. She hadn't seen it when she entered the house, but now she examined its surface. Stacks of *Picturegoer* magazines covered the tabletop, their covers graced by Barbara Stanwyck, Greta Garbo, Claudette Colbert and others that Trini didn't know. There must be at least fifty or sixty magazines.

She looked at Dottie who stood near the sofa. "I didn't know you were interested in movie stars."

"Oh," Daryl said. He rested his hand lightly on a stack. "No. Those are mine."

Daryl? A preposterous vision flashed before her: brawny, strapping Daryl Kerr with his child-voice, sitting in the frayed brown rocker with a movie magazine resting on his tree-trunk thighs, flipping through pictures of movie stars. A rude laugh stuck in her throat. Shame on her. Poor man. Maybe that's all he had in his life, but she bit her lip to keep a smile from her face. "Oh," she said. "How nice."

"I'm an official subscriber." His eyes shone with pride. "I get my magazines once a month through the mail. My favorite is Greta Garbo." He lifted the magazine with the star's photograph on the cover. "I'd love to meet her some day. You know, they say Hollywood, California, is the hub of the stars now. Everything is moving there. I'd love to go out there, meet the stars, maybe work in one of the studios."

Trini finally let her smile overtake her, but was careful to keep her voice soft with interest. "I had no idea you liked moving pictures, Daryl. Do you get to see many?"

He lifted his massive shoulders in a shrug. "I go to Pueblo whenever they change the feature. I was going to be an actor, but when they came out with the talkies, I knew they'd never take me on account of my voice."

Trini didn't detect any self-pity, just a statement of fact.

"Well. I really need to be going," she said.

She turned, gripped the doorknob and tugged a few times. The door was stuck. Daryl's hand reached in front of her. The muscles of his forearm flexed under a shadow of black hair, and she watched his giant fingers smother her own. He lifted her hand, set it carefully at her side, grasped the knob and turned. The door swung toward them on silent hinges.

She looked up, into his watchful blue eyes. "Thanks," she said.

Clamoring down the porch steps, she looked to the west. The sight of the umber prairie under a purple sky lifted her spirits, and she breathed in the cold night air.

"Drive careful."

Daryl's gravelly farewell caught her off guard. She turned to see him silhouetted on the front porch, Dottie standing in the house behind the screen door outlined by the dim light behind her.

Chapter Eight

Even as she drove through the empty grassland, a drive that would usually soothe her raw emotions, the unsettled feeling left from the Kerr visit festered. It was understandable that Dottie catered to her son; she'd been at the mercy of physical abuse for years and had seen her child suffer permanent damage. The guilt she must feel for being unable to protect her son from a brutal father had to be oppressive. And as for Daryl, Trini had a feeling that the teasing masked a smoldering rage at his mother. The relationship was awkward to witness, at best.

Trini swept her eyes across the dusky expanse of plain. What she needed was space and time alone. She'd like to just stake herself out in the grassland, without problems or interference, and let the wind and openness heal her for a while. But she knew she could not. She had obligations. People were depending on her.

And now, she had a difficult task before her. She had to convince Roy to help her call in a marshal, and she wanted to tell him what Katherine had said about her father feeling like Mallis was deep in his pockets. Trini didn't know what kind of reception she'd get from the man who got fired on her account, but she had to try. For Parn's sake.

She turned into the dirt road that led up to Roy Eastman's property and pulled to a stop in front of the white farmhouse Roy had inherited when his father died. A light glowed from one of its downstairs windows. A sprawling brown barn with open doors stood about fifty yards behind the house. In an attached corral, Roy worked a large dappled gray on a lead. She climbed from her truck, walked over to the fence, rested her arms on the wooden slats and watched him guide the animal. When he reversed the horse, he caught sight of her and waved. He led it back into the barn, and a few minutes later, strode through the open doors.

His long-legged stride didn't hesitate as he approached, but Trini couldn't decipher his expression under the Stetson. When he reached her, he touched his finger to the brim. His lips compressed in a non-committal line, and the dimple remained hidden.

He greeted her with a nod and her name.

Her mind froze. She'd intended to talk business: tell him about Katherine's remarks, convince him to call Denver on her behalf. But now guilt charged through her; she'd caused him to lose his job. In this day and age, that was no small matter. And beneath the frozen shame, another emotion brewed, a surprising pang of regret—regret for what might have been between them, despite her vow to keep her life uncomplicated.

He stared at her, and just like it had in the sheriff's office, she became aware of Roy's presence and the amount of space it took; even the outdoors wasn't big enough to hold him.

She fumbled through her thoughts, then her words. "I . . . I wanted to see you. And I hope you'll talk to me, at least for a minute."

The dimple flashed. "Of course I'm going to talk to you. You honestly thought I wouldn't?"

"Well, not talk to me, exactly, but take some time with me. I mean . . ." Her words trailed away like those of a clumsy fourteen-year-old girl.

He held her with the steady gray stare a minute, then hung the looped rope on the corral post next to him. He pushed his hat up with a finger. "Look, Trini. I don't want to get into a big thing about today. It happened. I'm not going to waste time in regrets or blame."

Relief ran through her. He didn't hate her, thank God. He didn't hate her. "I'm glad to hear it."

His mouth slanted in a lop-sided smile, and the dimple stayed. "Is that why you came out here? To make sure everything was okay?"

"Yes, and I was hoping I could talk to you some more. About Parn."

She saw something move over his face, maybe anger. It made her talk fast to explain. "All I need is a name, Roy. Just a marshal to ask for when I call Denver, to get some help down here. Or if you could telephone for me." She cringed at her own brazenness. "And I wanted to tell you some things Katherine said."

He stared at her a moment, then grinned. "You're worse than a hound on a trail, aren't you? I remember Jim told me once, when you bit into something, you held on like a she-wolf."

She smiled and relaxed her shoulders. "He used to tell me I was like a pequin pepper—small but deadly."

He smiled back for a moment then sobered. "I don't know, Trini. This is the messiest business I've seen in a long time. I just wonder if . . ." He stopped and stared out to the horizon.

"What? Parn's life is in danger, you know that. You have to know that."

He took off the hat, ran a dirty hand through his hair and exhaled a mighty sigh. A brisk wind kicked in and swirled Trini's hair around her head. He studied her as she smoothed it back off her face and turned away from the blow.

"You want to come inside for a minute?" he said. "It's warmer in the house."

Without waiting for an answer, he turned and walked across the yard. She followed through the dust his boots kicked up.

When he got to the door, he held it open for her, leaning in, so that she had to brush her shoulder across his chest as she entered the glowing kitchen.

"Have a seat." He gestured to the pine table and chairs. "I'm going to wash up." He walked through a doorway into a dark room Trini assumed was the parlor.

Something similar to stew, but filled with some spice she couldn't identify, gave the room a foreign smell. Knotty golden pine covered the walls and cabinets, and a wooden bowl brimming with apples took the center of the oak table. Red-and-yellow print curtains framed a window above the sink, the only feminine accent in an otherwise masculine room. Copper pans, some polished to gleaming, hung from an iron ceiling rack. The electric light on the counter glowed through its red shade, and a tea kettle simmered on top of the gas range beside the large stewpot. The aroma made her stomach turn with hunger.

She heard his footsteps, and Roy entered the room buttoning a soft and faded flannel shirt. His hair looked damp, like he'd run clean, still-wet hands through the silver mass. He carried with him the piney odor that she'd smelled yesterday. Had it only been a day? It seemed like a lifetime.

"Is the kitchen different from what you thought?" he asked.

"Yes, yes it is different. I thought, I don't know, you being a bachelor and all . . ."

"You thought I'd be cooking in front of a campfire, maybe?" The dimple played on his cheek.

"Is the kitchen like your dad left it? Your mother died when you were little, didn't she?"

"Yeah. I was ten."

"Me, too. That's when my mother died."

"I knew that. I remember your mother. I remember my dad talking about your mother, how beautiful she was."

"Funny you should say that. You're the second person today

to mention my mother."

He turned from her and walked toward a closed door beside the stove. He spoke with his back to her. "Have you ever had wine?"

"No."

"Let me get you some. I think you'll like it."

He entered the pantry and returned with a dark bottle. Dried red wax covered the top and its drips stopped above the white label. He set it on the counter, opened a drawer, and took out a tool like an ice pick only twisted. From the cabinet above him, he withdrew two squat glasses. "I got these in France."

"Is the wine French? I don't recognize one word on the label."

He nodded. "I sent home fifty cases for my folks to keep when I was still in France. Before Prohibition set in. They only drank a few bottles. Just at Christmas."

"So it's still good? After all this time?"

"Yeah. By some standards, it's still young." He scored the top of the red wax with the sharp point of the tool, then peeled it off.

"Is that called a corkscrew?"

He darted his eyes at her, warm and intent, and smiled with the dimple. "Yeah. A corkscrew."

She watched as he jammed its tip into the circle of cork that plugged the opening. Gripping the wood handle, he twisted it and pulled. A small *pop* sounded and a cylinder of cork stained red on the bottom emerged. He poured a dark red liquid into the small glasses, and the ruby color twinkled through the facets. Suddenly, she felt a surge of hope at the promise of newness, and the thought, "Life after Jim," flitted through her mind. Her stomach did a small involuntary turn of excitement. Or was it guilt? She was supposed to be still grieving, wasn't she? And, she reminded herself, she didn't want any complications in her life.

But when she spoke, her voice came out low and husky, ignoring the reminder. "I remember now you were a soldier. Jim wanted to go overseas, but they kept him here. New York. How long after the war ended did you stay there?"

"About five years. I came home in '23. After my wife died."

She stopped with her hand in midair, ready to reach for the glass he extended to her. His wife? Roy had been married? Jim had never mentioned it. Had he known? Maybe Roy had kept it a secret. But why would he? She'd almost blurted her questions when he raised his glass and spoke.

"Cheers."

They clinked glasses and she watched him sip. She put the rim to her mouth and tasted. Not sharp, exactly, certainly not like the whiskey she'd tasted when she and Jim shared a glass. Smoother and better. It didn't taste like food, but it didn't taste like liquor, either. Something in between. She examined the liquid as she licked her lips. She lifted her eyes to find Roy watching her, smiling.

"It's good," she said.

"Glad you like it." He took another sip from his own glass keeping his eyes on hers.

She drank again, feeling warmth spread through her chest. "I didn't know you'd been married before."

"Yeah. Five years."

"Was she French?"

"Yeah. Let's sit down. I've got some stew with wine sauce on. You can have some if you'd like."

They took their glasses and sat down at the table. She wanted to ask him more. What his wife was like. How she had died.

Did he think he could love again.

But she didn't. He had changed the subject, asked her about staying for dinner. Maybe he didn't want to talk about his personal life. The last twenty-four hours had seen a lot pass between them, but, she reminded herself, she really didn't know him that well.

She suddenly felt nervous, like she was a stranger invited in for the sake of politeness. "I . . . I should be getting back to pick up Katherine and Jake."

She told him of her plans to stay at the Woodsons', the break-in a few days ago, and Lyle Butcher's visit.

"Butcher, huh? That's strange," he said.

"Yes. I suspect Merle Woodson had many strange things going on in his life. And I wonder if they're connected to his death and ultimately, to Parn."

He got up and walked over to the stewpot, lifted the lid and stirred. A burst of fragrance filled the room. The heady aroma combined with the wine and the sight of Roy's broad back made her world spin. She needed to leave . . . to get answers to her questions, then leave, but her words seemed to have their own purpose.

"The stew smells wonderful. I would like to stay."

He smiled as he walked toward her. He stopped in front of her, and she tilted her head back to gaze up at him. She felt his grip on her arm as he helped her to stand. A slight shadow of a dark beard covered his defined jaw, and his lips parted a little. She raised her eyes to the deep gray pools and felt like she was diving in. A word came to her: complicated. A complicated man. He leaned toward her and covered her mouth with his, warm and soft. In her lower stomach, a tickle set in, deep and delicious.

It was a long kiss. His lips moved over hers . . . taking her measure, studying her, feeling her mouth with his own as if he was opening the wings of an exotic butterfly, peering into the middle to examine how it was made. She rested her palm on his chest, on the soft flannel covering the hard muscle. Trini breathed in his fresh scent and heard his breath as it intensified along with the kiss. She wanted to sink into this man, this moment. Finally, he drew away and looked down at her, then kissed the tip of her nose.

"You probably won't believe this," he said, "but I've been wanting to do that for a long time."

She smiled a little. "I might believe it."

He smiled back and lowered his mouth to hers again. The tickle grew more insistent. She'd better stop. Much more and this would get serious. Very serious. She pulled back a little and he broke off. He held her by her shoulders and examined her face, then smiled.

"Okay. But I'm glad. I'm glad we did that."

"Me, too." She sank down into the chair, her thighs suddenly weak and wobbly. He sat facing her, his jeans-clad legs spread wide and her knees between them. He held one of her hands in his own, rubbed his thumb across the back and looked at her. The dimple was deep.

"I just didn't expect it, I guess," she said. "I liked it, but I didn't expect it."

"Yeah," he said. He smiled wider.

"I didn't come here expecting anything like that. I just wanted to talk to you about earlier today."

He leaned back in the chair and stroked the back of her hand again.

"Well," he said, "today, other than right now, was not a hallmark day for me."

"Oh, Roy, I feel so terrible about all this. And so guilty. I feel like I got you fired."

"Look darlin', you didn't make me do anything. I made my own choice. I knew something would have to give way with Mallis and me, sooner or later."

"I can see why. I don't know how you stood it as long as you did."

They were silent a moment. Roy sipped from his glass then held it with one hand, stared into the ruby fluid lost in thought. A realization came to her: She loved the feeling of being a companion. The feeling of being a part of someone's life. It dawned on her that this was what she missed the most since Jim died. Having a family. Being a part of a family. All she had left was Parn. And Parn was in trouble.

"Roy, I'm so worried. About Parn."

He set the glass on the table, squeezed her hand briefly, then rose and walked back to the stove. He turned off the gas and tilted the lid on the stew.

"Aren't you?" she asked. "Worried? That Mallis may harm an innocent man?"

He turned to look at her and leaned against the counter, then ran his hand through his silver mane.

"Well, now, you got me there, Trin."

"What do you mean?"

"I mean that I'm not sure which one is worse, Mallis or Parn."

She almost gasped aloud. "You can't mean that."

"I'm not saying Parn's as ruthless as Mallis, but, well, I gotta tell you, Trin, bootlegging is lethal business. Those fellows in Denver don't play around, and Parn and Woodson were right in the middle of it."

"I know. I know. But that still doesn't change anything. Parn didn't kill Merle Woodson. He just didn't."

He sighed, walked to the table and lifted his glass, dumped the contents into his mouth. He set the glass down and looked at her. "You're probably right. Or if he had anything to do with it at all, it was an accident." He turned, walked back to the counter and stood with his arms folded across his chest.

She felt her neck and face grow hot with a flash of anger. "I don't think so," she said. "He would have told me. And there was something else, something from the past that he tried to tell

96

me when I saw him yesterday, then couldn't because Mallis walked in. Evidently he knows Mallis from a long time ago. That might have something to do with all this."

His voice was flat when he spoke. "So you think Mallis is trying to frame Parn because of something that happened in the past?"

"I do. And Parn's worried that Mallis might arrange for an accident there in the jail. Something that would give Mallis a means to hurt or even kill Parn. And now with you gone, I'm worried, too."

He stared at her a minute then shook his head. "No," he said. "No, that's crazy talk, Trini. Look, I know Mallis has got it in for Parn for some reason or another, and maybe it does have something to do with the past. But Mallis is a charging bull, not a killer. He's not going to murder Parn in the jail or anywhere else."

"How can you say that?"

"I'm not going to jump to conclusions here. And Parn has made his own bed. He's been in over his head with the bad guys for a long time. And I have to tell you—I'm bothered about the hammer."

"Mallis could have planted that."

"I was there, Trin. We found it together."

"He could have gone up to Parn's earlier. Or when you went there with him, you weren't with him every second, were you? He could have put it in the woodpile while you weren't looking."

"Complete with blood and hair on the peen? I don't think so."

She stood up and found herself walking toward him, her hands clenched at her sides.

"But you surely can't believe Parn is a murderer."

"I don't know what he is, Trin. But I think a judge needs to hear it all. Hell, Doc Cockrell hasn't even seen the body yet. We found out this morning he won't get back from Pueblo until tomorrow. You're jumping to a lot of conclusions."

"So you won't help me."

"Whoa, now. I never said that. I want to help you."

"Then get Parn out of Mallis's reach. Get him away from that awful man."

He held his hands in front of him and spread his fingers, like he was pushing down on her rising dread. "All right. All right. Now just don't panic. Let me feel out the situation with Mallis. He'll talk to me once he has a chance to simmer down. Then when the doc gets back, I can talk to him."

"And meanwhile?"

"What meanwhile?"

"Meanwhile Parn is there in that jail, alone with Mallis."

He ran his hand through his hair again. "Trini, you make it sound like Mallis is going to go in there and slit the kid's throat. I think you're imagining things. Mallis is not going to do anything like that. Taggert's there. We're in the middle of town, for God's sake."

"Accidents happen all the time, Roy. And Mallis is a hateful man. I think he killed Merle Woodson himself and is framing Parn for it."

"Now wait a minute, Trini—"

"For the bootlegging. One thing Parn did tell me: Did you know Mallis was a bootlegger in Denver before he came here?"

He gave a short laugh. "I'd heard that. Bootlegger turned sheriff. The world has gone nuts. But that doesn't mean he'd kill to run liquor again."

"And another thing. The break-in at Woodson's I told you about? I think Mallis did it."

"Why?"

"Katherine said Merle made some comments about Mallis

being in his pants pocket. And Merle is in debt for over twenty thousand dollars. Mallis may have been extorting money from him. Woodson could have kept records about that. Records that would implicate Mallis. Mallis would want to recover those records, and he would break in the house to do it."

"You seem to know a lot about Merle Woodson's financial affairs."

"I told you, I'm staying there. Katherine needed someone to talk to, help her sort through her father's business. We discovered all of this together. I'm not just searching through Woodson's papers because I feel like it."

His voice was gentle when he spoke. "I know you're not, Trini. You'd never do something like that. But you're assuming because Woodson had all these financial problems that Mallis was extorting money from him. And then what? Mallis didn't get enough money, or he wanted all of the bootlegging route, so he killed Woodson and framed Parn for a past wrong? That's a very intricate plot."

"But Mallis has been absolutely driven to pin Woodson's murder on Parn, right from the beginning. And you said yourself he didn't like Parn."

"He doesn't. But look. I'm not saying Mallis isn't a bad guy. I know more than anyone how much control he has in this county. But there's a difference between being a bad guy and blackmailing someone, murdering him and then framing an innocent man for it."

She stared at him. She couldn't believe Roy didn't see the flow of events, couldn't see how Mallis had evidently manipulated everything. "Roy, listen. Parn and Mallis have some kind of history that Mallis wants revenge for. He also wants the bootlegging territory. He kills Woodson, frames Parn for the murder, and he's killed two birds with one stone, so to speak. It's so clear, Roy."

"Clear except that there's no proof to what you're saying."

"You can't deny that with Merle dead and Parn in jail, things are perfect for George Mallis." She visualized her brother alone in his cell, only a few feet away from the sheriff. Trini swallowed back tears, but her voice shook. "And Parn is at his mercy in that jail cell."

He placed his hands on her shoulders. "Please, Trini. We'll work through this. I promise. And nothing will happen to Parn. I promise that, too."

She glanced around the warm kitchen, now grown cold to her.

So. He'll watch over Parn. How? Her emotions churned. Disappointment in Roy. Fear for her brother's life. And underneath the thunder, remorse, pointed and centered, that there would not be another kiss.

She turned away from him, crossed to the table and returned the chair to its place. "Well. I appreciate anything you can do, Roy." She wanted to say more, but she didn't know what it would be. She started toward the door.

"Trini . . ."

"I've got to go now. Thanks for the wine."

The door clicked closed behind her.

CHAPTER NINE

The headlights acted as a shortsighted beacon as Trini's truck surged across the flatlands. As she drove, she leaned out the window for a moment, examining the sky for stars. None. She was alone in a dark universe. The cold night air and the black prairie magnified her twisting emotions.

Her disappointment with Roy gnawed at her. Yesterday in the office when he'd ignored Mallis's sharp commands, she suspected he was a coward, that he used logic and deductions to avoid action. One thing for sure, Trini would never allow herself to get close to him again. A sudden sensation assaulted her of Roy's hard arms and soft mouth, the sweetness of those few moments, but she slapped down the memory and scolded herself. She should be happy—happy she discovered his character before she let herself get emotionally involved.

Passing the mercantile as she drove through town, she glanced into the night-lit window. Jefferson had closed shop, exactly at five, as usual, and even the upstairs room where he'd stayed since he moved out of his house was dark. He must be away for the evening. She'd been hoping to talk to him tonight. She wanted to know if the banker, Gilbert Hardy, had garnered any information about Mallis. She'd have to wait until tomorrow. Right now, she'd pick up Katherine and Jake at the café. Matter of fact, she was hungry herself. A plate of Margie Snowfeather's pot roast would taste wonderful. A remembered aroma floated through her mind of Roy's exotic stew and the few tastes of promising wine. Unusual. Unusual and complicated. Just like the man himself.

Stop it, she chided herself. Stop thinking and fantasizing about him.

But even though Trini slammed an iron door on her thoughts, she couldn't lie to herself: A deep attraction for Roy lived under her anger. Well, too bad. She simply would not allow herself to dive that far down. After all, she was a dowser. She knew all about depth and hidden energy and secret sources. She could control her emotions, her clamoring thoughts, and God help her, she would.

A square of light beamed through the café window; she parked in front of it, got out of the truck and climbed the steps up to the boardwalk. Through the window and the black lettering of *Plainsman Café*, Trini surveyed the interior. The bright room warmed by honey-colored pine walls buzzed with activity. Several groups of customers ate and chatted at four or five small square tables, each spread with a red-checked cloth. At the counter in the back of the room, Margie Snowfeather reached through the pass-through from the kitchen to retrieve two orders from her husband, Sam. In the glass case below the counter, three varieties of Trini's own bread were stacked, ready for sale. She was sure Sam would have a sourdough loaf now on his cutting board, slicing hunks to accompany the roast.

Wearing a smile of relief anticipating the warmth inside, Trini pulled open the door. As the bells tinkled, several people glanced up but then turned back to their meals. She searched the room, looking for a table with two kids, passed over them briefly then riveted back to a table seating two children and a man. George Mallis sat with his back to the door, his elbows folded on the table, leaning forward, intent on talking to Katherine. Jake sat across from him. When he saw Trini, he smiled, revealing a mouth full of chewed bread.

Trini strode to the table and stood between Katherine and Mallis. "These children are under my care, Sheriff. I don't want them talking to anyone until their relatives arrive."

The buzz of conversation lowered a notch. Mallis turned his face to look up at her. His hat rested on the empty chair beside him, and under a film of the few brown hairs that covered his scalp, the creases on his face appeared more abysmal than usual. He pushed the chair back, stood slowly, deliberately tugged his pants up with his thumbs then looked down on her from his full height. A ghoulish smile split the wrinkles. "Well now, missy. I don't recollect anyone appointing you as keeper of anything."

"No one appointed me. The children shouldn't be left alone right now, and I'm seeing that they aren't. I'm taking personal responsibility for their welfare."

Mallis snorted and glanced around the room. "I think you need a little readjustment in your thinking, Mrs. Trinidad Bates. You do not have any authority to take personal responsibility for the Woodson kids. You do not have any law enforcement authority in this town. And you sure as hell don't have the authority to go out to the Kerr house and question Mrs. Kerr about me."

She caught herself from gasping in surprise. Dottie, or Daryl, must have telephoned Mallis and told him of her visit. It seemed unlikely that Daryl would have done it. From the way he talked, he didn't like or trust the sheriff. It must have been Dottie. But why?

"What's the matter?" he asked. "You think I wouldn't find out about that?"

She swallowed the lump of intimidation that had risen in her throat. "I don't care if you know about me visiting the Kerrs. You don't scare me, Sheriff, and I'll talk to anyone I please."

"You talk mighty big for a small wetback, missy. And I think you'd be well advised to keep your nose out of my investigation from now on."

"Your investigation?" She wanted to laugh in his face, but she listened to the small voice at the back of her mind: *Be careful.* "I'm gathering information to present to a marshal to prove you should be relieved of that so-called investigation."

He narrowed his black eyes at her.

Did a snake have light in the pupils, she wondered, the pinpoint of white that were in the eyes of human beings, the pinpoint that indicated a soul on its journey resided within? Trini studied Mallis's pupils, and a chill shook her shoulders: She couldn't detect that light.

He spoke. "Katherine here tells me the Woodson house was broken into last week. And seeings how she told you about it, you should have reported the crime to me."

"Well, Sheriff, I just figured you'd know firsthand about that break-in."

He took a step toward her. "Are you insinuating I broke into Woodson's myself?"

Trini lifted her chin, met his stare and tried not to flinch from the coiled evil.

"You know," Mallis said, "it occurs to me that you might be an accessory to Merle Woodson's murder. You found him, by using that whirly rock on a string, something I don't think most judges would be willing to accept as a valid method for finding anything. I think a judge might conclude that you didn't find Merle at all, that you knew right where the body was all the time because you helped hide it there. After your brother killed him, that is."

"That's preposterous. That's not even logical. Why would I deliberately lead you to my own brother's murder victim? It stands to reason I'd want to keep the body hidden, not take you right to it."

"Well. We'd just have to let a judge sort that out, now

wouldn't we? And that might take a while. Days and days, if not weeks." He picked up his hat and set it firmly on his head. His mouth tilted up on one side in a sneer, and he whispered as he leaned a little closer. "Yes, ma'am, your brother would have to stay in jail an awful long time."

With a defiant glance to the rest of the customers, he marched from the room. The doorbells jangled as the door slammed behind him, and the buzz of conversation intensified as the diners chewed on this latest event.

He'd threatened her with that last remark. Another piece of evidence for a marshal. Trini carefully sat down across from Katherine; her legs were shaking. Placing her hand on her chest, she took a deep breath. She was all right. She was fine. Her heart would stop banging in a second. Just breathe and relax. One more deep breath, and she turned to Katherine, who stared at her openmouthed.

Her gaze caught eyes that averted and the shaking heads of a few customers. "Well," Trini said, "that will give them something to talk about."

She was better now. Fear had threatened to overwhelm her, capture her with its paralyzing grasp, but she was fine.

"I'm sorry, Katherine," she said. "Did Mallis bother you?"

Katherine blinked and then smiled a little. "I can't believe you stood up to him like that. I could never do that."

The knots in Trini's stomach loosened, but she gripped her hands together to hide her trembling fingers. "Sure you could," she said, "if you believed in something enough."

Katherine looked to her plate and Trini was left staring at the infant-like scalp. "I'm not strong enough to do anything," Katherine murmured.

At last, Trini thought, a connection. She wished they weren't sitting in the middle of the Plainsman Café. And she wished she wasn't so preoccupied with George Mallis. Katherine was trying to tell her something. Across the table, Jake sat silent, concentrating on the piece of bread he was tearing in half.

Placing her hand over Katherine's, Trini focused her energy on the needy girl beside her. "I wish I could tell you that life is easy, Katherine, and that finding the strength to go on is only a matter of asking for it. But it's not. Sometimes doing what you have to do is the most horrible thing imaginable. Sometimes, it feels like it would be better to just let things go on as they are and suffer through it."

"I know," Katherine whispered. "But what if you can't take it anymore?"

"Then you must look inside and find a place within yourself to get the strength from. And Katherine," Trini bent her head so the girl was forced to meet her eyes. "That place is in you, whether you've ever been there or not. It is."

Katherine heaved a sigh, looked away and began to pull and massage her lower lip. The connection was broken. Trini couldn't expect Katherine to reveal her deepest secrets now, not in the middle of the café. But at least it was a start. With a little time, she might open up.

Katherine's voice held a note of defiance. "The sheriff was actually very nice just now."

"What did he want?"

"He was really, um, concerned about me and Jake. He just wanted to know if we were getting along okay. He said several people had asked what he was doing to take care of us, but I told him you were with us." She puckered her lips with her fingers.

"Mallis was obviously upset that I'd talked to Dottie Kerr about him," Trini said.

"So that's what the sheriff meant. You went to the Kerr's house?"

"Yes. I just wanted to ask Dottie if your father had ever said anything to her about Mallis. You know, since you said that your dad told you about Mallis having his hands in his pockets."

Katherine's brows drew together, her eyes filled with dismayed tears and her fingers dug into her lower lip, stretching it then letting go. She rested her fingers on her chin while she spoke. "But, Trini, I didn't mean for you to go to the Kerrs'. I never—why did you do that, Trini? Why?"

Trini grasped Katherine's arm. "What is it? What's the matter?"

"I just didn't want you talking to anyone about that. I didn't want that all over town, and now it is. Were they both there?"

"Who? Dottie and Daryl? Yes. And it's okay, Katherine. It's okay. I have to get to the bottom of this and to do that I have to ask some questions. I'm going to call the marshal's office in Denver, and I'll need some reasons for getting someone down here. Dottie and your dad were good friends. I figured she might know something that could help."

Katherine toyed with her lip again, then wiped her face with her napkin. A streak of gravy transferred to her cheek, and Trini reached up with a clean napkin and dabbed it away. Katherine ignored the gesture.

"I just wish you wouldn't have gone to Kerrs', that's all." She slumped and lowered her eyes to her limp hands resting in her lap. Her voice shook when she spoke. "But now, I guess it's too late."

"What do you mean? Too late for what?"

Trini waited, hoping for more, but Katherine kept her eyes on her hands. Had Dottie said something to Katherine, something about her father? Was that the reason she left so abruptly last night? Had they quarreled?

Trini wanted to probe Katherine for more information, but the empty chair scraped on the floor as Margie Snowfeather pulled it away from the table and sat.

"The kids had a good dinner," Margie said. "And that was quite a bit of entertainment you and Sheriff Mallis supplied to the patrons tonight. Had I known there was going to be a show, I would've charged admission."

Her broad brown face framed by two thick black braids broke into a smile. She tapped Trini on the arm, emphasizing her point. "You gave the old iron-face what for, all right. But Lord, Trini, you sure do barrel right into the middle of things."

"Sorry, Margie. But look at it this way: You won't be at a loss for customers. You could even raise your prices. People will pay a lot to get firsthand gossip."

Margie threw her head back exposing her meaty neck and laughed with her mouth open. "That's the Lord's truth." Still displaying her bucktoothed grin, Margie looked at Katherine. "I'm glad you kids came by tonight. I like to see you around here. Will you be coming into town for the Fall Festival in a couple of days?"

Katherine shrugged.

"You're both welcome back any night. It's no problem."

"Could we settle up the tab in bread, Margie?" Trini asked.

"Sure. I'll just add it on to the one I got going. It's a mile long as it is." She winked. "What with you and Parn both on there, I could buy the town when you pay up." She laughed again.

Parn?

"Katherine," Trini said, "since you and Jake are finished, why don't you go over to the counter and pick out a loaf of bread for us to take home tonight. I'll fix you kids some of my famous French toast for breakfast tomorrow."

Katherine stared at her a moment then stood. After fumbling and chair-clamoring, they left, and Trini turned her attention to Margie. "Parn's on the tab? Since when?"

"Oh, just a few meals over the last month or so. Not much."

"I'd heard he and Merle were in here a few days before Merle disappeared. Evidently they had some kind of argument."

Margie's face sobered. "Yeah. A bad one. Got to pushin' and shovin' and knocked over a couple of tables. I had a whole house full for lunch, too. Both of them cussin' like a couple of miners. I was about ready to call the sheriff when they finally let it go."

"Do you know what it was about?"

"Never could make that out. Parn was madder than a mule, though, and Merle was tellin' Parn he was a no-count dumb kid."

"I know Parn has a temper and a big mouth, but I've never known him to get physical."

Margie looked down at the tablecloth and traced the red squares with her finger.

"What?" Trini asked.

Margie sighed then met Trini's eyes, resigned to telling. "He got mouthy, okay? I didn't think anything of it at the time, 'cause I figured they were just two sore-heads ready for a fight, but Parn told Merle if he didn't quit messing up his life, Parn was going kill him."

Trini covered her mouth and closed her eyes, trying to keep the nausea from overwhelming her. Margie put her hand on her shoulder. "I'm sorry, Trini. And like I said, I never thought anything of it. He said it in the heat of the moment. But now since all this happened . . . you okay?"

Trini breathed deep and the nausea seemed to settle for a moment. She opened her eyes to see Margie's forehead creased in worry. "I'm okay. Thanks for telling me. I better go. I've got to drive the Woodson kids home and get them settled in for the night."

"Trini, you sure you're okay? You look mighty upset."

Upset? More like up-ended. What in God's name was Parn

doing, going around threatening to kill Merle Woodson? Roy's doubts came back to her: "If Parn had anything to do with Merle's death, it was probably an accident."

What if Roy was right? Her brother might not be guilty of murder, but what if he was guilty of manslaughter? What if one day last week, they were at Parn's cabin and they fought? What if Parn grabbed their father's hammer to defend himself and in anger, he drove it into the back of Merle's head? Then when fear set in, Parn drove the car into Dawson's Gulch to make it look like an accident? What if—

Margie gripped Trini's arm and gave it a small shake. "It was just a hotheaded comment, Trini. It really was. I don't think anyone could make anything of it."

She nodded her head. "Sure. Thanks, Margie. I've got to go." She stood, numb and heavy, and set her chair under the table. "I'll see you later."

"Trini, wait. You're upset. Wait just a minute and let's talk this out."

"No, I've got to go. Thanks."

Through a fog, she gathered the children and somehow made her way through the café, out the door and into the frozen night.

CHAPTER TEN

The next morning, Trini telephoned the marshal's office in Denver. She talked with a Marshal Connelly, who, though sympathetic, told her their office would intervene to investigate a sheriff's impropriety only if ordered by a federal judge. Her other option was to contact the state attorney's office and request intervention. He gave her a name, Roger Blaine, for a reference, but when she telephoned the attorney's office, she learned Mr. Blaine was out sick. Another lawyer would contact her within a day or so. She gave the man the Woodsons' number, then slammed the receiver into its cradle. A day or so. The world could end in a day or so.

She sat at the breakfast table and took another sip of cold coffee. Everything was wrong, from Parn to Roy, and even Katherine. Last night, she'd tried to talk with her about Dottie Kerr, to ask her if she and Dottie had fought, but Katherine only answered with a short, "No" and clamped her mouth into silence. Later as they settled in Katherine's bed for the night, Trini tried to address the topic of Katherine's trauma, hoping she was ready to open up, but the girl rebuffed the gentle probes, turned away from Trini and went to sleep. She didn't force it; Katherine might shut down completely. This morning in the kitchen, Katherine greeted her in her usual manner, but Trini sensed the distance.

Enough, she thought, of this wringing of hands. She set her mug in the sink and headed toward the bathroom. A good soak in the tub, then on with the day.

She dressed in the long-sleeved gray wool dress she'd sewn last winter, her heaviest socks and her black brogans. The thick shoes were heavy, but they were best for traipsing around on a frosty day. She made sure Jake was dressed and settled with a set of wooden play blocks, then said good-bye to Katherine, who looked up from the seam she was stitching on her new Singer sewing machine. Trini told her she'd return in a few hours; Katherine's smile was vague and hurried. Trini shrugged on her coat, wrapped her knitted muffler around her neck then patted her coat pocket; the dowsing crystal was still there. She'd leave it, just for the comfort, the feeling of something in her life being connected and permanent. She climbed into her truck and sped to town.

She wanted to talk to Jefferson LeClair. She hoped he had information about George Mallis that he'd garnered from his friend, Gilbert Hardy. Then, she wanted to see Parn, make sure he was all right. She remembered last night Roy promised he'd look in on Parn today, but she wasn't counting on Roy for anything. His disappointing reaction to her brother's predicament weighed on her. No, she'd insure Parn's well-being by herself.

Trini parked in front of the mercantile, closed the truck door behind her and looked across the street at the sheriff's plate-glass window. Herds of bulbous clouds running across the sky reflected in the large panes, and she had to shift a little to see through them. A movement of a shadow. Was it Mallis or Taggert? She ducked and shifted a little more and the cloud reflection moved from the window leaving her a clear view. Mallis stared at her with his jagged face, his hands on his hips. Undoubtedly he thought she'd slink away in fear, but she met his gaze for a moment before turning her back to him and mounting the steps to the mercantile. The doorbells jangled as she entered.

Jefferson beamed at her from behind the counter while he tied the strings of a fresh apron around his waist. "Trinidad, I'm delighted to see you. Delighted. I heard you were staying at the Woodson house, so I didn't know if you'd come into town."

Trini felt her spirits rise with his greeting. Dear Jefferson. Such a welcoming, good friend. His positive mood was catching. She surveyed the area. The store was empty except for them. Good. Trini was anxious to talk to him uninterrupted.

She walked toward the counter. "You seem to know a bit of everything that goes on in this town, Jefferson."

"Ah yes. The one benefit of being a store owner. If I wasn't such an honorable gentleman, I could tell you any number of tawdry details about tawdry lives."

She grinned. "Honor is your best trait."

"Well, you might get some argument on that from my wife." He forced a laugh.

Trini perched on the counter stool, and he turned to her with his relaxed attention. "Jefferson, did you get a chance to talk with Gilbert Hardy?"

"Yes, my dear, I did. He had several very intriguing tidbits for me." He leaned forward assuming a confidential air. "Merle Woodson had borrowed twenty thousand dollars from Gilbert's bank. Mortgaged the house and land and then borrowed more unsecured."

"Yes, I know. Katherine shared some of her father's papers with me."

"She did? I couldn't believe it," he said. "What would Merle Woodson need that kind of money for? Especially in light of his thriving illicit liquor business? Gilbert said Woodson agreed to the highest interest rate allowed."

Trini knew Gilbert Hardy would extract every cent he could from the situation.

"I'm surprised Hardy told you about Merle's loan," she said. "I know that bankers are known for their discretion concerning clients. Did he say what the money would be used for?"

"No. He didn't say, and I didn't ask. I knew I was lucky to get what information I had. But my sense is he wouldn't have loaned Woodson the money if he wasn't sure to recover very handsomely from it."

"I wonder where the money is now?"

Jefferson shrugged his shoulders. "Certainly not hidden under the mattress. Woodson would have to invest the money somehow to make sure he could pay the high interest Gilbert Hardy would charge him." He hurried to reassure her. "I don't mean any disparagement toward Gilbert, of course. You know that, Trinidad. Despite his reputation, he really is a fine man. And, he was also extremely informative concerning our illustrious sheriff." He lowered his voice. "It appears that Sheriff George Mallis has an interesting background. He had quite a bootlegging organization for himself, in Denver, until his wife and two sons were killed."

"Parn told me he was a bootlegger. But I didn't know he was married with a family. How were they killed?"

"He evidently was caught skimming the profits from the local gang boss. To teach him a lesson, they sent him out of town on business, then crept into his home in the middle of the night and shot his wife and two sons, point-blank, while they were sleeping in their beds. Can you imagine?"

She stared at him, numb with shock. Parn had told her he and Woodson had been a part of some incident involving George Mallis in Denver. Unfortunately, Mallis had barged in before she could get the details, but, oh please, don't let Parn be involved in something like this. Because if he was involved in the murder of children, he certainly had a black spot on his heart and enough darkness in his soul to murder Merle Woodson as well. The knot in her stomach that she'd lived with for two days grew a name: suspicion.

"Trinidad, are you all right? You look deathly pale."

"No wonder," she whispered.

"No wonder about what?"

"No wonder Mallis had it in for Merle Woodson, and Parn, too. Parn told me, or rather tried to tell me before Mallis stormed in the jail yesterday, that he and Woodson helped set up a situation in Denver that would catch Mallis in the act of stealing."

"Good God. Are you saying Parn was involved in the family's murder? And Woodson, too?"

"No. No. From what Parn said, he and Merle were asked only to arrange something. Oh no, Jefferson." She shook her head firmly. "Parn wouldn't have been involved in any killing. He just couldn't have. Maybe the incident he talked about wasn't this same incident that involved Mallis's family. I'm sure he wouldn't have participated in that."

Jefferson shook his head. His voice was low and serious. "I don't know, Trinidad. As your friend, I have to tell you that I just don't know. It could have been the same incident. Very well could have. I'm not accusing him or Woodson of murder. I don't mean they pulled the trigger, but their involvement could have been very deep indeed."

Could Parn, the boy she'd cared for as a child—her skinny, fidgety, funny little brother be involved in setting up multiple murders? The killing of a woman and her children? She imagined the possibility and felt her world spin and tumble end-over-end, into some dark place, a place that had no name, a place that scared her to death.

Jefferson hurried from behind the counter and put his hands on her shoulders, turning her stiff body to face him. "Now, now, come on, dear girl. All right now." His voice was low and intent, and he kept his eyes on hers. "Don't get carried away with this. I'm not saying Parn did any wrong. I'm just saying if Parn participated at all, he wouldn't have comprehended what his actions entailed." His eyes left her face for a moment as he thought. "However, that said, it wouldn't make any difference to Mallis if Parn had known what he was doing or not. He'd want revenge on anyone who was even remotely connected to the event. Mallis would be vindictive indeed."

Yes. Yes, Jefferson was right. Surely Parn had done nothing wrong. If anything, Parn would be someone's dupe, the pawn of a gangster who used silly, trusting young men with big dreams to carry out his plans. If Parn had been asked to help bring about the death of children, if he'd known fully what the scheme was, he would have turned and run away, run home. He wouldn't be a party to that.

"Jefferson, I just had a thought. The murder of Mallis's family happened years ago. If Mallis was carrying this vendetta all this time, that means he would have had to manipulate the sheriff's appointment and arrange everything from very high up in the state."

"What do you mean?"

"Mallis was appointed to the sheriff's job after Bud Carevich died, what, two years ago?"

"I think so. About that."

"His family was murdered sometime before that, and let's just say for argument's sake, that Parn was involved. So think of the progression of events. Mallis would have had to discover who participated in the scheme, where Parn lived, curried the sheriff's appointment from the governor, and actually gotten the appointment. I mean that's years of planning and manipulation. Do you think someone could actually do that? Doesn't that seem a little far-fetched?"

"No," Jefferson said. "People will go to amazing lengths,

Trinidad, in the name of revenge. No, I don't think that idea is far-fetched at all." He squeezed her around her shoulders, pulling her close to his side. "But we're assuming Mallis's hatred of Parn stems from what he thinks Parn did to his family, and that could be false. He may have other reasons for wanting to frame Parn for murder. But the fact is, it doesn't make any difference why Mallis is doing what he's doing; he's out for Parn's blood. Even if Parn offered Mallis proof of his innocence in the murder of his family, you know Mallis wouldn't believe it."

"Yes. You're right. It doesn't matter what the reason is now. I just don't know if . . ." Suspicion bit her again, and she finished her thought silently. *If Parn deserves it.* That's what she was thinking. *If he deserves to be found guilty, to be punished.* The words were too horrible to say, traitorous words uttered by his own sister who would believe her brother to be a monster.

Jefferson said, "But what about Parn's hammer with blood on it? How could Mallis arrange that?"

"I'm not sure, and there's something about that hammer that's so strange, something I can't remember—"

The door to the mercantile jangled open and a woman entered. Trini knew her by sight: Lydia Hardy, Gilbert Hardy's wife. She surveyed the store slowly, looking down her imperial nose. A crimson cloche framed a face of contempt: pursed scarlet lips, penciled thin eyebrows raised in placid distaste, and hooded eyes. She held a clutch bag close to the waist of her print dress. The silk stockings on her legs gleamed, and her smart black pumps stopped as she turned and saw Jefferson.

He started toward her with his hand outstretched. "Mrs. Hardy. What a pleasant surprise. It's not often that—"

"Spare me, Mr. LeClair, your stupid pattering."

Trini blinked in surprise, and she saw Jefferson flinch with shock.

"I've come here," Lydia Hardy said, "for a very specific

reason. And I'll need to talk to you about that." She darted a glance at Trini.

"You . . . you may come back to my office, Mrs. Hardy." He swept his hand to the rear of the store.

Trini watched as they retreated, then crept up the canned goods aisle and stood around the corner of Jefferson's office. Through the slit between the frame and the door, she could see Jefferson's back and most of Lydia Hardy's face. She leaned forward to hear.

"Mr. LeClair, your wife informed me last evening of your perverted affair with my husband." Her chest heaved and she drew her chin in tight. "It is a secret no longer. Did she tell you she talked to me about it?"

Jefferson have an affair with her husband? Trini must have heard wrong. Mrs. Hardy must have meant that Jefferson's *wife* was having an affair with her husband. It would be no surprise that Camille was having an affair, but with Gilbert Hardy? A friend of Jefferson's?

Jefferson sagged against the door frame and shook his head. "No," he murmured. "Camille didn't tell me she'd talked to you."

"Well, that's between you and her, I suppose. But what you and my husb—Gilbert have done is beyond shocking. It's disgusting and degrading."

Trini shook her head. Shocking and degrading? Trini's heart pounded. Oh God. Had she heard correctly?

Jefferson looked down as Lydia Hardy lifted her chin in righteous superiority. "I find your conduct morally reprehensible. To say nothing of Gilbert's. You're both criminals, you know. Perversion is against the law."

Trini leaned her hand against the wall to steady herself and took a deep breath to stop the room from spinning. Jefferson was homosexual? And Gilbert Hardy was his partner? Atlas had tossed the world into space, and it was spinning away from her, out of control.

Lydia Hardy continued, "And I have come here to tell you about what I've decided."

Jefferson heaved a sigh. "Have you told Gilbert that you know?"

"Gilbert has no idea about any of this, Mr. LeClair, and he won't until I'm ready to tell him. Right now I'm in the process of making arrangements for our move. We'll be leaving for Denver as soon as we're ready."

His head snapped up and Trini heard his intake of breath.

"Oh yes, you may well be surprised, Mr. LeClair, but I've had my own secrets. You see, I've secretly hated Ludlin and hated living here. Gilbert has refused to respond to my pleadings to leave. Now, he'll have no choice. He'll leave with me. I see by your expression you doubt me. But I know Gilbert so much better than you. You stand no chance of winning against my money and status. My father acquired Gilbert's position for him, but maybe you didn't know that. The money is mine, and without me, he'll end up like all the other has-beens, riding the rails. He'd never allow that to happen for some sick relationship."

"Are you sure about that choice, Mrs. Hardy?" Jefferson asked.

"Oh I'm sure. He'll leave with me. And in case he's tempted to make another decision, I'll warn him that I'll spread your filthy little secret all over town. Neither of you will be able to show your faces again."

Jefferson was silent for a moment and then he spoke low and threatening. "And may I remind you, madam, that neither would you."

She gasped and put her hand to her chest.

He straightened and took a step toward her. "If you spread

your poison about Gilbert and me, your reputation will be ruined also. After all, what group of society matrons would want the wife of a pervert in their company? In their charities and attending their functions? And make no mistake, Mrs. Hardy, I would personally see to it that all of Ludlin, as well as Denver society, knew of your circumstances. You couldn't show your face in the entire state of Colorado."

"How dare you," she whispered.

"However," he sagged against the door frame, and Trini saw him look away from her, "it would also ruin Gilbert. A woman like you can't understand that, Mrs. Gilbert Hardy, but I wouldn't do that to someone I love."

Love. Trini's wild emotions began to drift into place. It was simple, really, as simple as love can ever be. Jefferson loved someone, and now his heart was broken. Though she was numb with shock, Trini's eyes burned with sympathetic tears. The fact that Jefferson was homosexual didn't change what he was to her: a friend. And he was in pain. Oh, Jefferson. Poor dear Jefferson.

"Love?" Lydia Hardy's lips twisted into a sneer. "You're joking. Perversion is the word. And until we leave for Denver, I insist you and Gilbert stop this horrible behavior. I will not tolerate it."

Jefferson stared at the woman in front of him.

"Do I have your word that you won't see Gilbert again?"

"I'm surprised you would put any value on the word of a pervert, Mrs. Hardy." Trini could hear the amusement in his voice.

Lydia Hardy took a step forward then stopped when he didn't move. "I'm leaving now. I think I've made my position quite clear."

"You have indeed."

Trini scooted behind a stack of bagged fertilizer and crouched low. The sharp odor tingled her nose, bringing Trini a sense of reality, like a dose of smelling salts. What a horrible woman. To insult someone, and her own husband, to call them names. But Lydia Hardy must be devastated, to discover her husband was nothing like the man she thought he was. In a way, she deserved pity, too.

High heels tapped against the wooden floor as Lydia marched to the door, pulled it open to the clamor of jangling doorbells, then slammed it behind her. Trini jumped with Jefferson's tap on her shoulder.

"Well, I guess you got an earful, didn't you?" he said.

Poor Jefferson. But no time now for her to say so. Several ladies entered, ready for help with their shopping. Jefferson marshaled his attention for them, and with a squeeze to his arm, Trini left.

Walking across the street to the sheriff's office, Trini put thoughts of Jefferson's trauma from her mind and gathered her courage. Calm and strong, she told herself. She could do this. As she closed the door behind her, Mallis stood from his desk, crossed to the railing and waited with his hands on his hips. Taggert sat forward in his seat. Roy's desk stood bare and cold.

"What can I do for you, missy?" Mallis asked.

"I want to see Parn," Trini said.

He hooted with his head thrown back.

Patience. Patience and compassion for a man who thinks her brother has done a despicable deed. "You know, Sheriff," she said, "I know about the deaths of your family. And I'm sorry." Out of the corner of her eye, she saw Taggert's mouth drop open as he watched the scene before him.

Mallis stared at her a minute, stunned, then smirked. "You think you can come in here and say that to me, say that and expect to catch me off guard, so that you can get to that ratty bastard brother of yours. I'm smarter than that, missy."

"Sheriff, please. You've got the wrong man. Parn would never be a part of anything like what happened to your family."

He looked at her a minute, then turned and walked to his desk. He leaned back on it and crossed his arms over his chest. The creases in his face settled into their usual frozen pattern. "My past has nothing to do with here and now. And here and now I got a killer in my jail and he happens to be your brother."

"Sheriff, you have to listen to reason. You have to—"

"You got a bad habit, lady, of telling me what I have to do. Now I'm telling you. Get out of my office right now. Visiting prisoners isn't allowed on Thursdays."

A blade of rage tore through her stomach and chest. The man was a cold, vindictive monster. Jefferson had said Mallis wouldn't believe denials of Parn's guilt, and he was right. Mallis had set his sights on one thing: killing Parn like he'd killed Woodson.

"Your little games can't go on forever," she said. "If you won't listen to reason, you give me no choice but to act. I've been talking to Marshal Connelly in Denver. He'll be looking into this." She gave him a hard stare, hoping he believed her.

"Oh he will, will he? Connelly, you say? Humpf. Well, I just had a call from a Marshal Connelly this morning. He wanted to know what your telephone call was all about. I told him some Mexican woman got her sombrero filled with nonsense. Know what he said?"

Her mind froze. She wanted to yell, scream, charge him with her nails ready to rake his face.

"He laughed. He laughed long and hard."

All the frustration and fury that had been boiling inside her roared to the surface. "Parn!" she yelled. She brought the scream from deep within her, from the shard of fear that lived in her stomach. The echo bounced off the walls. "Parn, are you all right?"

"Holy God," said Taggert. "Cut that racket." He leaned his elbows on his desk and covered his ears with his hands.

"I will not cut anything until I know my brother is safe." She cupped her hand around her mouth. "Parn!" as loud as she could bellow.

Taggert got up from his desk and rushed to her. "You got to quit that now. Quit it. Jesus on the Cross. Can't we get the kid for her, Sheriff?"

Mallis looked at her, a sneer breaking the crumples in his face. "Naw. Let her scream."

"Parn!" she screamed again. A passerby on the sidewalk stopped in front of the windows and shaded his eyes to peer inside.

"I can't take that," said Taggert. "I gotta go outside if she's gonna keep that up."

"Parn! Answer me if you're all right!"

Mallis stepped toward her and grabbed her arm. "All right. All right now, missy, that's just enough of that. Get out of here."

"I intend to stay here for as long as I need to, Sheriff." She sat in a chair, tucking her dress under her and crossing her legs. She folded her gloved hands in her lap.

"Parn!" she shouted again.

"I can't take it, I tell ya," said Taggert. Again he covered his ears with his hands.

She had to know he was all right. Had to know now. "Parn!"

"All right, damn it. Just shut up," Mallis said. He turned and walked toward his desk, stopped and looked over his shoulder at her a moment, then opened the top drawer and withdrew the keys.

"Get the kid." He tossed the key ring to Taggert who caught it in midair and hurried down the hall. He inserted a key into the cell-block door, opened it and disappeared inside. Trini turned her attention back to Mallis and found him staring at her, his expression as unreadable as ever. In a few seconds, she heard the door open and set her eyes on her brother's grinning face. He stood in the hallway, Taggert beside him gripping his arm.

"I heard you, Trin. I'm here and I'm all right. I was calling back to you, but I guess you couldn't hear me."

She stood and smiled at him. "Okay. We'll go home soon, Parn. I promise."

He nodded and she saw tears brim his eyes. With a jerk on his arm, Taggert led him back through the door.

"You try something like that again, missy, and you'll pay a high price," Mallis growled.

"You can't do anything to me, Mallis."

"Oh? I told you last night I think a judge might be interested to hear about that dowsing business. I still think it's mighty queer you knowing where a dead body was. Seems to me that only an accomplice would know that. Maybe someone who helped her brother murder someone with a hammer. A murder weapon that I've already sent to Denver, by the way."

"I thought you were going to have Taggert drive up to Denver with the hammer. I've seen him here for the last two days. He hasn't gone to Denver or anywhere else."

The evil leer spread the fissures of his face and he stared at her. "The Department of Investigation people told me to send the hammer up by mail. Takes a long time with the mail. And we don't know when Judge Slaton will be over this way for the arraignment, either. Appears he's tied up in Fredricksburg with a trial."

Use the mail to send a murder weapon to be examined? Judge Slaton tied up in a trial? George Mallis's machinations were pathetic. But, she thought with a sinking feeling, they've accomplished his goal: Her brother was trapped in a cell and Mallis held the key.

He opened the top drawer of his desk and withdrew a red box of Torch Light tobacco. He opened the top, withdrew a brown gob, twisted off a hunk and poked it into the back of his cheek. The nodule smoothed the wrinkles above his jowl. He spoke as he carefully closed the box. "You got a lawyer for your brother yet?"

Trini watched him replace the box in his drawer and stayed silent.

"I guess that lawyer Stansbury is out of town for several days. Along with his lawyer son. Too bad. Everything's taking a lot longer than I expected. Yessir. A whole lot longer. Guess your brother will just have to wait it out. Here. In the jail. Hope he doesn't try to escape or anything."

Her stomach burned. Just what she was afraid of, what Parn was afraid of. She felt tears beginning to well and her throat closing. She swallowed it down then met his sneer. "I feel sorry for you, Sheriff. Sorry for such a pitiful human being."

"I don't need pity from you or anyone else."

"No, you probably don't. But you need prayers. Prayers for your poor, tortured soul, and for the souls of your wife and sons. I'll light a candle for them in mass."

She turned, walked to the door, then turned to face him again. "And, Sheriff, you can expect me back here tomorrow. For the usual visiting hours at two o'clock."

She turned and left, closing the door gently behind her.

CHAPTER ELEVEN

Trini clutched the steering wheel with white knuckles as she drove the county highway back to the Woodsons'. The morning had left her shaky: learning of Jefferson's homosexuality by overhearing Lydia Hardy abuse her friend; pushing Mallis to the limit by outrageously yelling in the sheriff's office; the rat-like gnawing in her stomach at the thought that Parn might have participated, however innocently, in a gangland murder. She'd like to go back to the house, brew herself a cup of tea and think. Right now, though, she had one more thing she wanted to do.

She turned off the highway and started up the half-mile gravel road that the Woodsons used as a driveway. About midway, another road forked to the left, away from the house. She made the turn and drove several hundred feet up a sharp incline. She pulled to a stop in front of the Woodson mine and got out of her truck. The house stood about a quarter mile away, at the bottom of the hill. She knew that Katherine and Jake were occupying themselves inside, but to a stranger, the house looked vacant; blinds covered the windows and not even a wisp of smoke curled from the chimney. She'd drive down there in a minute, but first, she wanted to look inside Merle Woodson's hole in the mountain. Parn told her years ago they'd used the space as a distribution point for their illegal liquor. She assumed that still held true, at least until Woodson had disappeared last week. Now, certainly Mallis had removed the liquor, probably right after he'd killed Woodson. Trini wanted to search inside to confirm her theory. She needed to ask Katherine if she'd seen the sheriff up here, although she doubted she had. Katherine would have mentioned it. Where would Mallis have taken the liquor? He lived on several acres east of town. She'd like to search his house and outbuildings. He probably planned on storing it there for a few months, until his scheme to frame Parn had been successfully completed, then he'd sell the illegal booty for a windfall profit.

Gravel crunched beneath her shoes as she hiked the few yards from her truck to the mine opening. A lantern and matches sat on a rock ledge, and Trini struck the match, set it to the wick and lowered the glass chimney, then entered the black hole. She lifted the lantern high and in front of her at arm's length. The circle of light illuminated the rocks and footprints along the dusty path. Lots of footprints, and she guessed most of them belonged to Mallis. It must have taken him numerous trips back and forth from the mine to his truck to remove the stash of liquor. She wondered how many cases he had taken and how much it was worth.

Dangling the lamp in front of her, she followed the light through the tunnel into the black maze for fifty yards or so, until it split in two directions. She'd examine the right fork first; it looked a little wider, like it was the main tunnel. Then she'd come back and take the other direction. The bootleggers might have had several places to store the whiskey, and since she was here, she wanted to check all the possibilities.

As she walked, Trini counted fifty-four steps. She came to a dead end, then turned a right angle. Following the rocky path illuminated by the yellow glow of the lantern, she entered a room of rock. She lifted the light high in front of her eyes and slowly walked the perimeter. Footprints swarmed over the floor of the cavern, and along the back wall she could make out the ridges of dust left by the crates of liquor. She could imagine the room, depending on the volume at any given time, cases stacked as tall as a man against the rock walls. Empty now.

She continued her exploration of the area, looking for another tunnel or a smaller room that connected to this one—any other space that would allow for more storage. She found a crevasse in the wall, a cleft just wide enough for a human. Squeezing her way between the jagged walls, the light showed her that the opening was only a few feet deep. Enough to hide a person or two, but not cases of bootleg whiskey. She turned back into the main chamber. Now to retrace her steps back to the fork, then explore the other tunnel.

A scuffle of rock sounded from the main tunnel just outside the rock room. She stopped and held her breath. Was someone there? She could have sworn she heard a crunch of gravel, like a boot stepping on loose pebbles. Trini held the lantern higher to extend the luminous circle.

"Who's there?" she called.

Her echo answered, then silence. Her heart pounded in her ears.

"Katherine?" she called.

More echoes and silence. How silly. Katherine wouldn't be up here. She'd have no reason to be here. But had someone else followed her inside? This mine was nowhere to be caught. The mazes and tunnels were decades old, littered with shafts that were black and fathomless. She listened again.

"Anyone there?" she called.

Silence. Must have been a bit of loosened rock. The inside of the earth and the mines were always shifting and changing, she knew, and her frayed nerves served to exaggerate every small sound. She blew out a breath of relief and traced her steps through the entry back into the main tunnel.

When Trini got to the fork she'd seen earlier, she stopped. A gray light from a dull sky showed through the mine opening to her left, about fifty yards away. She shifted her gaze from the arched entry to the tunnel she had yet to explore. She was tempted to head to the outside, but she hated to leave without exploring the rest of the mine. The scuttling noise a few minutes ago had spooked her, that's all. She turned and started down the dusty trail, following more footprints. No telling whose they were. Mallis's, Parn's or Woodson's—or maybe some of their customers would have come to the mine to pick up their illicit goods. Without wind or water to disturb them, footprints would stay imbedded in the pathway dust forever.

Holding the lantern high in front of her, the swinging circle of light bounced across the walls and ceiling and caught the glint of quartz scattered through the rock. She brushed the rocky walls with her fingertips. So much history here. So much history of men's desire for gold. The blackness yawned in front of her. Maybe this tunnel went on for a long ways. Maybe she should turn back and—

She stopped and jumped backwards. Just in front of her, the floor dropped away. A shaft, deep and black, opened into the earth. She inched her feet to the edge and leaned forward, holding the lantern out and over the yawning pit. Her light showed the ragged shaft walls, but no bottom. The pit must be immense. Had there been an elevator here? She examined the rocky walls, shifting her lantern for a clearer view, but didn't see any leftover cables or platforms. The owners of the mine must have removed the mechanism when they abandoned the mining operations. Someone should have boarded over the shaft opening. She was lucky to have stopped when she did. She turned and headed toward the half circle of gray light that defined the opening.

As she emerged into the dull daylight, she blew out the lantern flame, set it back on the ledge and walked out into a day that reminded her of cold pewter. She wanted to get down to the house, get warm, and see the children. She opened the truck door just as an engine revved to gear down to take the hill. A black sedan pulled to a stop behind her truck, the driver's door opened and Les Taggert climbed out.

"Hello there, missy," he said. In an imitation of George Mallis, he pulled up his uniform pants by the waistband to cover his jutting stomach and sauntered toward her on bird-like legs. A ridiculous caricature of a man.

"What are doing out here, Les?"

He tipped his hat back with a finger, and smiled to show crooked yellow teeth. "Well now that's no way to be friendly, is it?"

"I'm not interested in friendly. I'm interested in knowing what you're doing here."

The simpering grin fell from his face and a sharpness came to his eyes.

"I'm here as an officer of the law. That mine contains illegal contraband and it's gonna be used in a court of law." A malicious grin. "To prove murder against your brother."

"That's very convenient. Except there is no illegal contraband. It's gone. The mine's empty." A gust of cold air swirled around them, and Trini hugged the collar of her coat to her neck.

Taggert's grin dropped again and he stepped toward her. "What do you mean gone? I come out here to apprehend it."

"You're too late to 'apprehend' anything. I'm guessing your boss beat you to it and by now has a buyer. Matter of fact, he's probably sold it and has the profits stashed away. He's becoming a very wealthy man, you know."

Taggert shifted his eyes back and forth as if looking for answers in the air around him. She noted he didn't argue with her, didn't even insist on examining the mine himself. He knew what Mallis was. He knew what she said was true.

Finally, his mouth creased in a thin line. "Son of a bitch," he murmured.

"Precisely," said Trini. It occurred to her that Taggert's arrival just now was incredibly coincidental timing. She squinted at him with suspicion. "Les, you weren't just in the mine, were you? Just a minute ago?"

"How could I be? I just now drove up."

Her eyes flicked to his feet. "Your boots are dusty. Maybe you walked over the top of the hill there and came in that way," she pointed to the mound to the east of the mine entrance, "or maybe there's another entrance to this old shaft."

"I weren't in the mine and there ain't no other entrance. Just the one."

She studied his face, the dull-witted eyes. Was he lying? "You sound like you know the mine well. When was the last time you were here?"

He stared at her a minute, then turned his back and opened the car door. He draped his arms over the top edge and glared at her with a yellow sneer. "Mallis is right. You are a pain in the ass."

He climbed in the car and headed back down the hill.

She parked the truck by the kitchen door and took several cold deep breaths to steady herself. The more she thought about Les Taggert, the more she wondered: Was he really after the whiskey, hoping he could beat Mallis to the valuable liquor? Had he just happened to come by when she was there? Why else would he come to the mine? The questions left her unsettled. She needed a cup of hot tea and to sit in front of a warm fire to think.

When she entered the Woodson kitchen, she found Katherine rolling out pie dough. In the parlor, Jake sat cross-legged and openmouthed in front of the radio.

Katherine looked up as Trini shut the door behind her and

began to remove her coat and scarf. "Hi," she said. "Lyle Butcher came by again this morning. He waited out by the tree again."

Trini felt uneasy about Butcher's presence, but not alarmed. Mainly, she was pleased with Katherine's demeanor. Evidently she was back to her friendly self and had forgiven Trini for her probing questions last night. Good. She'd let it go for now, but Trini had every intention of opening the subject of Katherine's trauma again. No good would come to the girl by keeping it buried inside her.

She smiled and sat at the kitchen table. "Lyle Butcher, huh? How long did he stand there?"

"I went out to talk to him."

"Oh, Katherine. I wish you wouldn't have done that. He's probably harmless, but I don't like the fact that he thinks he can come and go on your property when he wants to. And I don't like you talking to him when you're alone."

Katherine smiled a little. "I'm not afraid of him. He's really a nice man, and he didn't try to come inside or anything."

"Did he ask to see your father's papers again?"

"Yes, but when I told him you weren't here, he didn't press it. I think he has a crush on you." She grinned and her face and scalp flushed pink.

Trini laughed. "And I'm supposed to take that as a compliment?"

"Well, he said you were as beautiful as your mother, and he'd do anything for Lucinda's daughter."

"As I said, coming from him, it's not much of a compliment. Did you tell him when I'd be back?"

"No. He said he'd find you somehow."

Speaking of unwanted visitors—"Katherine, did you see Sheriff Mallis up here any time last week? Up at your father's mine?"

"No. Why?"

"I was wondering. Parn told me once that he and your father kept the liquor in the mine. I was just up there and it's gone. I wondered if Mallis had removed it some time last week."

"I didn't see him or anyone else up there." She looked at Trini for a moment. "I know what you're thinking. You think Sheriff Mallis had something to do with Pa's death, don't you? That's why you want a marshal here."

Where was the balance? Trini didn't want to cause Katherine additional pain, but then again she didn't want to hide anything from her. Of course, right now, she wouldn't be hiding anything but her own suspicions. She had no facts to present as evidence against Mallis. She decided to take the middle road. "Let's put it this way: I think Mallis has a stake in having your father dead."

Katherine nodded and thought for a moment. "Hmm. Maybe that would explain the notes I found on Pa's maps."

"What maps?"

"The ones I found in his desk."

"I don't remember seeing any maps."

"Not in the rolltop. The desk in his room."

Trini had forgotten about the other desk. Maybe there was something in Merle's papers that would incriminate Mallis. A bolt of excitement shot through her. "May I see them?"

Katherine brushed the flour from her hands, covered the pie dough with a dish towel, and led the way into her father's bedroom.

Last night, Katherine hadn't offered her father's room for Trini to use, and Trini was glad. As she familiarized herself with the house, she'd briefly stepped into the room. A chill had passed through her, like a brush of Merle's odor and something of his presence still lingered there. She felt more comfortable sleeping with Katherine than she would have in Merle's bed.

Now, the room looked sad and bare. Katherine had removed all of the pictures and personal effects from the dresser top. The bed had been stripped and boxes filled with Merle's clothes, all neatly folded, sat on the blue-ticked mattress.

"Katherine, I'm sorry," Trini said. "I didn't want you to have to take care of your father's things by yourself. I wanted to help you."

"That's okay. I don't mind. The maps are over here."

His desk and chair stood under a window. A red leather journal occupied the center of the polished bare top.

"I kept this out because I wanted to ask you about it." Katherine opened the top desk drawer, withdrew a stack of folded maps and set them beside the book. "These are the maps. But first look in Pa's journal." She opened the cover of the journal. "What does all this mean?"

Trini sat in the chair and Katherine stood next to her, peering over her shoulder. In the script of a man who treasured precision, Merle Woodson had penned, "Dome Partnership Purchases, Coyote County" at the top of the page. In the left column, a date read six months ago, May 18, 1932. On the same line across from the date, Merle had written, "$1,250.00 DOME Partnership / Santa Fe RR. Section 8, Plat 6." There were several more entries on the page: two for June, three in August, four in September, three in October. The latest entry was for November 9—the week before Merle disappeared. Each entry was for differing amounts, plats and section numbers. Fifteen entries. Trini flipped to the next pages. They were blank. Evidently, the purchases began six months ago.

Katherine's hairless brows creased with confusion. "What does this mean?"

"It looks like DOME Partnership, whatever that is, bought land from the railroad," Trini said.

"But what does that have to do with Pa?"

"I don't know," Trini said. Merle worked in the land claims department for Coyote County. When land or mineral rights were bought and sold in the county, Merle—or Dottie—recorded the transaction. Maybe Merle had brought this ledger home from work, something he couldn't finish during his regular hours.

Trini looked up from her seat to see Katherine biting her lower lip with worry. "Did your father ever bring home his record books from the office?"

"Not that I know of," Katherine said. She thought a minute. "I remember he told me they're like legal documents and can be used in court and with lawyers, so only certain people can write in them. I don't think anyone is allowed to take them out of the courthouse, either. Not even him or Dottie." She withdrew a stack of ledgers from the side drawer and placed them in front of Trini. "Look at this."

Trini opened the book on top of the stack. On the first page, Merle had written, "DOME Partnership Purchases Freemont County." Trini flipped through the book and two pages of the same type of entries, ten in all, written in Merle's neat script.

She took the next ledger from the stack and saw the same heading, only labeled Pueblo County. She quickly scanned the stack of ledgers and found each with a different county heading: El Paso, Douglas, Freemont and more, all accompanied by dollar amounts, plat and section numbers, in the same method as the ledger for Coyote County.

"I wonder why your dad would have records from other counties? Maybe Coyote County was involved in a joint project with these other counties."

Katherine opened a map, smoothed it and pointed to the bottom right corner. "See where he wrote 'Mallis'? What do you think that means?"

Trini stood to get a better look and leaned her hands on each side of the large document. Mallis's name, definitely in Merle's handwriting, filled the bottom corner. "I'm not sure what it means," she said.

From the boldness of the stroke and the splash of ink underneath the name, Merle had pressed hard on the pen nub. In anger or frustration? The map was of Elbert County, and was marked in several places with X's followed by a slash, then the word "DOME." Katherine handed her another map, Arapaho County, marked the same way. There were several more maps, each from different counties and each with "X-DOME" labels scattered across the surface.

"How many maps are there?" Trini asked.

"Twelve."

Katherine opened each one and laid one on top of the other. Mallis's name didn't appear on any of the other maps, but all of the maps contained at least three "X-DOME" labels, one had seven, and two bore ten.

Katherine laid the final map on top of the stack, open and ready for Trini's inspection. "Here's Coyote," she said.

Trini scanned their own county map. It contained the same markings, and there were fifteen entries, more than any of the others. Fifteen entries on the map, fifteen entries in the ledger marked "DOME Partnership Purchases Coyote County." She was familiar with most of the sites. One X was at the corner of the county highway and the Digstown turnoff. She knew that area well. There was nothing there but scrub.

"How strange," Trini murmured. "Do all the maps have corresponding ledgers?"

"Yes," Katherine said. "Twelve maps and twelve ledgers. And you know the funny thing? I looked at the state map in my geography book. All of these counties are in a line. Some north of Coyote County and some south of us, like a row of counties going up and down the state with us in the middle."

A line of counties with Coyote in the middle. DOME Partnership had obviously purchased a trail of land. Why? A highway or a public works project? Roosevelt had promised he'd get the country back to work. Happy days and all that. Maybe whoever owned DOME knew about where the projects would be and they purchased land that the government would want later.

But who owned DOME? Trini had a hunch that Merle Woodson was connected to it. The maps and ledgers probably didn't detail official county business; the documents were too personal, all in Merle's handwriting, and it would be odd for him to keep documents like this in his personal desk. She would assume for now that Merle either owned the company or worked for the company. Who made up the partners in DOME Partnership?

Trini dug under the stack and withdrew the first ledger for Coyote County and set it on top of the Coyote County map. Did the descriptions in the ledger match the X's on the map marked DOME? She had no idea how to read the legal definitions of land using plats and sections and then find them on a map. She'd need to go to the courthouse to find Dottie; she could read the two documents and make sense of it all. And what if the ledger and the map did coordinate? Then what did that mean? She needed to find out what DOME was. If it was a company, a company that Merle owned or worked for, how was Mallis connected to it? And he must be connected because his name is scrawled in the corner of the Elbert County map. It suddenly occurred to her, did DOME have anything to do with Merle mortgaging the house and borrowing money? Would he have gone into debt to buy land through the DOME Partnership?

Trini folded the maps and replaced the ledgers in the drawer. "Katherine, I need to go in town for a while. I want to go by the courthouse. I want to see what the county records are for these areas. Can I take the Coyote County map and the ledger with me?"

"Sure."

"I also want to talk to Dottie. If this is something related to work, she might know. Will you be all right here for a while?"

"I stay here alone all the time, Trini. No one is going to break in. It's the middle of the day."

"I suppose not. I'll be back in a little while. If you need anything, ring the mercantile and tell Jefferson to come get me at the courthouse."

She grinned at Trini. "I could telephone Roy Eastman. He'd help me."

Trini gently pinched her cheek. "Don't get a smart mouth, young lady."

The redbrick Coyote County Courthouse occupied the center of the town square. Climbing the wide steps flanked by two white columns, Trini glanced at the few dry leaves waving forlornly from the limbs of the cottonwood and aspen trees surrounding the building. The oak doors slammed behind her, and the soles of her brogans clumped on the limestone floor as she walked through the atrium. She turned down the first hall to her right and at the first door, read the sign on the glass window: *Coyote County Land Claims Office.* She entered and stood at the counter. A man wearing round wire glasses and as thin as a picket finished his notations on a map. He stretched to his full height and surveyed his customer.

"May I help you?"

"Hello. Is Dottie around? I'm Trinidad Bates. I was hoping to talk with her."

The man's Adam's apple bobbed above the tight collar of his shirt. "No, she went home. She said she needed to take care of some things today, so she just worked until noon. Something I can help you with?"

"No. I guess I could try her at home."

"Okay. I'll tell her you came by."

She stopped mid-turn. Even though she wanted to talk to Dottie about her possible knowledge of DOME, Trini didn't need her especially to read the map and ledger. This man could help her with the documents she had tucked in her pocketbook. "You know, there is something I'd like to look at. Do you have recent land purchases, say from the last six months or so, I could look at?"

"O-kee-doke. Where?"

"If I wanted to see if some property sold outside of Digstown, how would I look that up?"

"Well, you wouldn't, but I would. These are official legal records for Coyote County. Only authorized personnel may have access. I'm Miles Henry. Supervisor of Land Claims for Coyote County." He snuffled a little through a pinched nose.

She didn't recognize the man, but she wondered if he belonged to the Henry family that lived over in Denton. Since she had no personal acquaintances in the family, she decided to stick to business. "Nice to meet you. Could you please look up some property outside of Digstown?"

Mr. Henry crossed the small space to an oak cabinet with wide, shallow drawers. After much tugging and heaving, he opened a drawer and withdrew a large book with a green canvas cover. It landed with a flop on the counter and he flipped it open. "Oh-kee-doke. Let's see." He scanned the inside cover. "Dad-gum-it. This isn't what I want," he mumbled. He peered at her from behind the thick lens of his glasses. "I'm not responsible for this mess. These records are all misfiled and mislabeled."

"How did they get that way?"

"Well, I'm not going to speak ill of the dead, but that's the way I found them."

"Oh," she said. "I gather you're talking about Merle Wood-son. Did you know him? Were you his supervisor?"

"Oh no," he said. "No, I worked upstairs in water manage-ment. No, they brought me down here to work with Dottie after Merle was killed. Terrible thing, isn't it? Terrible. But I hear they caught the guy, so that's something. I swear, this county used to be such a nice place to live. Everyone so friendly. Now you just never know about people, do you? Seems like everyone has just turned cold-hearted and nasty."

Trini stopped herself from blurting out a statement in Parn's defense; a waste of time in this situation. "I suppose. Yes, it's a shame. So you think Mr. Woodson was responsible for the disorganization of the record books?"

"Like I say, I won't talk ill of the dead. All I know is that it's going to take me weeks to get this sorted out. And no telling how the records themselves have been treated. I've been finding duplications in some, and some records are completely missing. As I said, these are the official records, able to be subpoenaed by a court of law and everything. Very important." He sniffed again and reached under his chin to straighten his bow tie.

"Then I assume since the records contain legal information, no one could remove them from this office. Like take them home to work on or anything?"

Henry's eyes widened in shock. "Heavens no. Strictly against the rules."

"And do all the record books look about like that?" She pointed to the large green ledger Miles Henry still rested his hands upon.

"Oh yes. Everything uniform and in legal order. Why did you want to know?"

"No reason. I was just marveling at the order of the system." It was a silly answer, but one that she had a feeling Henry wouldn't challenge. Trini was not about to tell him about the records she'd found in Merle Woodson's private desk. She had her answers. The records Katherine had shown her were Merle's personal records. DOME Partnership was a part of Woodson's business, not the county's.

She smiled at Henry as she spoke. "So could you check about the property outside of Digstown? To see if it's been sold recently?"

"Sure. Sure," he said. He returned the ledger to a drawer and crossed to another cabinet with the same type of wide, shallow drawers. He opened the top drawer, shook his head and clucked his tongue in disgust and closed the drawer. He opened the next drawer down and after lifting the top ledger from the drawer, returned to the counter wearing an expression of smug satisfaction.

"Not where it should be," he said, "but I found it."

She waited while he placed the ledger on the counter in front of her and opened the cover. "First we'll look at the coordinates for that area, then see if there's been any transactions."

He flipped through several pages and leaned over the open map. A twig-like finger pointed to Digstown. He peered down at her over the rims of his glasses. "Where outside of Digstown?"

"Right where the county highway intersects Digstown Road."

"Um hm. Yessir. O-kee-doke. Got it."

He reached under the counter, withdrew a brown leather book labeled *Coyote County* in gold letters, and placed it on top of the map and opened it.

"That's fifty-two north by twenty-eight west," he mumbled.

He trolled through a column of numbers with his knobby digit and stopped toward the bottom. "These are the transactions, and it's just as I suspected: that land hasn't been sold, nor is likely to be." He stabbed his finger at the numbers several times and ran his eyes back and forth between the two documents. "Yup. All that land is owned by the Santa Fe Railroad. Has been for decades. Never been sold."

"All of it?"

"Yep. Every single mile."

"Would you check another one for me?"

Trini opened her handbag and drew out the Coyote County map she'd taken from Merle Woodson's desk and gave him several other locations. The Santa Fe Railroad owned every "X" marked spot labeled "DOME."

"What you got there?" He wiggled a finger at the map as Trini folded it and wedged it back into her bag.

"It belongs to a friend of mine."

He stared at her a minute and blinked. The Adam's apple moved again. Trini smiled at him. "Could you check something else for me? Could you see if a company named DOME Partnership has purchased land? This would be anywhere at all in Coyote County."

She watched his face for any reaction to the words "DOME Partnership," but saw none. He reached under the counter and brought out another ledger, this one black, opened it and flipped through pages. "Don't see anything about a DOME."

"Could I ask you something else, Mr. Henry?"

He blinked with his mouth open. "Well, sure. Sure go ahead."

"If a person forms a partnership with another person, where do they register the company? To make it legal?"

"Oh, you don't have to register it."

"Not at all?"

"Nope. Not with no one."

"But is it still a legal partnership?"

"Oh, sure."

"Well then, how would someone else, an interested party let's say, find out who's in the partnership?"

"They don't. The partnership can just be an agreement

between two people, just a spoken agreement. Although, if you're really going to do some big things with it, any sensible person would draw up papers."

"So they'd go to a lawyer."

"No. Not necessarily. Don't have to, certainly. Let's say you and me wanted to form a partnership for something. We could just write it out on this piece of paper here," he picked up a blank page from a stack on the counter, "and both sign it. That's a partnership."

"And you say that's legal?"

"Oh sure. Legal and binding. And we make all the rules of the partnership like we want them, buy anything we want with the partnership and nobody needs to know we have it."

"So then, it's basically a secret."

"Yup, unless someone challenges something the partnership has done, like in a court of law or something. Why? You forming a partnership with someone?"

"No. No. Just curious. Thanks."

"Oh-kee-doke. No problem. Glad to be of service. That's what the tax payers pay me for."

Her mind tumbled as she walked down the hallway and out the front doors. She'd go to Dottie's house right now and ask her about Merle's DOME Partnership. And this time she'd pressure Dottie a little more, demand some of the answers she was sure Dottie had. Why had Merle borrowed twenty thousand dollars? Did he use the money in connection with DOME? She thought about the small key in the bottom of one of the drawers in the parlor rolltop desk. She had asked Katherine at the time if Merle had a safe deposit box at the bank, and Katherine said she didn't know. If there was a safe deposit box, maybe it stored papers—partnership papers for DOME. Mr. Henry said papers weren't necessary for legal partnerships, but that a smart person would draw up documents to protect himself. Merle Woodson certainly was smart. He was juggling a lot of schemes: bootlegging, some past business dealings with Lyle Butcher, and now this DOME Partnership.

And what of Mallis? He must have been involved somehow with DOME because of the scrawled name on the map. And if DOME wasn't buying land, which according to Mr. Henry it wasn't, then what did Merle's ledgers and maps mean? What did all the legal descriptions and all those X's stand for? Did DOME have anything to do with the bootlegging? She needed something concrete, in writing, proving Mallis was involved with Woodson up to his wrinkled eyeballs. She could—

"Trini, wait! Wait!" Jefferson was running toward her, waving his arms.

He halted in front of her huffing with exertion. "I'm glad I caught you."

"Jefferson, what is it? What's the matter?"

"Please. Please help me. Stephanie has run away."

CHAPTER TWELVE

"Run away? When?" Trini asked.

"Today. Now. Oh, God, Trinidad." Jefferson choked through desperate tears. "She's gone. My little girl's gone."

Trini placed a hand on his arm. "Tell me."

He dabbed a white linen handkerchief to his lips, then wadded it between his hands. "Evidently about six this morning the Standard Oil truck made a delivery to the gas station. Jay Austin told me he didn't know the driver; the usual delivery man was sick. Austin said Stephanie walked right up to this driver, bold as brass, and asked him to take her to Colorado Springs with him." His eyes darted behind him. "Here comes Camille now."

Camille LeClair stopped in front of Trini and stared at her with red-rimmed eyes. The flaming red hair magnified her white face, and her pale lips moved to speak, but she made no utterance. Her aggressive demeanor had been cowed; she was too devastated to bully anyone. Despite Trini's dislike for the woman, she felt desperately sorry for her. Her child was gone, and if there was one thing Trini could identify with, it was the wrenching of a mother's heart for her missing child.

She placed her hand on Camille's arm and felt her trembling, though probably not from the cold, even though she wore no wrap over her thin housedress. "Camille, let's go inside the courthouse. I'll use one of their maps to dowse with. We'll find her. You have to believe that."

The trio climbed the granite steps and entered the court-house. As they hurried through the lobby, she dug in her coat pocket and pulled out her crystal; thank goodness she'd left it there this morning when leaving the Woodsons'.

"I blame myself," Jefferson gulped. "She did this because of me and . . . everything." He glanced at Camille, who met his look with hollow eyes.

"She never said a word," said Camille. "Last night she was fine, went to bed as usual. I woke up this morning thinking she was sleeping in. When I went in her room to wake her, I found a note."

Trini stopped in front of the land claims office door. "May I see it?"

Camille handed her a scrap of paper with shaking fingers, and Trini read the note from the twelve-year-old woman-child who now roamed the countryside teeming with desperate men.

"Mama, I have to leave here. Don't worry, I will call you later from my travels. Love, Stephanie."

Trini raised her eyes to Jefferson's. "Have you talked to the sheriff?"

"Yes. He said he'd start calling to find out the route of the truck. We were on our way to get our car and drive to Colorado Springs when we saw you. But I don't know if Mallis will do anything. Do you imagine he would help?"

"I honestly don't know," Trini said. She looked at Camille's frantic eyes. "But I think you should do everything you can."

Jefferson nodded as he pulled open the door. "You're right. Let's see what you come up with."

The group entered the room, and Mr. Henry raised his head from a map spread on the top of the counter. "Well, back again, are we?" he said.

"Mr. Henry," Trini said, "these are the LeClairs. We'd like to use your maps. Could I see one for the entire state?"

"Well now, this is highly irregular. Highly irregular." He bobbed his head and his throat vibrated. The eyes bulged behind the wire spectacles. "Like I said before, these are official property of Coyote County." He lightly patted the map he'd been studying. "No one's supposed to be using these but authorized personnel. And as the supervisor—"

"Mr. Henry." Trini leaned forward setting her nose as close as she could get to his own without vaulting over the counter. "We have an emergency. You're welcome to stand here and guard the map with your life, but we need to use it now."

He ran a finger between his neck and his collar. "Well, it's not that I don't want to help, nosir-ee, not at all, but I'm legally responsible for these documents, you know. Can be called up any time in a court of law and—"

"Mr. Henry," Trini said. She took a deep breath, smiled and tucked a piece of hair behind her ear. "You've been so helpful to me this morning. I'm sure you wouldn't mind, would you, if I just used your maps for a minute more? I'm sure you wouldn't mind."

He gave her a half smile. "You won't hurt them, will you?"

Trini smiled wider. "I won't even touch them."

He bent down and disappeared behind the counter, then rose hefting a large leather book. It thudded as he dropped it onto the countertop.

"Everybody wants to look at my maps today. First Sheriff Mallis, then you," he nodded to the LeClairs, "now them. I can't imagine this office is always this busy. If it keeps up, we'll have to hire another clerk, I can see that right now. I've got work to do, important documents to—"

"Sheriff Mallis wanted to look at your maps?" Trini asked.

"Yup. But just the county and townships. Not the state."

"What was he looking for?"

Mr. Henry tucked his chin in creating folds of thin flesh

above the Adam's apple and regarded her with an indignant gaze. "Well now, I reckon that's police business wouldn't you? Besides, he didn't tell me. And even if he did . . ." He stared at her.

Jefferson leaned forward and spoke. "May we see the maps now, Mr. Henry?"

Mr. Henry placed his hand on the book. "State of Colorado and all counties, townships, municipalities—about anything you want."

"Just the state map, please." Trini swiveled the book toward her and opened the cover. The map spanned the first two pages. "Camille, may I see Stephanie's note?"

Trini took the crumpled paper then reached into her pocket for the crystal. Holding its string between her thumb and index finger, she let her beacon dangle a fraction above the map.

"What's this business?" Mr. Henry scowled behind his glasses.

Trini glanced up at him, then back to the map. "I'm going to use the map to dowse. The LeClairs are looking for their daughter."

His knobby hand slapped the page. "Here now. That's state property, you know. You can't damage that."

Trini closed her eyes and said a quick prayer for patience. "This won't harm the map. It won't take long."

"I've never heard of anything like this. I—wait a minute." He squinted at her. "I heard about you. You're that dowser witch."

Trini sighed. "Mr. Henry, dowsing is not witchcraft. It's a technique for finding things."

He covered the book with his wiry arms and pulled it toward him. "No, no. No, you don't. You're not using my maps for anything like that."

Jefferson gently laid his hand on the man's arm. "My dear sir. Mr. Henry. You know me, do you not?"

Mr. Henry's Adam's apple quivered with his nod.

Jefferson continued, "I received your order at the store yesterday. You know. The order from that exclusive publishing house in San Francisco. The publishers who print particular pictures for clients with particular tastes. I have the package right now, in my office, locked in the safe. At least I hope I still have it. I'll have to check and make sure it hasn't disappeared, possibly added to someone else's order, by mistake naturally. But if that's the case, whoever had it would surely return it. Your name is on the material. There could be absolutely no question as to the owner."

Behind his lenses, Mr. Henry blinked deep and slow several times, then darted his eyes to Trini and Camille.

Jefferson's smile oozed sophisticated charm. "May we use the map? Please?"

"Well," Mr. Henry said, "I suppose if you don't damage it, it'd be all right."

"Good," Jefferson said. "Thank you. And you may rest assured that your satisfaction is guaranteed from Ludlin Mercantile."

Trini studied Jefferson. She was discovering a lot of new things about her friend, from his sexual orientation to the special services he offered his customers. She felt her perception of him shift. She briefly marveled at how truly private people were. Just when she thought she really knew someone, she'd discover another feature of his life, his personality. It had happened with Roy last night, when he had disclosed his marriage, and now Jefferson.

Trini refocused and pulled the book toward her. Again she dangled the crystal over the map. Let it come, now, let it come. "Where's Stephanie?" she whispered. "Find the girl."

The muscles between her shoulder blades knotted, but under the gray sleeves of her dress, her arms remained smooth and calm. The crystal hung static, the light in the room giving it a purple cast. She was under pressure. Just give it a second.

Trini breathed deeply and closed her eyes, waiting for the whorls on her fingertips to quiver with sensitivity. "Show me the girl," she murmured. "Where is she?" The crystal dangled lifelessly from its cord. Trini withdrew it and rotated her neck and shoulders.

"Should we leave the room?" Camille asked.

"No," Trini said. "No, it's all right. The crystal can be a little slow when it's cold outside. Just give me minute." The radiator hissed with a new burst of heat, and the room bore close and dry. Trini stretched her arms in front of her and repositioned the crystal.

"Show me Stephanie LeClair," she said.

A biting tingle wiggled through her shoulders, but then evaporated, and the hand of apprehension gripped her throat. Not now. Not today. Please don't fail today. She frowned in concentration and clasped the note tighter in her palm.

"Where is the girl?" she whispered.

She waited for the veins to transform to the small sharp ridges and stretch the skin in the top of her hands with their swelling, but they remained smooth and invisible. Nothing. Not a tingle. She might as well be holding air, for all the response she was getting. A flame of panic burst inside her.

"Show me the girl," she commanded.

"Maybe you need something other than a note," said Jefferson. "I have one of Stephanie's sweaters she left at the store. Would that help?"

Trini withdrew her hand from the map and rubbed her palms together. "Yes. Yes. Let's try that." Of course. Clothing or jewelry, an item that carried a person's skin particles, was always the most effective guide for dowsing. She should have thought of it earlier.

"I'll go get it." He hurried from the office.

Trini took off her coat and draped it over the counter beside the atlas. She kept her eyes on the map, but behind her she felt Camille's intense stare and heard her small gasps of stress. Trini massaged her arms and then rolled the crystal between her palms. Maybe if she relaxed a minute.

"So what's the matter?" Mr. Henry asked. "How come the thing isn't working?" He stood back from the counter, as if stepping out of harm's way of the dowsing crystal.

Camille spoke softly, "Mr. Henry. Would it be too much trouble for you to leave us alone for a minute? I'd appreciate it."

"Oh, no. No. I'm sorry, ma'am," he came forward and patted the page in front of him, "but I'm responsible for state property. I'm the one who'll pay if anything is damaged."

"But as you can see," Camille continued, "no property will be damaged. I think it would help matters if you leave."

Trini was surprised at Camille's diplomacy. It would be her usual style to demand Mr. Henry immediately withdraw on pain of her creating a public spectacle.

He heaved a sigh and stared at Camille. "I guess I could go in the mineral records room over there." He jiggled a knobby finger at Trini. "But don't try anything funny. I can see you from the doorway." He turned and entered a small room lined with leather volumes. He looked at them over his shoulder. "I can see you fine from here."

"That's fine, Mr. Henry. Thank you," said Camille.

Trini continued to massage her hands together as she spoke to Camille. "He's taking Merle Woodson's place here."

A sneer lifted the corner of Camillle's mouth. "Merle Woodson," she muttered. But in the next instant, the disdain was replaced by the frantic eyes of a desperate mother.

What did that comment mean? Obviously she was scornful of Woodson, but why? What had he done to her? She'd like to ask

Camille about that, but just then the door opened, and Jefferson entered carrying a blue sweater.

"Okay," he said. He handed the sweater to Trini. "Let's try this."

She rubbed the sweater between her palms, and concentrated on merging her energy with Stephanie's. She gripped the garment in her left hand and dangled the crystal over the map with her right. Why wouldn't the knot inside her relax? How could she dowse if she wasn't relaxed? Trini breathed deeply. Okay. Don't think. Just dowse. She hunched over the book.

"Show me Stephanie LeClair," she whispered.

The crystal hung motionless. She shifted her weight. "Where is Stephanie? Show her to me. Show me."

Of all the times for her to fail. Why not when she was dowsing for Merle Woodson's body? Or for a water source under the dried grassland? But not now. Please don't lose the power now.

"Show me the girl," she insisted. The crystal remained limp and dead, a rock hanging from a cord. She raised her blurry eyes to Jefferson.

"I'm sorry." Her voice cracked as she spoke and she shifted her eyes to Camille. "I'm sorry. It's just not going to work. I can't do it."

Jefferson placed a hand on her shoulder. Camille put a handkerchief to her damp eyes and turned toward the door.

Mr. Henry trotted to the counter, his arms extended to claim his property. "Well, then, you won't be needing my maps anymore I guess. Right?" No one answered him as he slammed the cover closed and lifted the book from the counter.

Jefferson surveyed her face. "I want to talk to Mallis again. Maybe he's heard something. We'll find her." He squeezed her shoulder.

"Jefferson, I'm so sorry."

He held the door open for her. "You tried your best, Trinidad, and I thank you. We'll find her."

As they descended the courthouse steps, Trini surveyed the street and caught sight of Roy Eastman's truck parked in front of the sheriff's office. Roy got out, slammed the door behind him, then climbed the steps to the office. As she walked to her truck, she watched him, watched Camille and Jefferson trotting toward the sheriff's and felt like she was floating somehow above it all.

Her dowsing was gone. When she'd failed at it years ago, with the child in the snow, it'd been different. The message had come then, but garbled; first one location, then the next, but at least there had been some movement of the crystal. Later, she'd found out she was pregnant. The failure had an explanation. Her body had evidently adjusted to the condition, though, because she dowsed several times while she carried her child, when she was in Kansas City. Never in all her life had the crystal been dead.

Trini climbed into her truck, exhausted, leaned her head back against the rear window and sat with her eyes closed. She drifted off, mentally traveled into her beloved prairie that stretched before her, going nowhere, surrounded by golden space. The fantasy of leaving, running away, drifted through her thoughts as it always did in particularly hard times. Leave Parn and Katherine and Jake. And Roy. Just pack and leave. She could drive to St. Joseph, Missouri, find her child, somehow explain to the adoptive family that the child needed her mother and—

A tap at the window, and she opened her eyes. Roy. In spite of herself, her stomach flipped a little in excitement. He opened the passenger door and climbed in beside her, filling the truck cab with his piney scent. His eyes seemed to change to a dark gray as he smiled. The dimple didn't appear, and he scrutinized her face.

"Do you have time to take a drive?" he asked.

She nodded. Her mind was numb, and she was past caring about anything. If her dowsing was gone, then she'd lost herself.

"Good. Let's go down to the river," he said.

Trini drove through town and turned down the river road. They wound their way through bare-limbed elms, fluffy cedars and brown brush. She pulled into a small grove of pines and turned off the ignition. The waterfall, several feet upstream, roared low in the background and a few birds called from the trees around them. The water cooled the air noticeably, and Trini pulled her coat close around her neck.

Roy took off his hat and hung it on his knee, laid his arm across the back of the seat and cupped his hand around her shoulder. She turned her head to find his gray eyes intent on hers, and she noted his ruddy cheeks above the angled jaw. He looked manly and healthy and strong.

"Cold?" he asked.

"A little, but I'm all right."

He leaned closer. She smelled the coffee on his breath and realized his eyelashes were brush-thick and velvet black. She let her eyes roam to the lush silver hair.

"Does premature gray run in your family?" she asked.

He smiled wide, the dimple settled in and he examined her face with a thoroughness that made her stomach squiggle.

"Yes," he said, "it does, as a matter of fact. My mother's brother was gray by the time he was eighteen. I saved mine until after the war."

"Did going through the war make it turn gray sooner, do you think?"

He sobered but continued to study her. "I imagine. A lot changes during war. Inside a man."

"What changed inside you?"

He leaned away from her and gazed out the windshield. "Oh,

more than I like to think about. But not who I was, or how I chose to think about my life. Those things had to do with me, not some war."

"But did war change you forever?"

"Yes, but not as profoundly as love."

"When you met your wife?"

"And lost her, yes."

"I know what you mean."

He looked at her again and smiled. "I know you do. And in a way, it's good that we have that in common."

"Why?"

He looked at her a moment more and leaned forward. She knew the kiss was coming, didn't want it to, but thought she might die if he stopped. He covered her mouth, warm and soft, and searching with his lips as he had a moment ago with his eyes. The melted feeling came again, in the bottom of her stomach and between her legs. It was a thorough kiss, long and deep, and towards the end of it, he brushed the tip of his tongue between her lips sending a jolt up her thighs. When he drew away, she found herself gulping for air.

"I've been thinking about you," he murmured. "A lot."

She stared at him.

"Probably too much," he said.

She smiled.

"And you," he said as he moved away a little, "have been thinking about Parn. And about Stephanie LeClair."

The names brought her back to the real world. Reluctantly, she released the delicious sensations. "Oh, Roy. You heard then?"

"Yes. I was in the sheriff's office when the LeClairs came in."

"Did Jefferson tell you I couldn't find her by dowsing?"

"No. What happened?"

"I wish I knew. I couldn't get any response."

He kneaded her shoulder and leaned forward to kiss the tip

of her nose. "Sorry," he said.

"Me, too." She closed her eyes and leaned her head back on his arm. "Me, too." She turned to look at him. "You've never told me. What do you think of my dowsing?"

"I'd seen you dowse before the sheriff's office, remember, at Warneski's place for water?"

"Yes, I remember. But what do you think about it? I mean, what's your opinion of it?"

He combed through his hair with his heavy fingers and looked out the window again. He stayed silent a minute and spoke without looking at her. "During the war, I saw a good number of things I never believed could have happened. Things I don't want to think about."

"It must have been awful."

"It was." He sat silent and staring out the windshield. "I reached one conclusion: Nothing's impossible. Not when it comes to what people can, or will, do." He looked at her and smiled. "And the thing is, see, I believe in you. I think you're one of the finest people I've ever known in my life. When Jim Bates told me he'd got you to marry him, I was so envious I couldn't talk to him for a month." He grinned at her. "So if I believe in you, I guess I have to believe in what you do, including your dowsing."

She was choked with emotion. She had no idea Roy Eastman had even known she was alive, except as a friend's wife. And here he was telling her how much he thought of her. A fine person, he'd said.

"Thank you," she whispered.

"And I was impressed, very impressed, when you found Merle Woodson."

"You know Mallis accused me of knowing all along where Merle's body was. Said it looked like to him I could have been an accessory to the murder."

"Trini, don't take him so seriously. He's a blowhard with a bad temper."

"I think he's more than that. I think he's dangerous." She studied his face a minute. "You certainly are tolerant of a man who just fired you."

"I don't like the man, that's true, but that doesn't mean I think he's some kind of monster. And just now, when the Le-Clairs told him about Stephanie running away, he was very concerned and started telephoning right away."

"Well, you'll pardon me if I don't put as much faith in the man's intentions as you do."

He was silent and she leaned her head back against his arm again and closed her eyes. She could sleep for a week. Mallis and Parn and Roy and Stephanie and Katherine—too much. Where would she get the energy to deal with them all? All she'd wanted to do, all she'd ever wanted in the months since Jim had died was to be left alone. If she could just be left alone to heal and be quiet and think. Why had she been pushed into the middle of this maelstrom? And now, without her dowsing, how could she go on?

Roy's whisper brought her from her reverie. "You're carrying a big load on your back right now."

She opened her eyes and rolled her head on his arm to look at his face. She smiled a little. "Feels like the world."

His thumb rubbed her shoulder. "Lot of people counting on you. You should be proud of what you're doing for Woodson's kids, Trin. And even though I think you're jumping to conclusions about Mallis, I know you're fighting hard for Parn. And I hope I can help, at least a little. What I wanted to tell you, why I wanted to see you, is that I got ahold of a Marshal Steadman in Denver. He or a deputy will be here in three days to look into Parn's arrest. They have another case they're finishing up and will come down then."

He'd called Denver for her? "We don't have to wait for a state's attorney? How'd you do that?"

"I know a couple of guys that are marshals. I asked them for a favor."

She scanned his face, watching his expression, and saw frank admiration in his eyes. "You did a favor for me by letting me see Parn yesterday and it got you fired. Now you're doing another one for me. I'm surprised you did that, called a marshal in."

"Why?"

"You just don't seem that concerned about Mallis, that he'd be doing anything wrong."

He heaved a sigh. "I don't know what to think. I'd like to wait until the judge gets here before I draw any conclusions. But I knew you'd feel better knowing a marshal would look into this, so I called. Meanwhile, I think Mallis will come around, as far as letting me have my job back. And until he does, I can make myself visible around the office. I'll keep an eye on Parn. He'll be all right."

She smiled at him. "To tell you the truth, I'm just so tired I don't care about anything. Tired and discouraged and feeling like I want to run away."

"Well, please don't. I just found you. I wouldn't want to lose you now." He lowered his mouth over hers again. She rested her hand on his chest and felt the kiss meld into her weary heart. His fresh scent traversed through her senses and she became acutely conscious of the soft hide of his sheepskin coat under her hand. He was gentle, but as the seconds passed, she felt him lean into her, press his energy on her. Finally, she broke away, gasping to catch her breath.

"Roy, I don't . . . I want to have some time. Jim just died eight months ago. I need time alone before I get involved with . . . with all this."

He stayed close to her face and spoke low. "No rush, Trin.

No rush. I just want you to know you can count on me to be here to help you. But don't worry, I can restrain myself." He looked at her with serious eyes. "At least I can give it a damn good try."

CHAPTER THIRTEEN

She left Roy in front of the sheriff's office, drove south on Main toward her house and tried to bring order to her emotions. Roy had been good to call the marshal's office. He'd been better than good, but the obligation his act entailed sat inside her like a stone. It wasn't that she didn't appreciate his intervention, because she did. But she knew that although he'd asked for nothing in return, he desired her affections. If she was honest with herself, she knew the word "desired" was an understatement. She could see the hunger in his eyes, hear it in the intensity of his voice. All the signals that spoke far louder than words told her Roy craved her attentions. And she'd be lying to herself if she didn't admit that inside her heart, she felt the stirring of deep feelings—feelings she thought had died with Jim.

But her questions about Roy were too much for her to dwell on right now. She couldn't dowse, and her heaving emotions obscured any rational thought concerning him, or even Parn. If her dowsing was lost, she was lost. She would be as handicapped as if she'd lost a limb.

She needed to go to her own home for a while, be in familiar surroundings to think, and to try the one thing that might recover her lost ability. In the top drawer of the old scarred desk in the attic, there was a map, a map that she'd used countless times to dowse for her child. Maybe, oh God please, maybe, her dowsing would return by enacting the familiar rite. She turned right off the blacktop onto the dirt road named Aspen. At the end of the block, she saw the corner of the yew hedge that marked her driveway. Trini parked in front of the shed she used for a garage, and gazed around at her property. It seemed like years since she'd been home.

The tidy house stood several yards from the garage, across the brown lawn, and was framed by mature cottonwoods. Her garden, between the house and the garage, lay dormant. Next spring, she'd plant flowers and vegetables and herbs and anything else she could plunk into the ground. Next spring. The thought of burying her hands in warm soil brought a new wave of tears. She loved to garden. The earth and the growing things soothed her sensitive hands and acted as a balm to the large tendons and muscles. She closed her eyes briefly, sealing the vision. She would spend hours in her garden and wouldn't think of Parn or Roy or George Mallis. She'd just work the soil and grow things.

She climbed from the truck, walked across the yard and up the wooden steps to her back door, the same door where only three days ago, Parn had stood with Mallis and Roy, asking for her help. The key turned sounding the familiar click, and she entered her kitchen.

Yesterday evening, when she'd come home to pick up some clothes and her personal items to take to the Woodsons', she'd closed all the curtains and drawn the blinds throughout the house. She'd turned off her oil heater as well, so a dense cold now clamped around her. Still wearing her coat and carrying her purse, she walked across the kitchen to the attic door, opened it and climbed the narrow wooden staircase to the top. The musty air assaulted her, and after she turned the desk lamp's key, she saw the clouds of her own breath. She reached into the top drawer, pulled the frayed map from its place, unfolded it and brushed her hand over its top to smooth it flat. She withdrew the crystal from her pocket and stretched out the attached string, then checked the knot that held the rock. Still good. She ran the string through her fingers. Smooth and undamaged. It wasn't the twine that was defective. The string had nothing to do with the dowsing. Actually, neither did the crystal. The talent was within her, or rather had been in her. She wrapped the cord around her fingers and let the crystal drop down a fraction above the dot of St. Joseph, Missouri. She pleaded to the universe. *Please come back.*

Trini bent close to the map and whispered, "Where is she? Where's my daughter?"

Cold and dead. Not even a quickening of the nerves, a shimmy on her flesh. Hot tears blurred her vision. "No," she whispered, "no. Please."

She repositioned the crystal, closed her eyes and focused on the back of her neck. She'd always envisioned the talent as residing there, largely because that's where the prickles started, like a curled and sleeping animal that stretched awake at her command. But now, rather than becoming aware of the white heat of her power, she shivered with the cold. And fear. Unbidden, a thought invaded her consciousness: The dowsing was dead.

Desperate for her talent to reveal itself, she commanded the crystal, and her voice reverberated through the frozen space. "Show me my daughter!" But the power inside her lay inert. Maybe it had just died and dissipated through her body, out of her lungs and into the air like a flock of birds scattering over the prairie. Whatever had happened, it was gone. The dowsing was gone. The tears came then, large and powerful, from the middle of her soul. Tears for herself. Tears for Roy. Tears for Jim. Tears for Parn. And tears of useless longings for her child and for her dearest possession, the power to find the unseen.

She didn't know how much time had passed, but it couldn't

have been more than an hour. Through the small attic window, she saw that the sky still displayed the same slate gray it had when she'd pulled into her driveway. She should leave now. She should get back to the Woodson children. She pulled herself out of the desk chair, her legs heavy as tree trunks. One step at a time. Fold the map. Switch off the desk lamp. One step in front of the other to climb down the stairs. She closed the attic door, crossed the kitchen to the back door and left.

Her tires buzzed on the blacktop as she sped along the county highway. The winter air from the plains thrust itself into the truck cab, through her coat, and into her bones. Trini glanced up through the windshield at the mat of clouds. Snow weather. No flurries yet, but any day now, a blizzard could blow down from the mountains and dump enough snow on Coyote County to bring life to a standstill. And if that happened, Parn would be isolated in jail. With Mallis standing guard. A shiver went up her spine. And what about Stephanie LeClair? If there was a blizzard, roads would be closed and Stephanie would be stuck wherever she happened to disembark from the fuel truck that had carried her away from Ludlin. She shivered again. Maybe it wouldn't snow. Maybe something would go right.

About two miles outside of town, Trini approached the turnoff that led to Parn's cabin. It was only a few minutes out of her way, and she hadn't been there in months. Mallis and Roy had been here right after they'd recovered Woodson's body. Mallis had found the incriminating hammer in Parn's wood stack, and Roy was careful to tell her two times now, once when they first showed her the hammer and again last night at his house, that he'd been with Mallis when they'd discovered the murder weapon. But buried in the woodpile? Even if Parn was guilty—please God, don't let him be guilty—would he be so stupid as to hide the murder weapon in his woodpile? She almost laughed aloud. Certainly not. She didn't know how he'd planted that hammer, but she'd find out. Yes, she decided, she'd like to see Parn's place. It might yield some information to her, something she could use against Mallis. Besides, there was one thing she wanted to look for up there: Parn's bootlegging loot. That damned bootlegging. She had never voted for a Democrat in her life, but when Roosevelt ran on repeal of Prohibition, she didn't have to think twice. She would have voted for the devil himself to end this horrible bootlegging.

Trini glanced in the rearview mirror, slowing her speed and preparing to brake for the turnoff. A black sedan that had been behind her some distance since town approached her from the rear, and she could see the outline of a hatless driver. It could be anyone on the well-traveled highway. Despite her rationalization, a small twist of apprehension turned her stomach. Was she being followed? She swiveled the wheel and made a sharp left turn onto a dirt road, her truck lurching from side to side through the ruts. Trini glanced in the mirror again. The sedan stayed to the blacktop speeding on its way. Nothing. Just her jumpy nerves. She started her drive up the hill.

The last time she'd been to Parn's was in May. Let's see: She'd just put in her peppers, Jim had been dead a month, the mountain trees were bursting with new growth, and . . . she'd been a dowser. The weight of her devastating void pressed on her again. She wouldn't let herself think. She'd reach deep inside and control her emotions. She wouldn't be idle. She wouldn't think about dowsing.

The truck waddled along, and when she crested the hill, she pulled over and turned off the ignition. She climbed out of the truck and walked a few yards ahead, crossing her arms to keep herself warmer. She surveyed the land below. The white trunks of naked aspens and birch lined the valley like sentinels guarding a paradise. No matter the season, Trini loved this valley. The town of Meadowland stood at the far end, and she could make out the roofline of its main street. She looked to her left and up; Parn's property sat at the top of the rise. Just below her, and to her right, the fenced pasture and tumbledown shed marked the center of the Fatzer property. Decades ago, the railroad bought the acreage from family. They'd long since left the area, but the name still designated that particular piece of land—land that now bore one of the "X-DOME" designations on Merle Woodson's map. She searched for the railroad tracks and finally found them outlining the valley below, weaving in and out of the trees, then disappearing into the hills. Railroad land. According to Mr. Henry, railroad land for decades.

What was DOME for? If DOME didn't own land, then what did the X's on the map mean? Merle's ledgers said that land had been purchased from the Santa Fe Railroad. Yet, county records said it hadn't been sold. Had Merle worked a private deal, buying land secretly from the railroad? Was he looking to develop? And what did Mallis have to do with it all? Why was his name on one of Woodson's maps? Puzzled, she walked back to the truck. She put the truck in gear and drove the last quarter mile up the hill to Parn's property.

When she stopped the truck in front of his cabin, she had to swallow hard. Her brother's rustic little home looked forlorn and lonely. The blinds were drawn over the windows and a sludge-gray dust coated the stone stoop. She found Parn's key under the rock by the sage bush, inserted it into the keyhole and turned the knob. The old wooden door screeched open.

Despite the cold, dim interior, it was evident the room had been searched. An earthy Navajo rug covered his log-framed bed, but it was rumpled and the bottom sheet was pulled out. Someone had searched under the mattress. The stack of folded rugs that usually rested on the floor at the foot of his bed was now scattered, as if someone had shaken them out and tossed them to the floor. One of the birch chairs reserved for the hewn wooden table lay on its side in the middle of the room. Ashes littered the floor; someone had searched in the hearth, too. Someone indeed. She'd bet her dowser's crystal that Mallis had been the interloper.

Trini meandered across the room, examining the fireplace and the rough log mantel. Several lanterns, a box of matches, and some iron fire tongs occupied its surface. She pushed aside the muslin window shade for more light to better survey the kitchen area. A can of kerosene sat on the floor beside the dry sink, and on the shelf above it rested a tin of flour, a can of baking soda, and a butter crock. She lifted the crock lid. Empty. An open bag of coffee rested on the counter. Spilled beans scattered themselves across the surface. She knew Parn would have taken care not to leave coffee to spoil. Mallis had been thorough. He wanted the bootlegging money and he'd searched every nook and cranny to find it.

She allowed herself a smile of satisfaction: The money wasn't in the cabin. When she'd found out years ago about his bootlegging, the first time, when Parn swore to her he'd never do it again, he'd shown her where he kept the illegal loot. While pleading for her understanding, he had rationalized his actions by telling her how useful the money would be to them, just in case. She knew what he'd been thinking about: Jim had just suffered his first heart attack. And Parn was concerned about his sister's welfare. Did he still use the secret hiding place? She turned and walked out the back door.

A gust of wind swirled her coat and dress around her legs, and her brogans kicked up dust as she hurried over the rise to the north of the cabin. She walked down the hill and across a dry gully where she was sheltered a little from the biting wind. The land started to rise again and a few feet up the incline, Trini started looking for the faint trail. It wound among the rocks, heading east for several hundred feet. Where was the marker? There, just to side of the trail where Parn had showed her, a pile of small boulders rested, some in a natural formation, and some that Parn had stacked in order to make his stone vault. She went to the far side of the mound and squatted on her haunches. The small hole she expected to see was still there, between the darkest rock and the boulder shaped like a squirrel hunched over a nut.

God forbid she was invading a rattler's nest. She took a deep breath for courage, pushed her coat sleeve up, and reached in. She could get her arm into the crevice, but even though she could feel the rough burlap at her fingertips, she couldn't grasp hold of the fabric. She lay on her stomach, and stretching as far as she could, finally clutched a handful of burlap and pulled. It squeezed partway through the fissure. She sat up and, using her other hand, shifted the contents, then tugged once more. It snapped from the opening, taking her backwards with the force. Trini sat the bag on the ground in front of her and unknotted the top.

Inside were packages of bills, each a few inches thick and some of the top ones crinkled from being shoved into their hiding place. She lifted one of the packets and fanned through it. A bundle of twenties. She flipped through the other four stacks and found they were like the first. There had to be several hundred dollars here. Was this all? Or had there been more that Woodson had kept in his own secret place? She'd like to ask Parn about that. She pulled apart the top of the bag and peered inside. Nothing else. No letters or documents or testimonials. Nothing written that would incriminate Mallis or help Parn.

Parn and his big dreams. And look where it got him: He sat in jail, in danger of losing his life, and his sister held a bag of buried money. Bitter anger welled up in her. Was it worth it? she wanted to ask him. Was all your scheming and dreaming for the big score worth it? She retied the top and stood up, brushing the loose dirt from her coat. The lower button had popped off, and her dress had been torn, obviously in her search between the stones. She bent to retrieve the button beside the pile of rocks then fingered the gash in her skirt. A perfectly good dress, ruined. Well then, she could just use her brother's booty to buy herself some wool and make a new one. She'd make it blue and soft and warm. Maybe she'd treat Katherine to a length of cloth as well. They'd both look stunning in new winter dresses. She smiled at herself, chagrinned at her own human nature. Just a while ago, she was cursing the illegal activity that led to this money, now she was planning how to spend it. What odd, contradictory creatures humans were, rationalizing all manner of actions. She shook her head at herself, and holding the sack by its knot, started back toward the cabin. It seemed to her—

Smoke!

She ran across the gully and up the embankment, then stopped at the crest of the hill and looked down at the cabin. Fumes clogged her nose and throat. She coughed and held her hand over her mouth. Orange flames shot out the window and door, and through the gap of a destroyed wall, she could see Parn's table and bed engulfed in fire. Suddenly, a blast and the back half of the roof blew to the sky. The kerosene in the kitchen. A black cloud rolled from the front door enveloping her truck in a thick haze.

Her truck. She'd parked it only a few feet away from the door. Oh please no, not the truck. She bolted down the hill and tripped, falling to her hands and knees. Her dress caught and ripped as she staggered to her feet. Stumbling her way through the acrid fog, she threw the burlap sack through the open window, jumped in, turned the key and ground the gear into first. She U-turned in the small clearing and headed down the hill. When she got far enough away from danger, she pulled over. Climbing from the cab, she watched the ash and smoke circle in the sky. She hurried to the top of the nearest outcrop and scanned the area. The roof of a black sedan disappeared around a bend. Was it the same sedan that had been behind her earlier? Had it doubled back after passing behind her on the blacktop? Whether it was the same one or not made no difference now. And she'd never find out; half the country owned black sedans and she hadn't seen anything but the flash of the roof anyway. Not one distinguishing detail. There was only one fact that mattered: Someone had torched the cabin hoping she was inside.

CHAPTER FOURTEEN

When she opened her eyes, Trini knew she'd slept for only about an hour; the pattern on the wall of sunshine through lace curtains told her the sun was almost where she'd left it when she'd collapsed onto Katherine's bed. How wonderful it would be, she thought, if she could awaken to a new life, swept golden and clear like a thunderstorm across the prairie. But even as she thought it, while pushing herself up on the feather pillow, all of her demons at once scrambled for attention. They'd been waiting for her: her lost dowsing, the mystery of DOME, the attempt on her life in Parn's cabin, now burned to ash.

God help her, someone had tried to kill her. Her intuition told her that whoever was driving the black sedan she'd seen from the top of the hill was responsible for the fire. The sheriff's car was a black sedan. So was the Coyote County deputy's car, the car Taggert had been driving when he came to Woodson's mine. Did Taggert want her dead? Unlikely. She didn't think he was working under Mallis's orders. He'd been at Woodson's mine, ready to beat his boss to the illegal liquor. He had no reason to wish harm to Trini. The only person who'd like to see her dead would be the person who she most bothered by being alive—George Mallis. She'd never be able to prove that he set the fire, but in her own mind, she was convinced her guess was right. A beam of insight flashed. If her suspicions were true, then Mallis didn't know she'd escaped. He thought the pesky gnat was gone. For all he knew, she was lying charred and dead inside the cabin while her truck sat out front, waiting for an accidental discovery. For a while, she was invisible. How could she use that?

She wanted to jump in her truck right now, drive to Roy's place and tell him she'd been right about Mallis's evil intentions. Together they could go into town, and Roy could witness firsthand Mallis's look of horror when he saw Trini approach him, alive and well. The moment of surprise would be to her advantage. She'd go to Roy now, prove to him once and for all what a ruthless man Mallis was.

She sat up on the bed, ran her hand through her tangled hair and then looked at her ruined dress, tattered and stained with dirt and soot. Where were the children? Now she remembered. She'd somehow managed to drive home, her grip on the steering wheel holding the blackness of shock and exhaustion at bay. Finally, she'd stumbled into the kitchen. On the table was a note telling her the Nortons, the Woodsons' neighbors to the south, had picked up Jake and Katherine and taken them back to their ranch to see a new foal. They'd return after dinner.

Trini's muscles screamed in protest as she stood. She felt like she'd been in an avalanche and carried down a mountain on a shower of boulders. Her arms were tender and bruised. And her hands. She turned them over in front of her. Her dead, empty hands. A river of despair swelled inside her. Her dowsing was gone. Where to go, how to go from here was impossible for her to see. Why had she lost her dowsing? Was it the anxiety and horror of the last few days? Was it the thought of Parn, his life truly in danger, that dammed her sensitivity to the vibrations of the earth she received during dowsing?

She reached under Katherine's bed and her hand found the burlap bag of cash she'd hidden there before she collapsed into an exhausted sleep. She withdrew the sack and opened the top, once again peering into its contents. The stash of money from

Parn's "hidey hole" disturbed her. His wild greed had led him into the world of gangsters and mob men, extortion and murder. He'd been living a secret life. And as much as she loved her brother, and feared for his safety near Mallis, she admitted to herself she resented him. All this time he'd been living nothing like their parents had taught them to live. He was spoiled. Like a child crying for his toy, he demanded things immediately and would not be refused. The niggling doubt that had made its home in the back of her mind seemed to be maturing daily: He might be guilty. What if he and Woodson had argued, fought, over the bootlegging run, or maybe fought over whatever Merle Woodson was involved in with the DOME Partnership? What if Merle had denied Parn what he wanted, more money or more control in the liquor trade, and Parn, in anger, had lashed out? What if Parn *had* accidentally killed Merle Woodson? They could have been drunk on some of their own nefarious product, their tempers hard and white-hot. What if Mallis had not planted the hammer at all? What if it really *was* a murder weapon?

Even though she fought them, tears came, and they rolled down her cheeks like the river falls where Roy had kissed her. She sank back onto the bed. It was too much. Too much for her. She'd done this to herself. She'd pushed and shoved so hard, she'd pushed the dowsing talent right out of herself. Her gift. Her specialness. She'd lost it. Roy was right. She couldn't just charge through this alone like a bull through a rodeo gate. What was the matter with her? In her mind's eye, she saw his face: the heavy silver hair, flashing dimple, the searching gray eyes. She'd like to see him right now, feel his hard chest under her hand, hear his breath in her ear, feel his lips on her own. She bent over and wept into her hands, then stopped in mid-sob.

"Anyone here? Hello?" A woman's voice from the kitchen.

Trini quickly retied the top of the bag, knelt down beside

Katherine's bed, and shoved it toward the wall. She pulled a folded quilt in front of it. Satisfied, she stood, grabbed one of her work shirts from the box she'd brought from home and wiped her face on its sleeve.

"Just a minute," she called. "I'll be right there."

She hurried across the room stopping in front of her image in the mirror that hung over Katherine's dresser. What a mess. The tangled nest on top of her head proved difficult to run her fingers through, and she only managed to straighten a couple of the worst knots. Using the shirtsleeve, she once again wiped at the dark smudges on her cheeks. That would have to do. She hurried from the room smoothing the front of her torn dress, but stopped in the hallway. She couldn't see anyone like this. She had to change.

"Hello?" the voice sang.

"Who is it?" she called.

"Hello? Anyone home?"

Her visitor was long on shouting and short on listening. That didn't sound like Corda Norton. Maybe one of the ladies from the church delivering a casserole for the children. "I'll be right there," Trini answered.

She hurried back into Katherine's bedroom and changed quickly, dropping the filthy dress on the floor. She pulled on her blue print housedress, fumbled through the buttons and then yanked on a clean pair of white ankle socks. She laced up the battered brogans and folded her socks over the tops. The shoes were scuffed beyond repair, but nothing could be done about that now. She could always use some of Parn's ill-gotten gains to buy new ones. New shoes and a new dress. Come to think of it, she just might do that. She needed new brogans anyway. And a pair of dressy pumps. And she could—what in the world was she doing, thinking about shoes? She must be going insane.

"Hello?" the woman called. "Are you coming?"

"Yes. Yes, sorry. I'm coming now."

While fastening her belt, Trini trotted down the hall and through the parlor. She halted at the kitchen threshold. Daryl Kerr stood outside the screen door, peering into the kitchen, his hand on his brow to shade his view.

"Oh, Daryl. Hello. I thought you were . . . I didn't know it was you." She never would have guessed it was Daryl with his poor, damaged voice.

"Hi, Trini. Sorry to catch you at a bad time. Where are Katherine and Jake?"

She supposed she'd get used to that falsetto if she was around him all the time, but it certainly would be difficult to live with.

"They're at the Nortons' for the day." She stopped at the screen door but didn't open it. In her rush to collapse on the bed when she'd returned, she must have left the main door ajar. She wished she'd closed it so that he couldn't have called through the screen. She really didn't want to talk with Daryl now. She had more pressing concerns. "Sorry, Daryl. I was just on my way out."

He smiled, the charm spreading across his wide face to the cap of black curls on his head. The green eyes studied her. "You don't look like you were on your way out. You look like you just got through a cat fight. And the cat won."

She felt the blood rush to her face and neck. She wasn't going to tell him about the fire. And she certainly didn't want Mallis to know she was alive and well. She had a sinking feeling of disappointment; Daryl was a gossip. Now that he'd found her here, she supposed it was too late. She thought briefly of asking him not to mention his visit to anyone so that she could surprise Mallis with her survival, but she dismissed the idea immediately. Asking him to do that would only provide one more morsel of news he'd want to share.

"Why did you stop by?" She grabbed her coat off the floor

where she'd flung it on the way to the bedroom and pushed her arms through the sleeves. He stepped aside to let her open the screen door and join him on the cement stoop. She closed the door behind her, gathered the coat at her throat and looked up past the oak-like chest into his face.

"I came over to bring some firewood." He gestured to the pickup whose bed was stacked with cut logs and thick branches. "I cleared out the brush and a good-sized pine from the back of our lot. I thought maybe Katherine could use the wood. You know, for when the relatives come for the funeral and all."

"How nice. Thank you, Daryl. That's thoughtful of you. The woodpile's around back."

"I know. I'll go ahead and unload it."

He lowered the truck gate. Using one hand to clasp the logs, he stacked the lumber against the thick bicep of his other arm. Trini watched silently as he emptied the load in three trips. When he was finished, he brushed his bear-paw hands together loosening the dirt.

She fought her impatience. It was only polite to offer him something for his trouble, but she wouldn't make the offer too welcoming. Maybe he'd refuse.

"Would you like a cup of coffee? I think there's still some left from this morning."

"Great. Thanks."

She knew her face fell with disappointment, but she couldn't help it. "Oh, okay. Come on in."

She led the way and he eased the screen door shut behind him. He started to close the main door, but she stopped him.

"Oh no. That's fine. Let's just leave it open." She spoke a little too quickly. "I mean, it's not that cool out, and the sun's shining." He was making her nervous. It was his voice. Something about being secluded in a closed room with him and that voice.

He sat at the table and rested his forearms on the yellow oilcloth. Trini poured coffee into a crockery cup, placed it on the table and then sat in the chair opposite him.

"Aren't you having any?" he asked.

"No. I'm fine. Do you want milk or sugar?"

He shook his head and sipped.

She could use this opportunity to ask about his mother. "Is Dottie okay?"

"Yes, yes of course. She's fine. Why wouldn't she be?"

"I went by the land office a while ago, and Mr. Henry said she'd left around noon. I was worried she was sick or something."

"Oh no. She never gets sick. Must be in her blood. I'm the same way. Strong as an ox and never sick. I tell her all the time, she'll work forever, won't need money to retire. I think she left work early to get some things done today. She's very upset about Merle Woodson, you know. Why did you go by the land office?" The schoolgirl lilt of his voice grew more pronounced the longer he spoke without stopping.

"I just wanted to talk with her about something that's come up. Just double-check about something."

"What?"

She hesitated. Typically Daryl, he was nosey, but there was really no reason why he shouldn't know about the DOME Partnership. Besides, maybe Dottie had mentioned it to him. "A partnership."

"What partnership?"

"There were just some things in Merle's papers that mentioned a partnership. I thought Merle would have said something to your mother about it."

He shook his head slowly, thinking it over. "Oh, I don't think so," he rasped. "She wouldn't have had anything to do with that."

"I don't mean she had anything to do with it. I just wanted to ask her about it. Maybe Merle mentioned it to her."

"Oh. Well, she never said anything to me, and I think she would have."

"That's okay," Trini said. "I'll catch her later." She thought for a minute. "Daryl, did Sheriff Mallis come by your house after I left the other evening?"

Pursing his lips, he regarded her a moment. "Yes. Why?"

"What did he want?"

"Nothing about this thing with Woodson's death and Parn. He just stopped by for a minute."

She'd like to ask him exactly what Mallis did want, but didn't. Sometimes, she wished she could be as brazenly inquisitive as Daryl Kerr, but she couldn't bring herself to do that. The politeness she'd been schooled to practice by her refined mother guided her. She waited for him to continue.

"He's really a stupid man, you know."

Again she waited, but he only looked at her, his scornful opinions about Mallis still evident on his face.

A surge of nausea threatened to overcome her for a second. Must be a delayed reaction from the panic of the fire. It settled as fast as it had appeared. "I just thought Dottie might have telephoned him," Trini said. "I thought maybe she'd been upset that I'd questioned her about Merle and had complained to the sheriff about it."

"No, she wasn't upset."

Trini wondered about that. She assumed that Dottie had telephoned the sheriff to complain about Trini's visit, but according to Daryl, Mallis's visit wasn't connected to hers. That order of events seemed odd to her, but she didn't have another theory.

She started to press him again for details when he spoke. "I guess you're just waiting for Judge Slaton to get here, to do the

177

arraignment."

"Yes. I'll be glad when it's over and done with." She lifted her hand to the back of her tight neck and rubbed through the soreness.

"I can see why," he said. He cocked his head to one side and his voice almost squeaked with his question. "Do you think Parn will be put to trial? How good are his chances of getting out of this?"

She rubbed her elbow and felt a scab there. She must have scraped it while digging for Parn's money or her fall down the hill. "I don't think he murdered Merle Woodson, if that's what you mean."

"Oh, no. No, I didn't mean that. But I know you suspect Mallis of manipulating this whole thing. I just wondered if you thought he might get away with it. It sounds like he has a good case against Parn. I heard about the hammer."

Trini squirmed in her seat a little. She supposed the whole town was talking about her vendetta against Mallis. She hadn't exactly made a secret of it, and after the scene in the café yesterday evening, Trini was sure their mutual rancor was well known.

"I'm just hoping for the best." It was a lame response, she knew, but her nervousness was increasing. Daryl was pointed in his questions and observations; Trini had the feeling he was only garnering information in order to satisfy his own ego. She could just hear him now, claiming to anyone who would listen, that he'd recently spoken to her, had the real story. It rankled that he took the liberty to ask her anything he wanted to.

She stood and lifted Daryl's cup. "You finished with this?"

He stood up and gently took the cup from her grip. He smiled, then tipped his head back to drain the contents, and she saw his rough black beard on the white of his throat. A white patch of scar tissue, probably from his injured vocal cords, covered the small indentation at the base of his neck and moved as he swallowed. He lowered his head, met her eyes and extended the cup to her. "Now I am," he said.

"Thanks," she said. She took it, crossed the room to the sink and set the cup inside. Facing him, she leaned against the counter behind her and hugged herself with her arms. "Thanks for the wood. Katherine will appreciate it. I don't mean to rush you, but I really need to . . ."

He waited for her with a placid smile.

"I need to go back to town. I need a couple of things at the store. Baking powder. More coffee, I think. A couple of other things. Small items."

"Okay, Trini," he rasped. "That's no problem at all. Glad to be of help." He turned and finally left. Trini breathed a sigh of relief.

She'd told Daryl she was going to town, and she would in a little while. First, though, she wanted to go by Roy's and tell him about the fire.

She changed from her housedress into her brown wool. She donned her thickest socks and the beat-up brogans, pulled on her coat, and wrapped her long red muffler around her neck. She grabbed her purse and keys and headed out the door.

As she drove, Trini rolled down both windows and let the cold prairie wind whirl through the truck cab. It felt good, like a slap in the face that she needed after a bout of hysteria. She slowed as she saw the sign for Digstown Road. This was the intersection that Merle Woodson had marked with X-DOME on his map. What had he wanted this scrub land for? The railway didn't run through this area, although Mr. Henry had assured her the Santa Fe owned this entire parcel. If Merle hadn't purchased land, then what had he purchased?

An idea boiled to the top of her consciousness, like it'd been buried all along and took until now to reveal itself. Of course. Water. If Merle wasn't buying the land, then he must be buying water rights. He must have knowledge, private knowledge, of water. She could drive into town and ask Mr. Henry to show her more purchases, this time for water rights instead of land. Or she could prove it to herself right now. She grinned with excitement. Maybe her dowsing could be recovered. Maybe all was not lost. And she hadn't tried the dowsing rod yet. Maybe it would be the one thing that would reawaken her sleeping talent. She dared to feel a trickle of hope.

She turned off the blacktop at Digstown Road, drove down a quarter mile or so then pulled over among the sparse weeds. The road curved down into a small gully and bent behind a shelf of boulders out of sight. Merle's map indicated DOME Partnership was to her left, on the east side of the road.

Wrapping her muffler around her neck, she got out of the truck. A gust of wind stung her eyes, bringing tears, and she squinted against it. A thin layer of dust settled on her brogans as she walked across the road and peered into the gulch below. The DOME spot looked unremarkable. Boulders and rock pierced the earth, and beyond the gulch, flat dusty land spread toward Kansas.

For a minute, she watched a hawk weave a circle in the distant sky, then she crossed the road back to the truck. She opened the driver's door, reached under the front seat and felt for the apple-wood branch she always kept there, her mother's dowsing rod. Lifting it from its place, she rubbed her hands over the smooth wood and examined the handles darkened by sweat stains from her mother's hands. Her mother had used the rod as far back as Trini could remember, and Trini was glad now for this comforting familiarity. After she'd died, her father had given it to her, made a special presentation of it. She only used it for water dowsing; other times she used her crystal. A heaviness pressed on her heart. Please let the rod work.

She walked across the road, and holding the branch with one hand and using her other hand to balance behind herself, she half-skidded, half-scooted down the side of the hill into the gully. She stood, and brushing the dust from her backside, walked toward a protrusion of boulders several feet in front of her, the knee-high weeds grabbing at her hem and scratching her legs. Maybe now. Maybe she'd get back her dowsing after all. Wasn't that a tingle in her fingers? Yes, she was sure. She held the two prongs, one in each hand, and extended the end of the Y straight out from her stomach. After taking a deep breath, she began. "Show me water," she said. "Where's the water?"

She walked slowly, carefully measuring out a twenty-pace square. Her mother had taught her this, the way of many dowsers, to pace a square, then the next square from there to be thirty paces, then forty and so on, widening the search as she needed. She'd get the pull when the rod found the source.

"Show me water," she whispered.

A sudden cold gust of wind brought the smell of coming snow, and the shrubs that covered the bottom of the gully vibrated in response. A faint whistling, the wind moving through rock formations, registered in the back of her mind. Trini focused on her physical sensations. Her fingertips held the small tingle, but the rod remained motionless. Dear God. Make it come. She continued to pace out the square, each step bringing her closer to tears. Nothing. Her hands, the rod, were dead.

"I seen your ma do that a time or two in her day, let me tell you."

Trini whirled around to see Lyle Butcher standing several yards behind her, the fringe of his buckskin jacket wafting in the cold wind. Beyond him, his mule stood tethered to a low shrub. She lowered the rod to her side and walked toward him.

"I didn't hear you come up. Your mule is quiet. Or sneaky."

She smiled to let him know she was teasing.

The creases around his blue eyes deepened, and yellowed teeth split the snarled gray beard in a grin. "That's Canary. Best transportation a man's got in these parts."

"Do you live around here or were you just passing by?"

"Little of both." He grinned, and the brim of his battered leather hat lifted with another burst of wind. He nodded toward the rod she held at her side. "I been watching you for a spell. Looks like you ain't having much luck with that stick."

She bowed her head and stared at her rod, fighting back the tears. "No. Not much at all."

"Sometimes your ma would only use her hands, you know. You ever tried that?"

"No. That's very difficult, and right now I'm having trouble with just the crystal and the rod." She held up the dowsing branch for him to see. "If this won't work, nothing will. It was hers. It's never failed me. Until now, that is."

"Maybe the failing's not in the rod."

"I know that. I'm not stupid." She eyed him for a moment. "What do you want, Mr. Butcher?"

"Oh, so it's back to Mr. Butcher now, is it? You get mad then you get all stiff and formal like."

She stared at him in silence.

"You makin' any progress on gettin' me my fair share from Merle Woodson's holdings?"

"I told you nothing in the estate would be settled until the children's relatives get here and that won't be for a few days, until after the funeral. They have to come from Nova Scotia. What business did you have with Woodson, anyway?"

"Merle Woodson owed me money from a gold mine we owned together a long time ago. The mine went bust and so did I. Woodson landed on his feet. I told him all these years I wanted my money, and he said he'd pay. Then just before he was killed, he told me he had a new venture going, that's what he always called his slick-handed schemes—ventures. And anyways, this venture would give him more money than he ever dreamed about and I could have double what he owed me then. Now he's dead, but I figure I still got money coming."

"I guess that's all you care about isn't it? Not that Katherine and Jake are orphaned."

"I ain't all that cold-hearted." His face softened. " 'Fore she was married, your ma always told me I had a heart as big as a canyon."

"You were in love with my mother, weren't you?"

"Yes. Yes, I was, and Edwin Shannon knew that until the day he died."

"But my mother picked my father instead of you."

He nodded. He looked down and his beard spread as it touched his chest. "I never was set up to give Lucinda what she deserved." He heaved a sigh. "Guess it worked out better this way. But I never forgot her." He looked at her. "And seeing you, ever bit as beautiful as she was, well, just makes my poor old heart break. Yessir, break clean away."

The faded blue eyes filled with tears. Trini took a step closer to him and laid her hand on his arm. "I'm sorry."

"Ain't nothing but the ramblings of an old fool." He wiped a buckskin sleeve across his eyes and mouth. Another puff of wind brought cutting cold and wafted the fringe on his jacket. They were silent a moment then he narrowed his eyes at her. "I got to say, you look like you're as worn down as ol' Canary at the end of a long trail. What have you been doin' with yourself?"

She thought about telling him about the fire at Parn's cabin, but she didn't. Talking about the ordeal would make her even more exhausted than she was now. She shook her head and looked away from him.

"Well, if you don't want to talk about that, at least tell me what you're doing out here, sides tryin' to get that stick to work."

"I'm trying to get my brother away from George Mallis before he kills him."

"And bein' out here's gonna do that?"

She told him about Merle's maps, the DOME Partnership, and the suspected tie with Mallis.

"So you're tryin' to find out what's around here that Woodson would want?"

"Yes. And what Mallis wants, too, is my guess."

"Well, hell, that's easy. You don't need no dowsing rod for that."

"What do you mean?"

"Oil. Them oil companies have been buyin' the mineral rights from the Santa Fe all over these parts. The railroad needs that money if it's gonna survive the Depression."

"Oil? But what does that have to do with Merle Woodson? He couldn't have been buying oil rights."

"Why not?" Butcher asked.

"Because the oil companies have already claimed every drop of oil around here, I'm sure. They've had their geologists swarming over the county, and most of southern Colorado from what I hear."

"You ain't givin' Merle enough credit for brains. That ol' conniver could think of more ways to mine a nugget than anyone I ever knew. He worked at the land claims office, didn't he? He knowed all about who was buying what claims and where they was buying them."

"So?"

"So." He laughed and his beard shook. "Just think about it for a minute. If Merle knows where all them oil companies have bought mineral rights, maybe he figured out some place where no one had bothered to look yet."

Could that be possible? Could Merle Woodson have discovered oil rights that no one else had purchased? What was it that Mr. Henry had said about finding the records in a mess, with duplications in some areas and missing records in others? In recording the oil claims, maybe Merle had seen places the oil companies had missed. Or maybe they'd made a mistake in their own calculations and Merle had seen the mistake. She remembered how all twelve counties that Merle had maps for were located in a north–south line. What had Katherine said, all the counties running up and down the state with Coyote County in the middle? What if the oil companies had left an entire corridor of oil rights unclaimed? She simply had not thought of asking Mr. Henry to show her mineral rights' purchases.

"So you think Merle discovered some available oil rights? Oil rights that the big oil companies missed?"

"Couldn't say."

Trini had a thought. If Merle had discovered oil rights through his job at the land claims office, then Dottie would surely have known about it. They worked very closely, and they had been the only two people in the office. It would be difficult for Merle to keep something of this magnitude a secret. Matter of fact, Dottie may have been privy to Merle's scheme. She must know something. He must have shared something about the oil rights and his plans for buying them.

She turned her gaze back to Butcher and thought aloud. "This whole thing would tie into Merle borrowing from the bank and mortgaging his house. He needed money to buy those mineral rights. He must have formed DOME to do it. That way he could keep his purchases anonymous."

She remembered what Mr. Henry had said about how a partnership didn't have to be registered anywhere. No one would know that DOME belonged to a county employee who had direct access to information about oil rights.

"Merle would want his plans kept secret," Trini said. "If it got out what he was doing, I'd imagine he'd have to face some severe consequences. And after he'd purchased the oil rights, he wouldn't care if the county or anyone else found out. He'd be rich."

Butcher pulled his hat down on his brow to set it against the wind. "I don't know what you're talkin' about with all that about Merle borrowing money and mortgaging his house, but the rest of it makes sense. That's why he was tellin' me how rich he was gonna be, and why he could afford to pay me off double. He was gonna be an oil baron."

Trini nodded. She'd like to know for sure if there was oil here. She debated the idea to try her dowsing again, this time asking for oil. No. The dowsing was dead. She'd go back to Mr. Henry and ask to see the county records for purchases of oil rights.

"What I can't figure," she said, "is how Mallis found out about this. And how he wormed his way into Merle's little oil 'venture.'"

"What makes you think Mallis knows anything about this?"

Trini told him about Woodson's ledgers and Mallis's name scribbled in a corner of a map.

Butcher shook his head slowly. "I don't know. But what worries me is if you're right, and Mallis thinks you're onto him, he may be getting scared. And scared people do stupid things. If Mallis is as dangerous as you think, you got to be more careful than walkin' into a den full of mountain lions."

She thought of Parn's cabin lying now in a heap of ashes and how she, by all rights, should be dead. "You're right. I'll be careful, I promise. Thank you, Lyle. Thank you. I have to go now."

She hurried back up the hill, clawing with her fingers as she slipped over the loose dust. When she got to the road, she turned back to the gully and searched. Lyle Butcher and his mule were gone. Where on earth did he live? Strange old man, but no doubt, he'd helped her see what she'd missed. She opened the truck door, set the dowsing stick under the seat and closed the door behind her.

It was getting late; a gray dusk colored the eastern sky and the sun hung like a glowing coal in the west. Talking with Butcher had taken more time than she'd planned. She needed to get back to the Woodson children. If the Nortons dropped them off and Trini wasn't there, Katherine might panic again. She decided not to go to town and confront Mallis. Instead, she'd pick up the children and then go to Dottie's. The theory about DOME being involved in oil rights was intriguing, and she was anxious to hear what Dottie had to say. If Dottie Kerr knew about Merle's shenanigans, and she probably did, that would explain her nervous behavior the other day and why she avoided talking about Merle's business. This time, Trini would be more insistent with her.

CHAPTER FIFTEEN

The evening bore close as her headlights cut a swath through the deepening prairie night. The air was cold now, and an occasional burst of snow flurries darted through the truck's light beams. She turned off the blacktop and drove the half mile up the rutted dirt road of the Woodsons' property. As she made the last hairpin turn over the ridge, her headlights illuminated a truck, Roy's truck, parked in front of the house. Oh please, let the children be fine. Don't let anything happen to them. Guilt swelled within her. She jerked to a stop and dashed through the back door.

"Katherine?" she called. "Roy?"

Roy's voice carried from the parlor. "We're in here, Trini."

She crossed the threshold into the parlor as Roy rose from the sofa, his craggy face drawn and tired. Katherine smiled at her from the chair beside the rolltop desk. Jake sat in front of the radio, his head cocked to one side to hear the low volume.

"Oh thank God," Trini said. She closed her eyes and pressed her palm on her heaving chest. "I saw your truck out front and I thought something had happened to the children. I didn't mean to be this long."

"We're fine, Trini," said Katherine. "Would you quit worrying about us? Me and Jake stay here all the time by ourselves."

Trini decided not to remind her that only two days ago, she'd flown into Trini's arms in a fit of terrified crying. But if Katherine and Jake were okay, then—Trini put her hand to her throat and looked at Roy.

"Is it Parn? Is he okay?"

Annoyance pinched his face for an instant, but he smiled and nodded. "He's fine, Trini. I just came from town, not more than an hour ago. He's fine. But I do need to talk to you." He darted his eyes to Katherine.

"Let's go in the kitchen," Trini said.

Katherine nodded with a smug grin as she picked up a dress she was hemming. Honestly. The girl lived in romances.

Trini removed her coat and hung it on an empty hook by the door. Her own wool cardigan that she'd brought from home rested on the next hook over, and she pushed her arms through the sleeves and gathered it to her throat. She sat at the table facing the parlor and crossed her arms on the oilcloth. Through the doorway, she could see Katherine's elbow moving as she sewed and hear the drone of the radio.

Roy sat in the chair beside Trini, leaned toward her and rested his hand on her arm. His thumb lightly rubbed her sleeve, and her stupid stomach flipped again. She tried to keep her breathing even. She found herself examining the frown of his black eyebrows. Her eyes drifted to his full lips and then his jawline, darkened by the shadow of his beard. Despite herself, she inhaled, searching for the fresh scent of him. She wasn't disappointed. Another tingle started low in her body and she covered his hand with her own. It was good to see him.

"Would you like a cup of coffee?" she asked.

"No. Nothing. Trini, something has happened. Dottie Kerr is dead."

"Oh, no."

"Just a few hours ago."

"But how?"

"She evidently was stirring the fire in the fireplace, and a log rolled out and caught on her dress. She died right there. I guess it was pretty bad."

Her thoughts reeled. Dottie dead, in a fire? First someone had tried to kill her in a fire, and now Roy was telling her Dottie died in one. Was Mallis the perpetrator? She'd bet he was the fire-starter at Parn's cabin. But why would Mallis want to kill Dottie Kerr? Did she know something that would incriminate Mallis in Merle's death? Trini wouldn't put anything past Mallis. He was dangerously ruthless. But would he really feel threatened enough by a middle-aged widow to kill her?

Another thought came to her: Now she'd never know if Merle had confided to Dottie about DOME and the oil rights. It was too late. What could she do now? Parn was still under Mallis's devious watch, and she was running out of ways to—she blinked in embarrassed shame. Could she not spare one moment to remember the poor dead woman? And what about her son? It must be dreadful for him. "Did Daryl find her?"

"Yeah. He phoned the sheriff's office and got Taggert. Mallis was out somewhere."

"Yes, I'm sure he was. He's been somewhere most of the day."

"What do you mean?"

"Roy, I went to Parn's cabin today to find his stash of bootlegging money. While I was searching for it, the cabin caught on fire. It burned to the ground."

He gripped her arm. "Trini, my God. Thank God you weren't hurt."

"Yes, but don't you see? Someone followed me there and set the cabin on fire, hoping I would be inside. Parn buried his money behind the cabin, far behind, like several hundred yards and down in a gully. So when I went to look for it, I went out the back door. Whoever started that fire had no way of knowing I was gone from the cabin. My truck was parked outside, so they would have naturally assumed I was inside."

He was silent a moment, regarding her. He leaned back in the chair and his voice was low. "What are you saying?"

"I think you know. Someone deliberately tried to kill me. You said yourself Mallis wasn't around. I think he followed me. And I think he set fire to the place hoping I'd—"

The chair scratched across the floor as Roy bolted to his feet. He stared at her a minute, then rubbed his hand through his hair. "Jesus Christ."

Keep your temper, she reminded herself. Don't push. She waited for him to come to grips with what she was saying. He had to see, had to understand how dangerous Mallis was. "I know you don't want to think Mallis would do something like this, but you've got to see the truth."

He stared at her a minute more, then sat down again.

"All right," he said, "for the sake of argument, let's say you're right. Let's say Mallis followed you and thinks you're dead in that fire. I know what you're thinking. You're thinking if Mallis torched Parn's cabin to kill you, maybe he used fire to kill Dottie. But that's just crazy. Why would Mallis want to kill Dottie? What possible reason would he have?"

She started to speak, but he held up his hand. "Now just let me finish. Trin, Dottie's death was an accident. I'd bet my life on that. I saw her. Mallis wasn't around, so Taggert telephoned me because he didn't know what to do. He had to stay there because if someone's in the cell, we always have to have a deputy stay at the office. I went out to the Kerrs'. Doc Cockrell got back from Pueblo this afternoon and he went with me. She looked real bad, but there's no way it was anything but a terrible accident. Besides, Daryl was home. No one, not even Mallis, could have sneaked up to the house, gotten inside and started the fire, then left without Daryl seeing him. He was working in the shed just beside the house. Unfortunately, he had the power saw going, and he didn't hear her screams for

191

help until it was too late. But Dottie's death is an accident, Trin, make no mistake."

She sighed and relaxed back into the chair. Maybe Roy was right. "What time was the accident, do you know?" she asked.

"Just a few hours ago. Maybe around four or so. Why?"

"Daryl came by here earlier today and delivered some wood. That was around midday, maybe two or three. The fire must have happened just after he left here and went home."

"Sounds like it."

"How's he taking it?"

Roy shrugged. "He seemed okay. More in a daze than anything."

Roy was always so logical, and this time he was probably right. It would be incredibly brazen for Mallis to sneak into the house and start a fire with Daryl in the shed only a few feet away. If Mallis wanted to kill Dottie, he'd be a lot smarter about it than taking a chance he'd be seen.

"What next? All this with Merle Woodson and Mallis. Then Stephanie LeClair running away."

"They found her, by the way," Roy said. "Over in Waynesville. I guess the LeClairs went over there to get her."

"Thank heaven for that. I felt so bad. Jefferson and Camille both blamed themselves for her running away, because of the separation. And then when I couldn't help them . . ."

"Can't say as I can blame Stephanie for wanting to get out of here. There's some pretty rancid rumors going around town about Jefferson LeClair."

"I know all about it, Roy."

"You know?"

She told him of overhearing Lydia Hardy confront Jefferson about having an affair with her husband.

Roy snorted and shook his head. "That's some fairly nasty business."

"I feel sorry for all of them, Roy: Stephanie, who is watching her parents go through this; Camille LeClair, who will probably be alone for the rest of her life because no one would want her; and mostly I feel sorry for Jefferson. Because he's alone and lonely."

He regarded her a minute. "I can't see it that way. As I said, it's nasty business. And LeClair has shown himself to be someone I wouldn't want to be connected with. That doesn't bother you? What he is?"

"What he is? He's a friend of mine, Roy, that's what he is. I know his private life is something most people don't understand, but it doesn't change who he is as a person."

"Yes, it does. It changes everything."

She stared at him a moment, and disappointment nibbled at her. She expected intolerance from most people. From Roy, she'd hoped for more. "Well, I still feel sorry for him. He's going to lose everything."

He then leaned close and gripped her arm. "You know," he said. "You are the most compassionate person I've ever met. I love that about you."

She was stunned. *Love. I love that about you.*

"Trini?" Katherine stood in the doorway. "I'm going to put Jake to bed, then go to bed myself. I'll see you in the morning."

"Okay. Sure. Yes." Trini rose and went to Katherine and hugged her goodnight. She turned to find Roy fixing her with his deep gray eyes. She pulled the sweater close to her as she walked to the stove and lifted the kettle from the burner.

"It's getting colder outside. I think I'll make a cup of tea. Would you like one?"

He rose and came toward her to stand close. His voice was low and slightly hoarse. "No. No tea."

She sidled past him to the sink, turned on the tap and began to fill the kettle. She dropped it with a clatter when she felt him behind her and the heft of his hands on her shoulders. He turned her to face him. "Trini."

His mouth covered hers and she found herself answering. The melty feeling in her stomach swelled and rocked her world. The kiss lingered, sweet and demanding. His breathing deepened, and he forced her head back. She relaxed further into his chest, letting herself collapse there, rest, for just a moment. The smell of him, that unique fresh signature, held her and too soon he pulled his lips from her own. She looked into his eyes, teetering on the edge of their gray depths.

His arms held her tight against his body and his eyes roamed her face. "I'm not kidding about this," he rumbled.

"I know you're not."

He rubbed his thumb along her jawline. "So beautiful," he whispered and lowered his mouth over hers again.

He pressed in on her, and she could feel his hardness through his denims. She surprised herself when a small desperate sound escaped her throat. She wrapped her arms across his solid yoke of shoulders and felt her torso respond to him as he brought one hand from behind her back and rubbed her side, his fingers gliding over the outside of her breast. The tickle inside her bloomed.

She had to fight this. She was in mourning. As much as she was attracted to Roy, she didn't love him. Not yet. And making love without love would be plain wrong. As much as she savored the delicious feelings, as much as she was tempted to just let go and let come what may, she pulled back from him. Staring into his eyes, she panted as she spoke. "Roy. Roy, not here. Not like this. And if we go further, it'll be . . . I'll feel . . . I don't know, I'm just not ready."

He searched her face for a minute, then answered in a rough whisper. "I need you to be ready, Trini." He opened his lips and came down on her again.

She didn't know if she could resist. She felt so thick and liquid and the knot of fear that had lived in her stomach for so long began to loosen a little. With her sensitive fingers and palms, she ran her hands along the swells of his shoulders and the firm biceps.

One long, one short, and another long ring sounded from the telephone, and as she lingered with him, tempting the desires of her body, it rang again. Roy pulled back and stared at her, smiled with his dimple, then kissed the tip of her nose. She smiled back as she broke away from him and went to the telephone, swaying with dizziness as she walked. She had to clear her throat before she spoke. "Woodsons'."

"This is Les Taggert. Is Roy Eastman there?"

"This is Trinidad Bates. Is Parn all right, Deputy?"

"He's fine. I need to talk to Roy if he's there."

"Hold on."

Trini extended the receiver to Roy. "It's Taggert."

He took the telephone from her and made a few grunts of acknowledgement, then hung it back in its cradle.

"I better go. Taggert is all in a flutter because Mallis hasn't come back yet."

"Where'd he go?"

Roy shrugged. "Taggert said he wanted to look at something out by Digstown."

"Digstown? I was just out there before I came back here. Merle had indicated something on a map I wanted to see about. DOME Partnership is the name of it. Lyle Butcher was out there."

Roy took his hat from the hat rack and set it squarely on his head. "You know, Trin, I wish you'd come to me instead of doing all this investigating on your own. I worry about you. What was Butcher doing out there?"

"I think he must live somewhere out there, maybe in an old

mine shaft or something."

He stood close to her again and wrapped his hand around the back of her neck.

"I don't know about that guy. Just be careful will you? Just wait here at the Woodsons'. A marshal will be here in a day or two and you'll feel better about Parn. I just hope to God this thing will be over after the arraignment."

"Any more news on when Judge Slaton will be here?"

He shook his head. "Same as before. He's tied up in a trial and will be here as soon as it's over. Maybe within a week or so. Assuming Parn's innocent, he may be free inside a couple of weeks."

Assuming he's innocent. She fought down the doubt, but she found herself forcing her comment to Roy. "He is innocent, and I think I can prove it. Mallis not only wanted revenge for his family's death, and the bootlegging route, he also wanted a piece of this DOME Partnership. I think he's after oil."

"Did you dowse out there? Is that what makes you believe there's oil there?"

"No. I . . . the dowsing is gone." She looked down, wanting to hide the sudden tears flooding her eyes. She blinked them away. She didn't want Roy to see them. With all this tumult going on around her, with Parn's situation and Dottie's death, she felt self-indulgent mourning her lost gift. She was thankful when Roy continued talking without asking her about her evident upset.

"What makes you so sure oil is involved?"

"Butcher had the idea, said that the oil companies had been all around that area buying mineral rights from the Santa Fe. Roy, I think Merle Woodson knew of some unclaimed oil rights. That's why he borrowed all that money—to buy them."

He kept his hand on her neck. "You may be right. But please, Trin, just . . ." He bent down and kissed her again, long and deep, then put his cheek on hers and whispered in her ear. "I think I'd go crazy if something happened to you." He tarried for a moment, maybe waiting for words she couldn't say or promises she couldn't make.

He turned and retrieved his coat from the kitchen chair, then closed the door behind him as he left.

Chapter Sixteen

The next morning, a stone sky showed through the Woodson kitchen window. An occasional cold blast rattled the window-panes and sheared through the gaps of the back door. Trini entered the kitchen wearing one of her favorite dresses, a deep crimson wool she'd made last winter, and an embroidered black shawl. Her heaviest wool socks rolled over the tops of her newly cleaned brogans. The large copper teakettle simmered on the back burner, and Katherine stood at the stove, wrapped in a floor-length gray robe, stirring a pot of thick oatmeal. Jake hammered the oak tabletop with two iron soldier-toys, one in each warring fist, shouting unintelligible commands to his army. He looked up at Trini and grinned.

"Eggs," he said.

Katherine turned to look at him over her shoulder. "No, Jake. Oatmeal this morning." Her gaze bounced off Trini as she went back to stirring the oatmeal. So much for high hopes, Trini thought. Katherine was closed.

Last night, after Roy had left, Trini crawled between the sheets of Katherine's bed to be met with a question. "What does it feel like to be in love?" she'd asked.

Trini had settled herself beside the girl and pulled the quilt to her chin, taking time to formulate her answer. A profound question, and she dismissed as her answer the worn platitudes about love that encouraged girls to wait to be swept off their feet and rescued by a savior who would love and cherish them forever. Above all, she would be honest. "It hurts, and feels wonderful, both at the same time."

Katherine lay silent beside her, fondling the edge of the quilt like a child taking comfort from a favorite blanket. "Well, does it just happen to you? Or do you make it happen?"

"I don't know," Trini said. "It's as mysterious to me now as it was when I was your age. I can tell you this: As your friend, I hope one day you experience it."

Katherine wiggled under the covers, but didn't speak.

"Do you remember your mother?" Trini asked. "How she and your dad must have loved each other?"

"Umm. Kind of. But not very much. I was four when she died, and Pa never talked too much about her." She was silent a moment more, then came a small whisper from the dark, "I don't think I'd like it."

"Being in love?" Trini asked.

"Yes. Not if it means . . . I just don't want anyone near me ever again."

Something was happening here. Trini wanted to reach over and touch Katherine, stroke the little tufts of hair sprouting from her tender scalp, but she didn't. If Katherine was ready to open up, Trini wanted to be there for her. The situation called for extreme tact and sensitivity, and her intuition told her if she touched Katherine just now, she'd shrink away. Instead, Trini turned toward her and shifted up to one elbow. In the soft moonlight glowing through the bedroom window, she could see Katherine kneading the quilt with her child-like fingers.

"I'm here for you, Katherine, as a friend. If you ever want to talk to someone." Trini felt her stiffen.

"About what?" Katherine asked.

"Anything. If something has . . . if someone . . ." She decided to come straight from her heart. "I think I'm being too careful with my words, Katherine. I just want you to know that if someone has hurt you, and you're ready to tell me about it, I'm here for you." She thought a moment, then added, "And I won't go away. You can count on me. I won't let you down, sweetheart."

In the back of her mind, she was a little surprised at herself. Where was the young widow who wanted to be left alone to grieve? She was still there, clamoring for her desire to be granted. But despite her need to be alone, Trini found she was drawn to this orphaned girl. One part of her wanted to leave, go home to her house and her garden and all the familiar things that would give her comfort in her isolation. But another part was desperate to console Katherine. And now she'd made a promise—a promise to stick by Katherine, stay beside her as a friend. Odd, though, that she didn't feel cornered by her rash declaration. She didn't regret it. On the contrary, the thought of being there for Katherine gave her a sense of purpose she hadn't experienced since Jim died. Without thinking, she reached over and stroked the childlike hand. She had meant what she said. She wouldn't go away.

A choked sob broke from the back of Katherine's throat, and then another one burst from her chest. She turned on her side away from Trini, and her shoulders shook as she cried. Poor child. Trini rubbed her knobby back and boney shoulders, and gradually the cries subsided into soft hiccups. Trini tried to gently turn the girl back toward her, tried to get her to talk by gently calling for her, asking if she'd please talk some more, but Katherine stiffened and jerked her shoulder away.

Finally, Trini gave up. "Okay. Okay, honey. But if you need me, I'm here." With an affectionate pat, Trini sank back into her pillow, folded her hands on her chest and thought.

Katherine had been molested, no question. And, Trini decided, it had been going on for a while. She just hoped Katherine hadn't been raped. She knew that many times rape victims lived the remainder of their lives silent and scarred. While she lived at Florence Crittenden, Trini had met a girl, only a child really, who'd been raped. Helen: soft and lacy with filmy blond hair and a cupid face, attacked when she was twelve years old by her stepbrother, then sent away in disgrace to bear the baby. Her mother had blamed her for the pregnancy; if Helen had not tempted the stepbrother, he wouldn't have bothered her. Trini had tried to befriend her, even offered to bring the forsaken girl back to Ludlin, but Helen had remained detached and dejected. She had her baby, and a week later, hung herself with a leather belt from an exposed beam in her bedroom.

Yes, Katherine had been deeply injured. But by who? Merle? As much as the thought sickened her, she knew incest happened more frequently than whispered about. But she didn't think it was Merle. Katherine's reaction to her father's death would take a different tone if he'd been molesting her, Trini was certain. Mr. Norton? Barney Norton? Trini didn't know him that well, but Katherine would certainly be available to him. While Emma Norton took care of Jake most days, Katherine also would go to their house after school and wait for Merle to pick them up after work. Barney would have been able to approach Katherine every day if he had a mind to. Would he harm a young girl? Molest her? Trini doubted it. Katherine had spoken fondly of the Nortons, and she wouldn't have expressed that opinion if she'd been hurt by Barney Norton.

Trini didn't know who the perpetrator could be, but now that the seal of secrecy had been broken, she hoped that in the next day or so Katherine would confide in her completely. Trini gripped the hem of the quilt, and a hot anger rose in her chest. Whoever it was, Trini vowed, his pathetic life would never be the same.

But that had been in the privacy of Katherine's room, in the dark where secrets could be told in whispers. Now, in the morning light, some things were too awful to speak of, and Katherine stood at the stove, withdrawn and silent. Trini poured coffee into a tin mug, attempting to catch Katherine's eye and smile at her, but the girl's gaze carefully avoided Trini's.

Carrying her mug to the table, Trini sat in the chair opposite Jake. She sipped the steaming brew then spoke to Katherine's back. "You're not dressed for town. Don't you want to come in to the Fall Festival? It'll be fun, and Jake would enjoy it."

Katherine ladled the thick cereal into a bowl and placed it in front of Jake, who scooped the first spoonful as Katherine withdrew her hand. She faced Trini and crossed her arms over her broom-handle chest. Between the tufts of hair, her red scalp flushed crimson.

"Please, Trini," said Katherine. "Don't worry about me. I don't want to go to the festival. I'd rather stay here and read and knit. I'm not afraid in the daytime. Besides, no one will come out here. They'll all be in town."

"But I thought you wanted to go. Wanted to take Jake."

Katherine reached her hand up as if to pat her hair and stopped. She refolded her arms. "Well, I don't."

Trini had wondered when Katherine would consciously realize her altered appearance. She thought Katherine probably was in denial that she was losing her hair. But now, with the gesture toward her scalp and the fact that Katherine was hugging herself, protecting herself, Trini guessed that because they'd broached the topic of her molestation last night, Katherine had shifted the sordid experience from deep shadows into the harsh beam of reality. She didn't want to be seen in town, and Trini couldn't blame her.

"I wouldn't force you to go, but . . ." she stood and approached her, keeping her voice soft and gentle as if she was coaxing an injured animal to safety, ". . . I'd help you fix a scarf over your head. It's cold out, and everyone will be bundled to their chins—"

"I told you I don't want to go." Katherine whirled her back to Trini.

Jake's eyes darted between them, his mouth open, displaying a glob of half-eaten oatmeal. "Side," he said.

Katherine looked at him over her shoulder. "No, Jake. We're not going outside. Now eat your oatmeal."

He stared at her a minute, then clamped his mouth closed and went back to his bowl.

Trini decided not to pressure her about town. The last thing she wanted to do was alienate her. "All right, Katherine. I won't go to the festival if you and Jake aren't going. But I want to talk to a couple of people, so I need to go into town. Otherwise I'd stay here with you."

"It's not necessary." She faced Trini and again folded her arms across her chest, still gripping the wooden spoon in one hand.

Once again, Trini decided coming from her heart would be the best approach. "Katherine. Do you remember when we were talking that night in the café, about me standing up to George Mallis?"

Katherine stared at her. Trini briefly worried that she was being too aggressive. Maybe she should leave things alone. But Katherine relaxed her shoulders and uncrossed her arms. She nodded.

Trini continued, "Do you remember what I told you, about doing something that's really hard to do?"

She nodded again.

"What did I say?" Trini asked.

"You said if you believe in something enough, it gives you extra strength that makes you able to do hard things. And you said sometimes you have to reach deep down where God lives and bring up the strength and do things."

"That's right. No matter how hard something is, you can find the strength to do it."

An expression of comprehension crossed Katherine's face, and Trini knew that they'd connected again.

"Okay," Katherine said. "I'll think about it. But please don't make me go into town."

At least she's talking around the edges of her horrible experience. It was a start. "All right. I'll tell you what. I'll come back about noon. We'll have the rest of the day together. We can pop corn over a nice fire in the fireplace." Trini smiled at Jake. "Okay, Jake?"

Jake's eyes gleamed as he nodded his head. A bit of saliva drooled from the corner of his mouth.

Trini reached out and squeezed Katherine's shoulder. "Phone the mercantile if you need anything. Jefferson can get word to me." She was rewarded with the glimpse of a smile.

Katherine turned back to the stove, and Trini headed to the parlor, to Merle Woodson's rolltop desk. She opened the bottom drawer on the right, lifted the stack of papers and felt for the small gold key she'd seen when Katherine had shown her Merle's papers two days ago. She shoved it deep into her dress pocket and closed the drawer. She debated about telling Katherine that she'd taken the key and decided not to. It would serve to no end except cause her worry, and besides, she was protecting Katherine's interests, not planning to steal from the orphaned children.

She crossed the kitchen, opened the back door and leaned out. The day was hard and gray, but not as cold as it had been of late. She smiled to herself. Edwin Shannon's old saying came to her: Mountain weather was as fickle as an Irish girl. For the few hours she'd be gone, her embroidered shawl would be warm enough. She didn't want to bother with a coat and muffler. She grabbed her handbag, and with a final good-bye, left.

Trini drove through the town swollen with parents and running children followed by dogs with wagging tails. Laughter and shouts echoed in the streets as people dodged through the traffic making their way to the Fall Festival at the schoolyard several blocks south. The festival would offer games and hayrides, and a chance to gossip.

Trini found a place to park in front of the mercantile. She got out of the truck and looked at the windows of the sheriff's office, but she didn't see any movement. She'd go over there in a minute to check on Parn.

The doorbells jingled as she opened the door, and a throng of people stood at the counter where Jefferson, his face narrowed with concentration, rang up sales for hot coffee, soft drinks and last-minute needs of the festival-goers. Several dozen people milled through the aisles, and four children stood at the end of the candy counter comparing their selections. Trini caught Jefferson's eye as he finished a sale. He called to her over the mayhem, "I'll be a minute."

She smiled and waved to him. She'd go see Parn now, then come back. She left the store and trotted across the street in time for an *ooga*-horn to blare at her backside. The raucous laughter of teenagers followed as she jumped to the sidewalk. The door clattered open and Roy stood to greet her. In uniform.

"I don't believe it," she said. She surveyed the empty room. "Did he hire you back?"

"Not really," he said. He walked toward her, his dimple showing with a smile. "I hired myself."

"Sounds intriguing."

"Oh, intrigue is our specialty in Coyote County."

He looked good this morning. Fresh and wonderful smelling, solid and real. The emotions she'd experienced last night when he'd kissed her exploded to the surface: the luxury of physical desire, of leaning against a strong man, both physically and emotionally. Sometimes, it was tempting to be helpless.

"Are the Woodson kids at the festival?" he asked.

"No. Katherine didn't want to come into town. I think . . . well I won't talk to you about that now. But later I have something to tell you."

"Is it something I should know about? Are you snooping around where you don't belong again?"

Wait a minute. She wasn't some child, to be monitored and corrected. "Roy, it's not even about me. It's about Katherine."

"Okay, now. Don't get yourself all in a huff." He stepped forward, but didn't reach out to touch her. A small sizzle of anger stayed with her. The presumption that she had to answer to him galled her. The luscious feelings of surrender just a few seconds ago were forgotten. She wondered if she wanted to become part of a couple again. As much as she'd loved Jim, being partners was incredibly difficult. Maybe she did best on her own, answering to no one.

She decided to get down to business. "Is Parn all right?"

He sighed. "Yes, Parn is fine. Taggert is down at the festival, and Mallis, well, I don't know where Mallis is."

"He never came back?"

"No. And Taggert said he went out to his house and it was closed and empty, like he'd been gone forever."

"But where could he be?"

"I don't have a clue. But I figured I needed to just step in here. You want to see Parn?"

"Oh, thank you, Roy. Yes." She felt her heart swell with tenderness and the irritation melted away. He was so considerate, so sweet. Would she want to have him as a serious participant in her life? All this trying to figure out how she felt was confusing her. Right now, she needed to focus on Parn. She'd put everything else out of her mind.

The cell keys rattled as he led her down the hall. He opened the outer door, and they entered the small vestibule. Suddenly, she had the overwhelming desire to run. Bolt down the hall, out the door, get in her truck and drive into the vast flatland. She examined her feelings. It wasn't fear. She wasn't afraid for her safety or Parn's. It was an impulse, without reason. Why would that desire flash through her, so urgent and real?

"Trini!" Parn had been lying on his cot, but now jumped to his feet.

"I'm not going to open the cell door. Just a few minutes, okay?" Roy said. "Never know what can happen around here." He smiled at her and she knew he was thinking about the last time he'd let her visit her brother, when Mallis had thundered through the door, ordered her out of the building and fired him. Roy pulled the wooden stool out of the far corner, placed it in front of the cage and then left, closing the door behind him.

Trini set her pocketbook on the floor. She perched on the stool facing the bars while Parn grabbed the blanket from his cot, spread it on the floor in front of her and sat down cross-legged. He leaned his elbows on his knees and looked at her, grinning with his entire face. But despite his obvious joy in seeing her, dark circles under his eyes gave his face a haunted appearance. In the three days since his arrest, he'd aged.

"Are you okay?" she asked.

"I'm okay. I'm glad Roy's back. Taggert told me all about how Roy got fired. I guess now he's back because Mallis has been gone since yesterday."

"Yes, I know."

"You look pretty tired yourself," he said.

She nodded. "I am."

"Trini, don't worry so much. You'll see. I'll get out of here after the arraignment. They won't have any reason to hold me then."

"I hope not."

He stared at her a moment then whispered, "What do you mean, you hope not?"

She sighed. What could she say to her brother? *I have doubts about your innocence? I wonder about your secret life? I'm not sure who you are?*

"Trini? What did you mean, you hope not? Don't you think they'll dismiss the case at the arraignment?"

She lowered her eyes to her clasped hands. Her knuckles were white with tension. At a loss for words, she found herself stumbling to express herself. "I hope the judge dismisses the case. I'm just not sure . . . it's just . . ." She pushed ahead. "I can't dowse anymore, Parn. I've lost it. And I don't know why, but I think it might have something to do with you. With how I feel about you."

He stared at her.

"Stephanie LeClair ran away. Jefferson and Camille asked me to dowse for her, and I couldn't. It just didn't work. And I've discovered some things about Merle Woodson's business affairs that Mallis is involved in. I think it's about oil rights and a thing called DOME Partnership. I went out to one of the sites I'd found in Merle's papers, someplace I'm pretty sure there's oil. I couldn't dowse. Not even a wobble."

Parn's voice was high with desperation when he spoke. "I don't know what you're talking about with all this stuff about a partnership and oil. And right now, I don't care about that. I care about you. You're my only kin. Why do you think I have something to do with losing your dowsing? What's the matter? Are you mad at me for getting myself into this mess?"

The desire to flee roared through her again. She was ashamed of her traitorous doubts about Parn, and she didn't want to tell him. But she ordered herself to stay put, seated on the stool, tears flowed down her cheeks, and she had to fight not to break down. Her words came without her thoughts before them.

"Yes," she said. "Yes, I guess that's it. I'm mad at you. Angry that because you tried to make things easy, you got us here. Angry that you couldn't do things the way they should be done. You had to get the free ride." She felt her face suffuse with ire, and her voice gained intensity and speed. "Half the country is hungry and half the country is going without shoes and people are making sacrifices and working themselves into old age while they're still young, but you couldn't do that. You had to try to take the easy way out, and it makes me mad."

Taking a deep, calming inhalation, she folded her hands on her lap and waited for him. Shame and guilt converged in her. She shouldn't have said that. Looking at him with his head lowered, staring at his hands, she knew he felt terrible. She was about to apologize, excusing her outburst with the explanation of exhaustion when he raised his eyes to her. She was surprised to see they held fire, and he spoke through tight jaws.

"You were always so damned right, Trini. Always working so hard, trying to be the best. When Jim was sick you almost killed yourself taking care of him. Same with Dad. After his stroke, you were the one he leaned on, and you damn near killed yourself over him, too. Even after what he made you give up. Even after the baby."

She jumped to her feet and the stool clattered behind her. "I don't want to talk about that."

He stood up and grabbed the bars. "You never want to talk about that. Not once did you turn to me for help. And I've known all along. Even though I was only twelve, I knew what was going on. And when Pa drove Ethan out of town, made him so scared he had to leave, then made you go to Kansas City and give up the baby, you came back and still you did all you could for him. I swear to God, I don't know why you didn't let the brittle old man die in his misery."

She closed her eyes and covered her ears. She didn't want to think about this. She didn't want to hear it. She wanted to shout and scream for him to leave her alone. For everyone to leave her alone.

Dropping her face into her hands, great sobs tore from her. After a moment, she raised her head. "I can't help it," she said. "I just have to do what's right." She sobbed again for a minute while Parn stood silent. Eventually, she took a handkerchief from her pocketbook and wiped her face.

Parn's voice was soft when he spoke. "You're a good person, Trin. It's nothing to be apologizing for. But do you always have to do everything alone? Could you for once in your life let someone help you?"

"I . . . I don't like to be obligated to people."

"Trini, people helping you is not obligation. Not when they love you. Not when they just want to be a part of your life. God, you can hold yourself apart like no one I ever seen."

"I don't mean to be apart. I don't like being alone, really."

He waited in silence.

"I don't know," she said. "I'm just so confused about everything right now."

He stared at her a minute then whispered, "Maybe you're confused because you think I'm guilty."

She leaned her forehead against the cold iron bars and closed her eyes. He'd said it now. He'd brought it out in the open. Just like Katherine had let her own secret out last night, now it was Trini who was telling a secret. Yes, she doubted his innocence. God help her, she wondered if her own brother had committed murder. She opened her eyes to find him staring at her. She nodded slowly.

"Trin, it's okay. How could you not doubt me? I've been living one step away from riding the rails with the rest of the hobos. Like you said, I've taken the easy way out all my life."

"Oh, Parn. Don't."

"That's what you're thinking, deep down, isn't it? That's why you can't dowse. You think I might be guilty. And if I'm guilty and your dowsing helped to free me, then you'd be doing wrong. And you couldn't live with yourself."

"Oh, Parn. You make me out to be as hard as Dad."

"No, Trin. Not as hard. But every bit as driven as he was. Just thank God you got the one thing from Ma that makes the difference: You got her heart."

She smiled a bleary smile and wiped her face.

"I can't promise I'll change, but I can promise you this: I learned there's a big difference between wanting something, dreaming about something, and living like a dreamer. I don't know really what I have to do different, but I know it's got something to do with not expecting things to be easy." He smiled at her. "And, Trin, I didn't kill Merle Woodson."

She reached her arm through the bars and grabbed his hand. His smile seemed a little different to her. And as she searched his face, she realized what it was: The little boy was gone. In his place stood a world-weary man.

He kept going, almost breathless. "And Roy told me about what you found out about Mallis's past. About his wife and kids being killed. Trini, you got to believe me. Me and Merle had nothin' to do with that. We set it up so Colletti could prove Mallis stole from him. But I didn't know nothin' about the murders. That didn't happen until months and months later. Merle and me were nowhere near Denver."

"I believe you, Parn. It's all right." And she did. Of the two doubts she had about his guilt, murdering Merle Woodson or murdering Mallis's children, it was the death of the children that had weighed heaviest on her. She didn't think she could ever recover her love for her brother if he'd been a part of that.

"I'm glad you believe me," he said. "I'm real glad. And

besides that, I couldn't have killed Merle with that hammer."

"What do you mean?"

"Don't you remember? I lost that hammer over a year ago. I told you about it. Matter of fact, the last time I used that hammer was right here at the sheriff's office when the whole town helped to put on a new roof after the tornado. Remember?"

She did. That's what had been niggling at the back of her mind. She remembered the incident. She'd been upset that Parn had lost their father's tool, scolded him for his irresponsibility. She'd forgotten about it until now. So that meant the hammer, the supposed murder weapon, wouldn't prove a thing against her brother. It was all a fraud. She'd been right about Mallis manufacturing the evidence. And this meant Mallis had never intended to have the hammer's fingerprints analyzed.

"But," she said, "how did Mallis get the hammer?" She thought for a moment. "Maybe you didn't lose it after all. Maybe Mallis stole it with the intent of biding his time until he could kill Merle and then frame you for the murder. I'm glad Roy's here now. I honestly think Mallis planned to somehow kill you and then claim you died in an escape attempt."

"That could be," he said. "If he thought me and Merle had something to do with killing his wife and kids, he'd want to kill us both, that's for sure. That's one thing. And another is, I know from what you said you think Mallis was tied into Woodson somehow and that he wanted to kill him for some share of oil rights or something."

"I'm not sure about all that yet, and I don't want to go into it now. It's long and convoluted. But I know Mallis had some business situation with Woodson." She thought of Mallis's name scribbled at the bottom of Merle Woodson's map and what Katherine had said about Merle telling her Mallis was deep into his pockets. "Maybe Mallis thought of a scheme where he could kill two birds with one stone: He'd get revenge for what he thinks is your participation in killing his family, and at the same time he'd come into a lot of money. But I'm not going to let him get away with it. I'm collecting a lot of information that can prove my case. And I'll have something to show to a marshal that will not only get Mallis away from you, but charged with Woodson's murder as well."

He was silent a moment, and Trini could see that he was thinking something through. "Well, I appreciate that, Trin, I really do. And I hope you're on the right track about Mallis. But you know, there's a lot of people who didn't like Merle Woodson. A lot of people who hated him enough to kill him."

"Like who?"

He shrugged a little. "A whole mess of people in Denver. People who he stepped on to get where he was with the bootlegging. He made a lot of money you know, and he'd do anything to anyone to get what he wanted. He ran roughshod over me and everyone else. I only put up with him because I wanted to make a lot of fast money. Camille hated him. She said sooner or later someone would do him harm just to get him off the face of the earth."

"Camille? Camille LeClair."

He hesitated a minute. "Well, yeah."

Her thoughts jumbled over one another. Parn had talked to Camille? As far as she knew, they were casual acquaintances who would only greet each other in passing. "So when did you talk to her?"

"You mean the last time?"

"Last time? Parn, I feel like I'm stumbling around in the dark here. You sound like you two are good friends."

The door behind her opened and Roy leaned inside the vestibule. "The flurry's getting heavier outside, Trin, and I have a feeling it's going to get worse before it gets better. You might want to get going."

"Okay, thanks, Roy. Just a couple of more minutes."

He nodded then closed the door to leave them alone again.

Parn regarded her, one corner of his mouth slanted up in a smile, and his hands jammed into his pants pockets.

She stared at him in disbelief. "I'm just so shocked. I mean, I had no idea that you knew Camille LeClair any better than to say hi to her in passing."

"Well, I know her better than that." He looked at her a minute then took a deep breath. "Okay, look, Trini. Camille and I have been seeing each other for a couple of months. She's known about Jefferson for a long time. We just didn't want anyone to know about us. Her situation with Jefferson is messed up as it is. We figured to just keep it quiet until they're divorced."

"Seeing each other? You mean as in romantically?"

He nodded.

She stared at him, dazed and shocked. Another part of her brother's secret life. He certainly was not who she thought he was. And how could Parn be attracted to a bossy, domineering woman like Camille LeClair? Did they have anything at all in common? "She's old enough to be your mother, Parn."

His eyes flared with anger. "She is not. She's 34. Nine years difference. And she happens to be a very wonderful woman who's gotten a raw deal with Jefferson."

She almost shook her head in disbelief. "Good Lord. I had no idea. How? Why in God's name did you . . . I mean, Good Lord."

"All right, Trin. I think I'm pretty clear on how you feel about this. Stop with the 'Good Lords,' okay?"

She scrutinized his face. She knew he was innocent of Woodson's murder, but he truly was a man living a secret life. "Well," she said, "I don't happen to believe Camille got a raw deal with Jefferson as you put it. Jefferson discovered some things about himself that he needed to be truthful about—to himself and everyone else."

"Let's don't dance around the issue, Trini. He's a pervert and he's left his wife and daughter for another man."

"He is not a pervert." She took a deep breath and deliberately controlled her tone. "He is not a pervert. He's a good man in a very difficult circumstance."

"I'm not going to argue with you about Jefferson LeClair. Let's just leave it that we disagree."

They stared at each other for a minute. "So you and Camille have been seeing each other. Does Jefferson know?"

"No, at least he didn't know before I was arrested. I don't know about now, since this whole thing with him and Gilbert Hardy has come out in the open. Camille might have told him about us by now."

Trini thought about the last time she'd seen Jefferson. She would bet he didn't know about Camille and Parn. He would have said something to her.

"Matter of fact," said Parn, "as soon as this whole thing is over, Camille and Stephanie and me are heading to Oregon. She's got a sister there and her husband owns a saw mill. We're going to live there. And as soon as the divorce is done, Camille and me are going to get married. That's what I was bootlegging for, to get the money to get us set up proper. Camille didn't like it none, but she knew it was only temporary. Everything's been arranged."

"But what about Jefferson?"

"I don't know. I guess he can do what he wants to. I've been saving my money for Camille and Stephanie and me."

Speaking of bootlegging money . . . "Parn, I went out to your cabin and took the money from your hiding place. I have it at the Woodsons' for you."

He smiled. "Thanks, Trin."

"You should know, too, that your cabin is gone. Burned to the ground."

His eyes widened with shock. "Jesus Christ."

"And to make matters worse, it happened when I was there. I think it happened because I was there. I think someone followed me and, thinking I was in the cabin, set it on fire."

"Jesus Christ."

"I know."

"Trin, you got to be careful. I don't want you putting yourself in danger like this. Did you see anyone? Do you have any idea who did it?"

"I only saw the roof of a car from on top of the hill. A sedan like hundreds of others. But it could only be one man, Parn. Mallis wants me out of his hair. I'm sure he knows I'm onto him. He'd love to be rid of me."

"Trini, let Roy handle this. Please. I couldn't take it if something happened to you. I may be moving away with Camille and all, but you're still my only blood kin."

Tears clouded her eyes again. Only blood kin. Family. That was really the important thing, wasn't it? Family and connections and caring for people. Maybe Camille would be good for Parn. Maybe the responsibilities of being a stepfather would make him grow up.

The door opened and Roy stuck his head through. "It's starting to snow heavy out there now, Trini. You might want to get back to the Woodsons'."

"All right. I'd better leave. I want to talk to Jefferson before I go back to the children."

Parn reached through the bars and caught her hand. "Thanks, Trin."

She squeezed back and smiled, then followed Roy into the office and walked to the front windows. Fat white flakes drifted from a slate sky.

Roy spoke from behind her. "Everyone at the festival will go inside the schoolhouse, I'm sure, thinking the storm will blow through, but I'm not so sure it will. Taggert should be here in a few minutes. I'll have to go on down to the schoolyard and see if I can't convince folks to head home. What did you want to talk to Jefferson LeClair about?"

"Just a couple of things."

He put his hands on her shoulders and turned her to him. "Please don't. Let the judge and a marshal handle this. It'll only be another day or so."

"But I'm so close. I know I can prove Mallis had a reason to kill Merle. I even—"

He dropped his hands and strode away from her, then whirled on his heel back to face her. "I'm losing patience, Trini. You're putting yourself into dangerous situations. Enough is enough. You're not a deputy."

"I have to do something to help my brother. I have to. I just can't sit idle."

He searched her face a moment and relaxed against the desk. "All right. But will you just keep me informed? Please?"

She walked over to him, leaned toward him and stood on her tiptoes. She brushed his lips with her own. "Don't worry. I'll be all right."

She lifted her shawl over her head, opened the door and stepped into the lacy flurries.

CHAPTER SEVENTEEN

Trini trotted across the street, weaving her way through the snow-decorated pedestrians, and once more entered the mercantile. Five men stood around the stove in the middle of the room, but the buzz of activity that had been present a while ago had abated. Jefferson smiled at her from behind the counter.

"I'm glad I caught you at a slow point," she said.

"I believe the worst is over for now," he said. "Unless this snow keeps up. Then they'll all congregate here for shelter."

She grinned at him. "You just have that kind of personality, Jefferson. People are naturally drawn to you."

He cocked one eyebrow in disbelief. "They may be drawn to me now, but only out of curiosity. Since yesterday, I'd wager that most people are coming to the store so they can claim that they saw a pervert, in person."

She surveyed the group of men standing around the stove. Twitters behind hands that covered smiling mouths, shoulders jiggling in restrained laughter and sidelong glances to Jefferson illustrated his point. She wanted to march over to them and give them a piece of her mind, but a restraining hand on her arm and Jefferson's intense whisper stopped her.

"Don't," he said.

Her back loosened from its stiffness, and she covered the hand with her own. "Oh, Jefferson, I'm so sorry. I hate to see you going through this. And in a small town, unfortunately, its occupants provide entertainment for each other. Wasn't it Jane

Austen who wrote something about the purpose in life is to provide sport to our neighbors, and they to us in turn?"

He laughed. "Yes, I think so." He smiled at her a moment. "I'll miss our conversations."

"Miss them?"

He shifted his gaze to the men gathered around the stove, then motioned with his head for her to follow him to the far end of the counter. They stopped directly in front of the large front window, but at least isolated in a kind of corner. Trini had pulled the stool the few feet with her and now settled herself on it, leaning her forearms on the counter.

Across from her, Jefferson leaned on one elbow slightly facing away from the customers and lowered his voice. "They can't overhear us from here. What I'm going to tell you I want kept private, at least for a while. Trinidad, I've made a decision. But first, let me tell you of Camille's plans because that's where it all started. Now that Stephanie's back home, well, it's brought me a new perspective. She's a sensitive girl, you know, and I'm afraid that because of me, she'll be the object of horrible gossip for years. Camille's been in contact with her sister in Oregon who has offered a home for Camille and Stephanie. I'm encouraging her to accept their invitation."

So, Camille had not told him about her involvement with Parn. Should Trini tell him? He was her friend, and she hated for Camille to deliberately hide the truth from him. Little did he know that not only would Stephanie have an uncle to parent her, but his daughter would also be gaining a stepfather. On the other hand, it was really none of her business. And hearing about the affair from her rather than his wife would be humiliating for him. He was waiting for her response. She decided to take the conservative route and keep it to herself.

"That may be for the best, Jefferson. As much as I'd hate to think of Stephanie going through the upheaval of leaving her hometown, I understand. Gossips can ruin a person's life forever. There's no reason to subject Stephanie to that if you can avoid it. But you said 'they' will be going. You'll go out there also, won't you? Even though you'd be divorced, at least you could be near Stephanie."

"No." He looked down at the counter and shook his head. "That's the decision I wanted to tell you about, Trinidad. I'm going to leave. I'll be moving to Europe. Either Paris or Berlin."

She gaped at him.

"I know. I apologize for rather springing it on you like that, but I've decided. There's nothing for me here anymore. With Stephanie gone, and, well, with Gilbert moving to Denver, there's no reason for me to stay."

She threw a glance in the direction of the men around the stove. They'd moved on from the local gossip and were engrossed in a loud debate about the merits of Roosevelt's proposals to end the Depression.

"Jefferson, I understand how you'd want to leave Ludlin, even Colorado, but Europe?"

"I know, Trinidad, it's another world, a completely different existence. But, from what I've read, Europeans are so much more accepting of—they're more accepting of differences in people. And living abroad is very inexpensive, so I've read."

"But how can you bear to be so far from Stephanie?" Trini asked. She'd just reaffirmed her own family ties with Parn; she hated to see Jefferson sever his. And with a distance of an ocean and almost two continents, he wouldn't see his daughter for years.

He shook his head firmly. "No. She'll have her uncle, and he's a good man with daughters of his own. Besides, what could a man like me offer his daughter?"

Trini clamped her lips closed. She still thought she'd made the right decision by not telling him about Parn and Camille, but she was uncomfortable nonetheless for the omission. It felt like a lie.

Jefferson nodded with his certainty. "She'll be better off without me, and without the persistent rumors that are apt to follow a person from one place to another." He squared his shoulders. "No, my mind's made up. I'm leaving. I'd like to think I could find a buyer for the store right away, but I won't, I'm sure. I'll sell off the stock and leave before January. I'll stay in New York for a while and then sail in the spring."

"Well," she said. "You certainly have thought it all out."

"Yes, I have. And I thank you for your concern." He reached across the counter and covered her hand with his own. "And your dear friendship."

Trini squeezed her eyes closed, hoping to blot out the sick misery that rumbled in her chest. Why did everything have to change, be disconnected and foreign? She needed to catch hold of something, a rope, a lifesaving tether to anchor her to this world. She opened her eyes, blinked to clear them and glanced through the front window to the sheriff's office across the street. Roy was in there. An image flashed in her mind of herself running across the street, dodging the festival traffic, clamoring up the steps and into his arms, begging him to take her away, protect and hide her.

"Trinidad, are you all right?" Jefferson's low voice brimmed with concern. "I'm sorry. I didn't mean for this to shock you."

"No. I mean yes. Yes, thank you. I'm fine."

So. He was leaving. A friend, a good friend, would be gone from her life. A thought flashed through her mind: Things would never be the same. A few days ago, her dream had been to be alone to mourn Jim's death. Now that seemed like a childhood fantasy. Something had happened, some line had been crossed. Jefferson leaving, she and Katherine forging a bond, Roy's burgeoning presence—all too much, too fast.

And she still had to help her brother. She had a case to prove against Mallis that would convince a marshal that the sheriff of Coyote County needed investigating himself. And she needed to ask Jefferson about having Gilbert Hardy help her to do that.

A stab of urgency pierced through the fog of her exhaustion. "I have a favor to ask you, Jefferson. A big one."

"If it's within my power, I shall be happy and willing to grant it."

She smiled. "You may not be when you hear it. Jefferson, I want to see some papers, some partnership papers, that I think exist between Merle Woodson and George Mallis."

"They were business partners?"

"Against Merle Woodson's will is my guess. I think Mallis used the bootlegging business as leverage to make Woodson give him a part of his oil claims, basically blackmailed himself into a partnership. Then I think Mallis killed Woodson for it and framed Parn."

"Good Lord, Trinidad. That's the stuff of mighty spies."

"I know it sounds crazy, but I've been doing a lot of thinking about this and it's the only thing that can explain everything."

"So what's the favor?"

"I think Merle Woodson probably has a safe deposit box." She reached in her pocket and withdrew the small gold key she'd taken from Merle's desk before she'd left the house. "I'm guessing this is the key to it, and I want you to talk Gilbert Hardy into letting me search it."

"I don't think even I could do that, Trinidad. That's against the law. Now if Katherine wanted to look, that would be a different circumstance."

"Katherine's at the house. And besides that, she's a frightened young girl. And she's a minor. I don't think she can see that box until Merle's estate is settled, and that won't be until after her relatives are here and after the funeral. I don't want to wait,

Jefferson. If I have something to show the marshal when he gets here, it's all the better for Parn. I'm going to try to convince the marshal to take Parn into custody until the arraignment, get him completely away from Mallis, but he won't do that without solid proof of criminal activity from Mallis. Please, Jefferson."

"But Mallis isn't even around. I heard no one can find him; even his house was empty."

"I know, but I'm sure he'll show up here, sooner or later. Mallis is dangerous, and I'm afraid of what will happen to Parn when he returns. Once the marshal gets here, the situation will be better, if he believes me that is. I have to have some proof of Mallis's intentions. Please, Jefferson. Ask Hardy to help me."

He darted his eyes around the store then settled back on her. "All right." He smiled at her. "You've been a good friend, and I'd like to help you if I can. I guess I shouldn't be so worried about imposing on Gilbert. It's not like I'll be affiliated with him in the future anyway, what with he and Mrs. Hardy moving to Denver."

Trini briefly recalled the scene with the imperial Lydia Hardy and her prediction that Gilbert Hardy would choose money and stature over Jefferson. Obviously she'd been correct. Not only was Jefferson losing his daughter, his home, his store, but his lover as well. She felt a wave of pity for poor Jefferson, but kept silent. He was in the midst of huge changes. Pity wouldn't help.

Jefferson continued, "Yes, I can talk to Gilbert for you. I'll see if Ed Barnes can watch the store for a couple of hours, then I'll need to ring Gilbert at home. I can't promise anything, Trinidad."

"I understand. Thank you, my friend."

Trini stood in front of the bank building next to Jefferson and, through the thick snow flurries, watched Gilbert Hardy trundle towards them. Even though it was Saturday, he had dressed for business in a gray overcoat that swung open to reveal the bulge of his stomach under his pale gray suit and matching vest. A black bow tie rested under the folds of his chins. When he stopped in front of them, he removed his black bowler and revealed thin, dark strings crossing his bald pate. His eyebrows, like two thick sticks of cinnamon, drew together in a scowl as if giving his banker's disapproval.

"LeClair. This is highly unusual. And what's so secret that you couldn't tell me over the wire?"

"Gilbert, you know Trinidad Bates, I'm sure."

Trini extended her hand and the banker received it in his own black glove. "Thank you for meeting us, Mr. Hardy. Jefferson asked you here as a favor to me."

"Mrs. Bates." He inclined his head and his thick lips lifted in what Trini supposed was a smile to reveal small, slightly pointed teeth.

Trini had of course seen him before, but they'd never been formally introduced. As a schoolteacher, Jim hadn't maintained the kind of account, or owned the kind of land that had interested Gilbert Hardy. But now that she had a chance to examine Hardy closely, she grew puzzled about Jefferson's alliance with him. His air of self-importance was in stark contrast to Jefferson's handsome ease, and he appeared to be the last person on earth someone could love. A cruel thought, she knew, and obviously, Jefferson would disagree with her. Still, despite Jefferson's pain, Trini was glad he would be starting a new life elsewhere; he deserved better than Gilbert Hardy.

"May we go inside, Gilbert?" Jefferson asked. "Trinidad has something she'd like to ask you."

Hardy's eyes shifted back and forth between Trini and Jefferson assessing the situation. He seemed to reach a decision after a moment. The banker pulled his watch chain from his vest and inserted the key that dangled from its fob into the lock.

The door swung open, and he flipped on an overhead light. Jefferson and Trini followed as he led the way through the black-and-white-tiled lobby and behind the teller cages with gleaming brass rails. Their steps echoed through a back hallway, and stopped when they came to the last door on the right. Dignified gold lettering in the center of a mahogany door read, "Gilbert Hardy, President." Hardy pulled another key from his chain and unlocked it. They entered his office, and he flipped a light switch to reveal a massive oak desk occupying the center. Two wing chairs sat opposite each other, both in brown leather. Trini sat on the edge of one of the chairs, Jefferson sat in the other. Gilbert walked behind the desk and clicked on a brass desk lamp. Thick oriental carpet and dense red velvet drapes with gold fringe muffled his question about their comfort. The rich chair squished softly as he sat. A leather blotter covered his desktop and a fountain pen of richly engraved silver rested in the center.

"Now, what may I do for you?" His vest stretched at the buttonholes, and as he leaned back, he folded his hands across the mound of his belly. He looked at Trini, but Jefferson spoke.

"Gilbert, Trinidad desires to see some papers that she believes are here in the bank."

"Can the woman speak English?"

"Gilbert," sighed Jefferson, "of course she can speak English. Don't be absurd."

"Then let her speak for herself."

He stared at Jefferson, and Trini saw the snap of anger in Hardy's eyes. So, she thought, animosity lay between the two men. Trini wondered if they'd broken off their affair. She assumed they had since Hardy had plans to leave for Denver with his wife and Jefferson would be leaving for Europe. Obviously, the breakup had not been amicable.

"Mr. Hardy," she said, "I have reason to believe that Merle Woodson and George Mallis are involved in a business partnership. And I think Woodson may have kept the partnership papers here, in a safe deposit box."

He regarded her with flat eyes. "And you want me to give you access to that safe deposit box?"

"Yes," she said.

Trini watched as Hardy looked from Jefferson to Trini and back again. "LeClair, have you gone entirely insane?"

"Gilbert—"

"You know damned well that's impossible. I can't open that box for anyone but the rightful heirs and only then after probate is settled. I'm sorry you wasted my time and yours. Now, if you'll excuse me." He stood up and leaned his knuckles on the desktop.

Jefferson bounded to his feet. "Don't be a total ass, Gilbert."

Hardy's face reddened, and he started around the desk toward Jefferson.

"Wait, please," said Trini. "Mr. Hardy, may I be frank with you?" She charged ahead even though he gave her no indication of an answer except shifting his glare from Jefferson to her. "I'm sure you know all about it, as does everyone by now: My brother's life is at stake. I need those papers to help prove his innocence."

"Young woman," said Hardy, "your family problems cannot induce me to break the law."

Trini examined him. She knew what she wanted to say, and in a split second, decided to say it. "Break the law? Mr. Hardy, homosexual activity is against the law, isn't it?"

She glanced at Jefferson. She didn't mean to hurt him, to be cruel, but she had to see those papers. Jefferson slid his eyes to her. She hoped he didn't walk out in disgust, proclaiming he had no idea she'd resort to insults to get what she wanted.

She spoke again before either of the men could. "Please understand I have sympathy for your predicament. Jefferson is my friend. I want him to be happy and if being happy means you and he together, then that's fine with me. But your whole situation is changing now. I witnessed your wife's visit to Jefferson."

From the shift in Hardy's expression, Trini had a feeling Jefferson had told him that. She wondered if he was surprised at her candor about their relationship.

"I'm sorry," continued Trini, "and I wouldn't ordinarily ask this. But you letting me see those papers, just to know the existence of them so I can present that to a marshal, is not going to matter after you're settled in a new life in Denver and Jefferson is in Europe."

Hardy's face flushed, and he whispered as he stared at Jefferson, "Europe?"

Jefferson cut her a look of annoyance. "I'm sorry, Gilbert. There was no time to tell you." He glanced at Trini again. "But yes, I'm moving to Europe."

"When?" Hardy croaked.

"Soon. A couple of months."

"My God, LeClair. My God."

Hardy slumped back into his chair and stared at Jefferson. His eyes reddened, and a hush settled over the room. Should she leave for a moment? Give them some privacy?

Gilbert looked at his hands as he spoke. "We had a good thing, Jefferson. A good thing until you left Camille. Why couldn't you leave things alone? Just go on as we had?"

"It was intolerable to me, Gilbert." Jefferson flicked his eyes to Trini. "Intolerable to continue to live a lie."

A weary sigh surged from Hardy and he looked down, fumbling with the charm on his watch fob. Trini slid a look to Jefferson who was staring at Hardy. She wondered if Jefferson blamed Hardy, thought less of him for not revealing his true nature to the world as he himself had. So many secrets. Hardy and Jefferson. Parn and Camille. Merle Woodson. Katherine.

Gilbert Hardy rose from his desk and looked at them. He wore a resigned expression. Or maybe he was just tired. "All right. I'll be right back."

He left the room and Trini turned toward Jefferson. "Another favor, Jefferson, that you've done for me."

He smiled at her, though creases of pain framed his eyes. "Maybe one day you'll be able to repay me the favor, Trinidad."

She was about to answer when Hardy re-entered the office carrying a long, black tin box under his arm. He placed it on the desk, and found another key at the end of his watch fob. He inserted it into the keyhole and turned.

"I have the other key," she said. She held up Merle Woodson's gold key.

"No need," he said. "I've got a master. Haven't had to use this key in all of ten years as much as I've had to the last couple of days."

"On Woodson's box?"

He nodded.

Trini felt dread clutch her chest. "Who else? Who else has seen the contents of this box?"

"Sheriff Mallis," Hardy said. "Yesterday on official sheriff's business, which by the way, he's entitled to do."

"Didn't you have to wait for a search warrant or something?"

"Mallis said he was working on a hunch, wanted to get to the bottom of it. He said he'd take care of any legal problems. I knew I was covered under Mallis's protection."

Trini wondered how Mallis had talked Gilbert Hardy into doing something that violated the law. Although, even though he protested otherwise, Trini had a feeling that Gilbert Hardy was not as particular about obeying the law as he claimed to be.

Hardy lifted the lid and Trini and Jefferson sat forward in

their seats. A single folded paper rested on top of a stack of money.

"Not much here," Hardy said. "A lot of cash. Ridiculous not to invest this much cash." He raised his eyes to her and his voice deepened with authority. "Despite all claims to the contrary, Mrs. Bates, with proper guidance, money can still be made by investing." He looked at the contents of the box again. "Damn Merle Woodson couldn't manage money." He unfolded the single page and scanned the contents. "This is what Sheriff Mallis found so interesting. I guess you want to see it, too." He handed the paper across the desk to Trini. Jefferson got up from his chair and stood next to her. He leaned close to read over her shoulder.

Finally, she thought. Finally, she'd have something firm to prove Mallis's duplicity. She quickly scanned the document. It established DOME Partnership for the purpose of buying mineral rights from the Santa Fe Railroad. The profits were to be shared equally between the partners. It wasn't written in legal language, just Merle Woodson's plain talk. And at the bottom were two signatures: Merle Daniel Woodson and Dorothy Mae Kerr.

Dottie Kerr? But where was Mallis's signature? Trini flipped the paper over; the back was blank. She read the page again. This couldn't be right. She must have missed something.

"This doesn't say anything about George Mallis," said Jefferson.

She scanned the page two more times. This was the DOME Partnership? Mallis's name must be on another sheet. She looked up to meet Hardy's questioning gaze.

"Are you sure there isn't another paper in there about DOME? Maybe under the money?"

He lifted the cash from the box and showed her the bottom. "Just the money and that one paper."

"But I don't understand," she said. "Merle made a notation on the bottom of one of the DOME maps with Mallis's name. Mallis had to be a part of DOME."

Next to her, Jefferson spoke lowly, "Maybe not, Trinidad. Maybe not."

She darted her eyes to Jefferson, then Hardy, then back to Jefferson. "But he had to be. That's why he killed Merle in the first place, to take control of DOME. I don't understand."

"Maybe," said Jefferson, "you don't understand because you're wrong. DOME would be the first two letters of Dottie's and Merle's names. And from this paper, it would seem this is the one and only partnership."

"But what about the notations on the map I saw? Mallis's name on the bottom of the map?"

Hardy shrugged. "People make all kinds of doodles and scribbles when they think. Maybe Woodson was thinking of Mallis's complication in the bootlegging business and scribbled his name as just a random thought. I don't know. But I do know the only legal document is the partnership agreement. If Mallis's name isn't on that, it doesn't matter what Merle Woodson wrote on a map. Funny that Mallis was shocked about this partnership, too."

Trini collapsed back into the chair. Had she been wrong? All this time? Mallis had nothing to do with DOME?

"Then Merle wasn't killed for the oil at all," she said. "Mallis must have killed him for the bootlegging business. And as revenge for the death of his own family."

Hardy spoke from his seat, "What's all this?"

Jefferson glanced at him but directed himself to Trini. "If none of this DOME business had anything to do with Mallis, then you're back to where you started."

Trini sat in stunned silence.

"Did Dottie Kerr ever say anything about a partnership?" asked Jefferson.

Trini shook her head. "Nothing. I talked to her just two days ago and she never said a word. Of course, now it's too late."

Hardy spoke in his banker's tone, "That at least solves the financial situation for Katherine and Jake Woodson. If the DOME leases do in fact yield oil, the Woodson children will be wealthy."

Trini thought a minute. "That's right," she said. "With Dottie and Merle dead, the oil rights would go to their heirs. Katherine and Jake. And Daryl."

What was it that Daryl had said about Dottie? Something about Dottie not needing money for retiring? And now Dottie's dead. Burned to death in a fire. Just like the fire that had burned Parn's cabin to the ground.

Something cold and ugly squirmed up her spine. Fire and oil and Mallis and Woodson and Parn and Dottie Kerr. She couldn't make sense of it all logically, but her instincts told her that somehow the puzzle fit together differently than she had been thinking it had. Mallis had framed Parn, no question. He'd somehow manufactured the evidence of Parn's hammer as the murder weapon. So that meant in order to frame Parn, he had to have murdered Merle Woodson. Didn't it? And what about Dottie and Merle both being owners of valuable mineral rights and now both dead? The questions shoved and pushed for logical order, but she could find none.

She'd take one step at a time. First, she knew now who made up the partners in DOME. She needed to tell Roy about that. Maybe he could help her think it out, smooth the tangled threads of the events. And she wasn't sure why, but she felt an urgency, almost a panic, to do that. She bolted to her feet. "I have to go now."

"Where?" asked Jefferson.

"I have to leave. I have to talk to Roy."
She pulled the door open and ran out of the building.

CHAPTER EIGHTEEN

Trini slammed the door to the bank behind her and scanned the street. An ever-thickening layer of snow coated the sidewalks, vehicles and the granite window ledges of the shops. Flakes the size of silver dollars quickly erased footprints left by festival-goers as they still funneled their way to the schoolyard. Undoubtedly, people hoped for a quick snowfall and then for the day to continue uninterrupted. Trini wasn't so sure that would be the case. From the look of the dull sky, more snow would be coming, and it wouldn't take more than a few hours to seal the countryside as tight as a root cellar. She needed to get back to the Woodsons'. If this snow kept up, the hill leading up to their house would soon be impassable. But first, she had to see Roy. She had to tell him of her discovery of the partnership.

Trini started towards the sheriff's office, and then felt a hand press on her shoulder. Jefferson? She turned, and her nose caught the unmistakable odor of unwashed body and buckskins. Lyle Butcher squinted down at her. Snowflakes sprinkled his eyelashes and beard adding their whiteness to his peppery whiskers. He looked like a grizzly caught outside his den.

"Glad I got you, Trini. I need you to come with me."

"Lyle, I can't now."

"You better think again. I got something important to show you."

"I'm sorry, Lyle. I just can't right now. I've just learned

233

something about Woodson's oil leases, and I have to talk to Roy."

"That's what I'm aiming to help you with if you'll quit hollering like a branded calf. I got Sheriff Mallis up at the mine. He's alive, but just barely. And he's been asking for you."

"You have Mallis?"

"That's what I just said. You might be as pretty as your ma, but you got your pa's hard head."

"How? Where'd you find him?"

"Gutted and left for dead east of town, at the bottom of Cottonwood Gulch."

Jumbled thoughts clawed their way through the murk of shock. Someone tried to kill Mallis? When? Why?

"You gotta hurry," he said. "He's almost dead."

She clutched Butcher's buckskin sleeve and turned him toward the sheriff's office, two goals pulsing through her body: Get Roy, get to Mallis. "Did you see Doc Cockrell?" she asked. "We could take him with us in the truck. Maybe he could save Mallis."

"I already went over there. Doc ain't here. He's out at the Mauser's place birthing a baby. And we ain't going way out there. Mallis is almost dead as it is and we can't take the time to get the Doc. 'Sides, Mallis made me promise I'd bring you back fast."

"I want to get Roy first. He needs to talk to Mallis, if that will be possible."

They hurried down the sidewalk, Butcher talking as they went. "Well, hurry up. Mallis ain't gonna last for long. I left him barely drawing breath." He veered off from her to the blacktop, calling over his shoulder as he trotted across the road. "Pick me up at the gas station. I gotta put Canary in the shed out back. Joe O'Henley will take care of her. This blizzard's gonna be a mean one."

Trini broke into a jog and glanced at the hard sky. The wind had picked up. Rushing past the sheriff's window, she peered inside. Taggert sat at his desk reading the newspaper. She threw open the door and leaned through the threshold.

"Les, where's Roy?"

"Well, well, well. If it ain't Joan-of-the-rock-on-a-string, Miss high-and-mighty. You know—"

"Taggert," Trini interrupted, "where's Roy?"

"Down at the festival. Now don't get all in a snit there, missy, and don't go into one of them screaming fits again. I couldn't take that. You near 'bout—"

Trini slammed the door and dashed to her truck. She turned the key and backed onto the snow-covered blacktop. She had to get to Roy. Not only so that he could talk to Mallis, but she wanted him with her, his strength and comfort, for herself.

She eased her foot onto the gas, and her tires skidded a little. The truck crept along as the crowd zipped around her. The throng was unbelievable. The Fall Festival was usually a popular event, but it had been snowing for an hour or more; people should be packing up and going home. Lyle predicted it would be a full-blown blizzard, and she trusted the instinct of the old mountain man.

Trini turned the corner in front of the school, craning her neck, frantically searching the crowd for Roy. Her neighbor strolled on the sidewalk ahead of her. Trini slowed down to match her pace and tapped on her horn. She pulled to a stop, leaned across the seat and rolled down the passenger window.

Adeline Chase leaned over to peer inside and smiled. "Hello there, Mrs. Bates. I've heard you're staying with the Woodson children. I've been meaning to get over there with a pot roast. I know you—"

"Mrs. Chase," Trini said, "I'm desperate to find Roy Eastman. Have you seen him?"

Her neighbor's eyebrows drew together in a frown on her pretty face. "Why, no. I haven't seen him around here, but I've been at the pie booth all morning. Now that this snow seems to be getting worse, though, I think I'll round up my brood and head home. What a shame to—"

"Sorry, I hate to cut you off. But if you see him could you please tell him I'm with Lyle Butcher?"

She nodded. "Of course I will, but what's the matter? Should I tell him where you are?"

"I don't know where Butcher lives. Just give Roy the message. Please."

The woman agreed, and Trini pressed the accelerator as hard as she dared, slowly parting the crowd that spilled over from the sidewalk onto the street. She completed the circuit around the school, ducking and darting her gaze through the mob of people. No sign of Roy. She couldn't wait any longer. The prowling fear inside her had grown into a raging lion. She had to get to Mallis before he died.

She pulled to a stop in front of the gasoline station, and Butcher trotted around the side of the building, the fringe of his buckskins tangling in the wind and snow. He climbed inside, and they sped out of town as fast as the snow would allow.

Inside the cab of the truck, Trini had turned up the heater to full. The fan hummed over the whine of the engine, and she had to raise her voice to talk to Butcher. "I don't even know where you live."

He grinned at her, a yellow split through his beard. "You know the Garrett mine? Past the road to Pueblo?"

"I kind of know. You'll have to direct me. I thought you lived in an abandoned mine."

He shrugged. "Best place for an old miner."

Trini turned off where Butcher indicated and followed the road as it curved and bent into the rocks. Fifteen minutes later, she turned again at a dirt road, now resurfaced in frosty white, which led up a hill to the mine. She slowed as the truck lurched through the snow-filled potholes and ruts.

"I can barely see the road. I don't want to drive off the side," Trini said.

"I just hope Mallis is still alive. He'd been slit clean across his gut, and he was near frozen when I found him. If I'd had me a truck, I would have brought him in town myself, at least tried to get him to the Doc. But I knew if I tried to sling him over Canary's back, he'd die sooner. That's why I just thought I'd better get into town myself." He shook his head. "The man has gravel in his gizzard, ya got to give him that."

Trini smiled at Butcher's comment. Yes, Mallis was a gritty survivor, hard as the mountains. But as much as she'd hated Mallis, she now found the prospect of seeing him near death disarming. He would die the same way we all do, she thought. One last breath and his presence on earth would be gone forever. She just hoped she wasn't too late.

She stopped about twenty yards down the hill from the mine's entrance and jumped from the truck. The harsh wind cut to her skin. Knotting her shawl across her shoulders, she squinted at the black square that was the entrance to the mine and followed the mountain man up the hill. Her brogans slipped and skidded on the sheet of ice that glazed the rocky path, but Butcher clasped her wrist and pulled her along. She stumbled in a snow-covered gap, caught herself on one palm then staggered upright. When they got to the entrance, Trini glimpsed the details of his home: pots, pans, a few tools propped on a ledge just inside the opening, a cured deer hide mounted on the rock wall. She ducked her head under the rock doorway and entered.

Inside, Lyle's biting odor, oddly enough, was muted. Perhaps the odors of animal skins mingled with smoke obscured it. The interior was surprisingly well lit. Several kerosene lanterns sat on the rock floor, and three hung from iron hooks hammered into the granite wall. More deer skins and Ute-patterned blankets covered the floor, and in the far corner on a hearth of loose stones, a low fire burned. Trini followed the white curl to the smoke-hole in the ceiling. In front of the rustic fireplace, blankets and a bear skin had been heaped over the form of a man. Trini and Butcher knelt beside him. Butcher placed a hand on his shoulder and gently rolled him over.

Mallis's face looked to be made of gouged milk glass, hard and white, and the closed eyelids wore the chill of pale blue. Wispy white threads lay across his bald head scattered with dull age spots. His mouth was a thin gray line. One hand lay across the mound of blankets like a white shriveled spider. Mallis had grown old to get ready to die.

"Is he alive?" she asked.

Butcher leaned down and put his ear to Mallis's nose. "He's breathing, but barely."

Butcher swirled a cloth in a pan of water that sat on the ground by Mallis's head. He wrung it out and placed it on the dying man's mouth. The blue eyelids fluttered open and those eyes, still obsidian black, regarded Trini. She knew he was lucid. Lyle was right: Mallis had gravel in his gizzard.

He slowly opened his lips, and a croak emerged. "Wanted to tell you."

Lyle dabbed his mouth again with the wet cloth, then Trini bent closer. The odor of blood and innards assaulted her, and she covered her nose and mouth with the end of her shawl. She had hated the man, hated and feared him. Was it only yesterday that she wanted to claw his face, scrape that self-serving grin from her sight? Curse at him, beat him for making her brother, and herself, go through this? And now, he lay here, at her mercy, ready to die. The fate of us all, she thought, no matter how good or bad. She wished she had her rosary. No soul deserved to leave the earth without prayers. Not even George Mallis.

She had a thousand questions to ask him: Who had done this to him? How and why did he kill Merle Woodson? Was he a part of the DOME Partnership? Did he still believe Parn had killed his family? But she held back. She wanted to be open to all he had to say.

"What is it you wanted to tell me, Mallis?"

The cracked lips quivered and the croak broke through again. "Wanted to tell you." He swallowed. "Did not kill Woodson."

She leaned closer. "Who? Who didn't kill Woodson?"

"Me." His croak became more insistent.

"But Parn didn't kill Woodson, either. You know that, don't you?"

The head twitched in a nod and he shifted a little under the heap of fur and blankets. "I know it. I figured Woodson for dead when he went missing. Thought the gang up in Denver got to him."

The black eyes seemed to clear and the ravaged lips lifted in a smile. Trini had the distinct impression that just as he had when they found the wreckage of Woodson's car, Mallis was relishing the moment.

"Wanted to cause Parn Shannon lots of trouble, keep him for a while behind bars." He closed his eyes, brought his eyebrows together in a deep frown and coughed deeply several times. Butcher again dabbed at his lips with the wet cloth. The sheriff gasped for breath, opened his eyes and spoke again. "After you found the wreck, perfect opportunity to set up your brother." He closed his eyes again as if exhausted by his efforts. The smile stayed on his face.

So there it was. She wanted to be sure. "You set it up so it appeared Parn murdered Woodson?"

The white head nodded once and the blue lids stayed closed. Butcher once again held the wet cloth to Mallis's parched lips.

The eyes fluttered open again and the mouth moved to receive the moisture. Butcher removed the cloth, and a whisper came from the near-corpse.

"Used chicken blood." The lips curved in a smile. "Smeared it on the hammer."

What a hateful man. Rage once again surged inside her and she clamped her teeth together to restrain her curses at the brute. Railing at him would do no good now, but she had to know more. "You were planning to kill Parn all along, weren't you? Have him die during a so-called escape or an accident. Weren't you?" She wanted to shake the wizened old man, shake him enough to bring him back to health so she could hate him again.

The spidery hand clawed the blanket, and a deep frown line appeared between his white eyebrows. "Killed my wife and boys," he rasped. "My boys. My boys." A lone tear slid from the corner of one eye into the thin white hair at his temples.

"Mallis," she said. "Mallis. Don't go from this world thinking Parn had a part in that. He didn't kill your family."

He closed his eyes a moment then opened them again and stared at her. He choked as he spoke. "Killed my boys."

She almost insisted again that Parn hadn't been a part of his family's murder, then stopped herself. She'd never convince him now, and it really didn't matter. Let him cross to the other side believing what he did. He'd learn.

"Mallis," she said, "did you try to kill me in Parn's cabin? Did you set his cabin on fire?"

The eyebrows knitted together, but his eyes remained closed. He neither shook his head nor nodded. He was leaving fast.

"Mallis," she said. Trini had to restrain herself from shaking him. "Who killed Merle Woodson?"

She wondered if he heard her, or if he'd already gone. He stayed still, his face frozen in the pain. But after a moment, the thick creases relaxed, and he opened his eyes once again to meet her gaze. "Same man that's done killed me. Got too close to him. Knew I was onto him."

Trini leaned into his face, trying to command his last seconds. In her heart, she knew what she needed to know, but she wanted Mallis's confirmation. "Don't die, Mallis. Don't die. Tell me. It was Daryl Kerr, wasn't it? Daryl Kerr."

She placed her ear next to his mouth to take in the last syllable of his life. "Yes."

The eyes remained open, but the light was gone. Trini sat back on her heels and crossed herself. "At least he's with his boys now."

They stood and Butcher grabbed her arm. "Was it that Daryl Kerr? Is that who's been doin' all this killin' for greed around here?"

"Yes. Oh, Lyle, I feel so horrible. When I saw the partnership papers, I knew it, but I couldn't believe it. He wants those oil rights. He wanted them so bad he killed his own mother to get them."

Her stomach heaved with sick knowledge: He'd stop at nothing. If he could kill his own mother to assuage his greed, he'd do anything. And the only two people who stood in the way of Daryl Kerr inheriting the entire partnership were Jake and Katherine. But he'd never get away with it. The scheme was outrageous and Daryl must be insane to believe he could kill and kill again and escape the consequences. Numbing fear pumped through her. Apparently, he did believe exactly that. Trini knew as sure as Mallis lay dead at her feet that Jake and Katherine were in mortal danger.

"I've got to get to Katherine and Jake."

The old man regarded her with flint eyes, ready to do the bidding of Lucinda's daughter. "You think Kerr might kill them kids?"

Cold terror nestled inside her and made its home. She nodded.

"Okay, then. Let's go." He flipped a blanket over Mallis's glacier-like face.

Trini raced outside, and a frozen slap of wind hit her face. Heaven help them, they'd be lucky to make it to the Woodsons'. The roads would quickly grow impassable. The urgency inside her chest swelled to near panic, and she slipped and skidded down the hill. She stumbled to the truck and turned to see Butcher close behind her. They scrambled into the cab, Trini mercifully started the cold engine and the truck lurched forward.

She'd been ready to follow the trail of her tire tracks, but they were nearly obscured. In the best of circumstances, Butcher's road would severely jar the occupants of a vehicle as they traveled over the rugged terrain; but now driving across the snow-hidden ruts, the crown of Trini's head struck the roof of the cab as they trundled down the hill. She only vaguely registered the blows; the images of Katherine and Jake hovered above every turn of the road. Maybe Daryl wouldn't be at the Woodsons'. Maybe she was letting fear get the best of her. After all, Daryl didn't know what she'd discovered in the partnership papers. Maybe he thought since he'd killed Mallis that he still had plenty of time to implement his fiendish plan. Maybe he was at his house, comfortably sitting out the storm, biding his time, planning to conclude his nefarious scheme when the weather cleared. Maybe there was time to get Roy's help, then secrete Katherine and Jake away until Daryl could be arrested.

But panic pumped through her veins, and the engine whined its song: "Katherine and Jake. Katherine and Jake."

CHAPTER NINETEEN

Trini stopped at the end of the hill, where Butcher's dirt road met the blacktop, and surveyed a stark expanse of white. Landmarks of rocks and bare trees protruded through the pristine blanket; she'd use those to navigate by.

Butcher sat beside her, leaning out the open passenger window and shouting warnings to her. "You're going too far to the right. You got to stay on the blacktop. There's gullies and washouts all along here. Get over. That's it."

They sped down the deserted highway, enveloped in a white cocoon, spinning snow from the blacktop. The prairie spread to infinity around them. Trini felt like she'd been transported to another star in the solar system.

She glanced at Butcher and grasped for a wisp of hope, gulping every parcel of air while tossed on a pounding sea. "Maybe Daryl won't be at the Woodsons'. Maybe he's in no hurry to . . . to do anything. Maybe he figures he'll wait until the storm's over before he'll try anything with Katherine and Jake." She waited for Butcher's answer, hoping he'd agree, reassure her she was right, make the terror go away.

"Don't kid yourself," he rumbled. He was silent after that, a silence that hardened the truth of what she suspected: Daryl Kerr would be there.

Forty-five minutes later, Trini spied the mound of rocks topped by a mailbox indicating the Woodsons' turnoff. She took her measure of the distance and swung onto what she supposed was the driveway. The truck careened and skidded then plunged into a ditch. The rear tires spun in a defeated whirl.

She laid her forehead on the steering wheel. "Oh, Sweet Mary, Mother of God, I've done it now," she said.

"Couldn't be helped," said Butcher. "We're going to have to walk up to the house."

"I know. It's a half mile yet. We better get started." She reached for the door lever.

"Don't you have nothing but that wrap?" He indicated her black shawl she'd bundled around her shoulders.

"No. It looked warmer out this morning. I thought we'd have a nice day and I'd be back here by noon. It doesn't matter. We've got to get going." Nausea born of fear twisted her stomach.

"Well, you can't go out in that."

He tugged off the buckskin jacket and handed it to her. She briefly wondered if the stench had been frozen out of it and eyed it suspiciously.

"Go on now," he said. "Take it."

"But that leaves you only with your shirt."

"Don't matter. It's a nice, warm buckskin. Go on now. I knowed you don't want to, but take it now. You'll need it."

He was right. Now was no time to be finicky. She clutched the buckskin to her.

Pushing the door against a gust of wind, Trini climbed from the truck. Her feet crunched through the icy crust and covered the tops of her socks. She pulled her shawl over her head and wrapped it around her neck, then pushed her arms through the sleeves of Lyle's jacket. The odor nearly gagged her. She hurried around to the front of the truck where Lyle was waiting, and gripping his arm, they started the climb up the hill.

Trini had lived all her life in Colorado and had seen many winters that kept everyone indoors for several days, but she'd never stayed outside in weather like this for an extended period of time. The blunting cold sent a spike of fear through her, numbing her tendons and muscles and bones. She clutched the offensive coat to her neck, no longer squeamish, and ducked her head against the wind's frigid jaws; nothing stopped the assault. The iciness bored its way through the coat, up and under the bottom of her dress, down into her socks. After only ten minutes and still far less than halfway up the Woodsons' drive, she was weak and stiff.

Butcher stopped beside her. He yelled in her face through the howling wind, "Where are we?"

She squinted through the swirling mass to see his beard and eyebrows now caked with snow. Small ice bits dangled from his mustache. His bloodshot eyes squinted at her, and coins of red punctuated each cheek and the end of his nose.

"That stand of pines at the top of the hill marks the turn," she yelled. "That's halfway."

"Can we cut off the corner? Let's cut through here." He pointed toward the open meadow to their right, the same meadow she had imagined yesterday as it would appear in the spring, wearing a quilt of wildflowers.

She yelled again to raise her voice over the wind. "I don't know, Lyle. I've never walked it. It's too rocky."

She saw his mouth move, but a gust of wind caught his words, and Trini turned away from him to protect her face. She felt him pull away. He'd evidently answered that they should try the shortcut. She cupped her hand around her eyes as a shield against the onslaught of billowing snow and looked in the direction where they headed. The tops of the pines at the turn bent under the wind, and beyond them Trini made out through the white haze the small aspen and birch lining the roadway. As long as they had landmarks, and she knew the Woodson property well enough by now to know them, they wouldn't get lost. She pushed her way through the wind, keeping hold of Lyle's sleeve.

When they stepped off the roadway, Trini sank up to her knees in a ditch of new-fallen blizzard. She lifted one foot, and as she waded forward looking for a solid hold for her weight, Lyle's arm was torn from her grasp, and he went down. He lay folded on the ground beside her, holding his ankle.

"Oh, God! Oh, damn it, damn it, damn it!" he screamed.

"Lyle. Oh, my God, Lyle. What happened?" She pushed her way to his side and leaned over him.

He rocked back and forth on one hip, grasping his ankle. "I busted it. I busted my leg."

A flame of panic shot through her warming her insides for an instant. What should she do now? Dear God. If Daryl Kerr was at the Woodsons', how would she handle him alone?

"You got to go on," he yelled. "You got to get them kids."

"But, Lyle. I can't leave—"

He looked at her, his expression sneering, deadly earnest. "Don't be stupid. You got to go on. I can't walk and you can't stay here."

"But . . . but at least let me help you back to the truck. You can't stay out here."

"No. No. That'd take too much time. You got to get to them kids." Suddenly, he laid back in the snow and his face opened and he smiled. She leaned near him to hear. "No. You go on now, Little Lucinda. Go on. I'm a man of the mountains, you always said that. No harm will come to me."

Lucinda? Was he hallucinating? How could she just leave him here? "At least let me see the break," she said. "If it's not too bad, you can lean on me. We can make our way to the house."

He seemed to come back to himself because his eyes bore into her. He pushed himself to sitting. "No! We'll never make it. You ain't listening to me. My leg's broke. I can't walk and you can't drag me."

She couldn't leave Lyle to certain death. Surely there had to be something else to do, something she wasn't thinking of. She darted her eyes around her for an answer to come swirling out of the white.

No answer came, but a certainty did: She had to get to Katherine. Sacrifice Lyle for Jake and Katherine? How could she make that choice? Yet she had to, and when she felt the decision come to her, build a bridge to an internal line of hard acceptance, she knew it was the only decision she could make. She felt the steel of resolve set itself across the tops of her shoulders.

"All right." She surveyed the area, then gestured to a stand of rock a few yards from them. "Over there," she yelled. "There might be a windbreak in those rocks."

He wrapped his arm around her neck, and taking his hand to balance his weight, she let him push down on her as he heaved himself to his feet. They slogged through the gale until they reached the outcrop. He collapsed against the side of the mound in an indentation just large enough for his back, away from the direct assault of the wind, and fell to the ground.

"All right now," he said. He adjusted his weight on one hip and bent his knee to pull the broken leg on top of his good one. He began to pack it with snow. "All right. This will keep me."

Trini knelt beside him. Good God in Heaven, no one could survive in this blizzard. Was she committing murder?

Behind the small fortress, she was away from the fierce howling, but she leaned near his face to speak. She examined the deep lines around his eyes, his cracked and weathered lips, and the wiry beard. "Are you sure, Lyle? I can help you up the hill, or we can go back to the truck. I—"

"No more arguing. You get to them kids. When you can, get yourself bundled up good and get back down here with extra blankets and coats." He adjusted himself again, crossed his arms and jammed his reddened hands under his armpits. He focused on her. "Git now. And, Trini, you're gonna have to be as strong as you ever been in your life. You're up against a killer. You got to outsmart him. Go on now. You can do this. Any daughter of Lucinda's can do this. Every minute you waste here is a minute lost. Go."

She studied the rough old visage again and thought about Lyle Butcher and her mother. All those years ago. And here he was, right here in this frozen meadow, for her now. He was right. She had to leave. She had to dig deep inside herself and find that part of her where strength and cunning and iron will lived.

She shrugged out of the buckskin jacket. "Okay. But here."

"No, now. Don't." But Trini thought his voice sounded a little less insistent.

"Don't be a fool," she said. "I'll be moving, and you won't." She tucked the jacket under his chin and around his shoulders. She had to get back to him. Please God, give her the strength to get back to him. "Maybe I should leave my shawl, too."

"No," he said. "You need something. Go on. Git."

She nodded and stood. Gathering the shawl around her head and shoulders, she turned from him and headed up the embankment. After a few steps, she stopped and looked back, then cupped her hand to her mouth and yelled through the wail, "I'll be back, Lyle."

She saw him lift his hand in a weak wave. She turned and continued her climb.

Chapter Twenty

Step and breathe. Step and breathe. Stop and rest for a second. And again: Step and breathe. Step and breathe.

Trini's universe narrowed to the scalding cold of her feet, her hands, and her face. She stopped, turned her back to the force of the wind, hunched over, and let her shoulders and back take the brunt of the whipping for a moment. Then she faced the flogging again, ducked her head, and put one foot in front of the other.

Thank you for the snow being less than knee deep. Thank you for the wool shawl gripped tight beneath my chin. She'd ordered the wool special, three years ago. Was it three? Yes, just before Jim's first heart attack. It was the winter of '29. Step and breathe. Step and breathe. She'd seen the offer in one of Jefferson's catalogs. New Zealand wool, the advertisement had read. It was expensive, a dollar a yard, but Jim had told her to get it for her January birthday. The visions in front of her swirled through white: Jim, healthy and strong; Parn, grinning after a funny joke; Roy's warm gray eyes; her daughter, how Trini imagined her, scampering across a green hillside. Step and breathe.

She stopped and peered through the white haze. The oak. Grandma's Oak, Katherine called it, because it had been planted generations ago by a Woodson pioneer. Trini stumbled to it and collapsed against the coarse trunk swallowing snow and air. She squinted. The roofline of the Woodson house. A surge of hope burst through her. She'd made it. What awaited her, she couldn't guess, but she'd made it. She started her routine again. Step, breathe. Step, breathe.

She reached the yard. Oh for the warmth of the house, for a fire, a cup of hot tea. But was Daryl Kerr here? The house looked silent and deserted, and his truck wasn't parked beside the back door. A flame of hope shot through her. Maybe what she'd hoped for was true: He was at his own house, and Katherine and Jake were safe. Or maybe he'd already come and gone, and she'd find . . . stop it. Conjectures wouldn't help anything.

She started toward the house again, then halted midstep. At the side, parked behind a large evergreen almost out of sight, Trini spied the black fender of a truck. She inched closer, grimacing through the blasts of wind, until she was several feet in back of it. The rear gate was up, and several inches of snow coated the truck bed, but she recognized it. Daryl Kerr had delivered wood yesterday in this truck. Despite the cold, her face flushed red. She was too late. Dear God, too late. What should she do?

She should do what Lyle told her to do: Be strong. She inhaled an icy breath and thought. She had to see inside the house, figure out what she was up against. Tugging her shawl tighter to her neck, she waded through the knee-high drifts to the front of the house.

Bare shrubs lined the house, and she pushed her way through the hedge until she hugged the plank siding of the front wall. At least the structure provided some shelter to her frozen torso. The kitchen window and door was to her right, and to her left was the corner of the house. She let the siding brush against her as she followed the wall and turned the corner. She was on the leeward side of the house. The drifts here were gentle with edges that looked like ruffles. Out of the wind's direct assault, her breathing slowed to normal although her heartbeat was loud enough to echo in her ears. The front screen door, about twenty feet in front of her, thrust back and forth on its hinges with each gust of the blizzard. The thick pine door was closed.

That's odd, she thought. No one ever used the front door, not even company; only the back kitchen entrance. Maybe the screen door had jiggled loose in a burst of frozen wind. She eased herself behind a row of spindly lilac bushes, their tentacles now bare except for a ridge of snow that stuck to each branch as if someone had painted their tops with thick frosting. If she flattened herself against the siding, she could squeeze between the bushes and the house, and then scoot near the parlor windows a few feet away. Using her exhausted and frozen thigh muscles, she squatted down and eased her way to the edge of the casing. She carefully, slowly, stood up just enough to see inside.

Slam! She plummeted to the ground. What was it? Had he heard her? She froze in place, bending her head down to hide the cloud of smoke from her breath. She waited for half a minute or so. Nothing. Suddenly, she heard the front door open. She raised her eyes for a peek: a rolled-up flannel sleeve, a muscled forearm coated with wiry black hair, a mammoth hand grasping the screen door and pulling it shut. With a firm thud, the main door closed again.

Good God. The noise had been the screen door slamming closed, bouncing off the frame then swinging open again. And there was no question whose arm she'd seen latching it back into place.

She scooted up again to stand next to the window casement. She inched her way forward and carefully crouched in order to peek into the parlor. The heavy black window screen blurred a clear view, but she'd seen enough: Daryl Kerr sitting on one end of the parlor sofa, and Katherine, squeezed into a frightened ball at the other end.

A torrent of fury rose from her center. She knew what Katherine's posture meant. Trini briefly thought about Katherine's reaction the other evening at the café when Trini told her she'd visited the Kerrs; she'd been sick with panic. The mention of Daryl Kerr undoubtedly terrified the girl. And, now that she'd seen it with her own eyes, Trini knew what her instincts had told her from the moment she read the partnership paper: Not only was he a murderer, but Daryl Kerr was also Katherine's tormentor.

Trini began to tremble and she thought for one awful moment, as black spots floated in front of her, she might faint. Breathe, she scolded herself. Breathe and stay right here. Blacking out won't help Katherine.

After a moment, the world stopped spinning and sensation returned; the gnawing cold had cramped her muscles, and a spasm twitched her left shin. Now what? What should she do? Sneak in a window—Katherine's bedroom window at the back of the house? How could she do that? All the windows were closed and locked against the winter weather. She could break the glass, crawl in and overpower him. The insanity of the idea made her stifle a giggle. First of all, the breaking glass would warn him, and she'd lose the element of surprise. Secondly, even if she could surprise him, she would never be able to overpower a massive man like Daryl Kerr. Brawn would not work. She'd have to use her wits.

She stood away from the window and let the ideas swirl through her head like the snow around her. She wouldn't have to feign desperate exhaustion, but she would pretend she didn't know Daryl was in the house. She wanted him to believe she was unsuspecting of his murderous and lecherous behavior. She wanted his guard down. She'd tell him mostly the truth; her fear for Lyle Butcher who she left in the meadow at the bottom of the hill. She'd telephone Roy for help. She'd insist on taking the children with her to rescue Butcher. And if Daryl refused to let her, well, she'd have to somehow, some way overpower him.

Not much of a plan, she thought, but it was all she could come up with. The main thing was that Katherine would be safer with Trini in the house than standing out here wondering what to do.

Tucking the shawl around her head again, she sidled out from behind the hedge the way she'd come in and hurried to the back of the house. Using her shoulder for a lever, she thrust herself at the door, and with a sucking *swoosh,* it opened inward to the warm kitchen. For an instant, she registered the comfort of the temperature. Thank God. Thank God she was out of that cold.

"Oh my God," she called. "Katherine? I'm here. I'm home."

Daryl lumbered into the room. Surprise raised the black eyebrows and creased his forehead. Katherine stood behind him, her eyes red-rimmed, wide and sober, her fingers tugging her bottom lip. Where was Jake? Trini's heart pounded the walls of her ribs. She was scared. Scared to death.

"Daryl. Oh, Lord," Trini said. "I didn't see your truck." She threw her shawl across the back of the chair, and went to stand beside the warm stove. The large copper kettle sat on its usual burner, and she extended her hands over the swirl of steam that curled from its spout. "I can't believe it," she panted, "I can't believe I made it."

"What happened?" he asked. His feminine voice no longer evoked a wave of pity in her. Instead, she repressed a shudder of revulsion.

"I ran off the road at the bottom of the hill. I walked all the way up. Daryl, we have to get your truck and go back down. Lyle Butcher's in the meadow with a broken leg. I had to leave him." She hurried across the room and lifted a heavy coat from the coatrack.

"Lyle Butcher?" he said. "What was he doing here?"

She shoved her arms through the sleeves. "No time for questions. We have to go." She extended her arm, palm up, toward him. "Give me your keys. I'll go. Come on, Katherine. You and Jake need to help me carry him. Where is Jake anyway?"

She tried to reach behind Daryl for Katherine. The coat sleeve pulled up and he caught her bare wrist. "No one's going anywhere," he said.

Panic seized her, but she tried to keep her eyes wide and innocent as she looked up into his face. "No, you don't understand. Butcher's there, outside in the blizzard, now. We have to save—"

He gripped her wrist tighter and pulled her toward him. "I said no one is going anywhere."

"What's the matter, Daryl? Why wouldn't you want to help him?" She blinked, trying to keep the disgust from her face.

He squeezed her arm and jerked her enough to rattle her teeth. "Don't play that game with me, Trini Bates. You're just like Mallis, both of you asking too many questions. Sticking your nose into business that isn't yours."

Her throat closed with fear and she answered in a whisper, "What do you mean?"

He gave her wrist another jerk and spoke through gritted teeth, "Quit trying to play the little innocent. You've been stirring up trouble since Parn was arrested. You should have stuck to trying to prove Mallis murdered Woodson, Trini. That would have been the smart thing."

She tried to swallow, but her throat closed. Even to herself, her breathing sounded shallow and ragged. She must, above all, not panic. She must keep her wits about her. Her instincts told her that continuing to play dumb would only anger Kerr further. She tried to keep her voice neutral.

"I couldn't prove Mallis guilty of murder. Because he wasn't. He was only guilty of trying to frame Parn."

He snorted a high-pitched laugh. "That's true. His private history worked very well into my own plans."

"So did you know when you killed Woodson that Mallis had a history with him and Parn?"

"No. But as I got to asking around town and heard the story, I thought it fit in perfect."

"What were you going to do? Just hope that no one would find Woodson in his car where you'd left him?"

"Oh, I knew someone would eventually find him. But thanks to your dowsing, they found him in a few days rather than a few months. I was planning for him to be lost clear through the winter. By the time he would have thawed out in the spring, Ma would have been dead for months and Katherine and I would have been long gone. I figured everyone would assume Woodson died in an accident. With him being dead and frozen for months, there'd be no proving otherwise. But when Mallis arrested Parn for the murder and you got your sights set on proving Mallis a big bad man, I went ahead with my plans. Unfortunately for him, Mallis started talking to people down at the courthouse, found out what a mess Woodson had left those records and got to nosing around. I didn't know you'd stuck your nose into DOME until Mallis started coming around asking questions about that, too. Like I said, you should have stuck to proving him guilty."

"So you broke into the house here and tried to find anything that Merle would have written down, anything about DOME that you could use."

"There was only one thing that could have saved my poor, stupid mother. If I could've found them partnership papers, I could have changed the ownership myself and gotten Ma to go along with it."

"You mean threatened her to go along with it. Then you would have killed her later."

"Who knows? But Merle hid them papers, which I found out last night was in the bank, of all places. Sheriff Mallis told me that. Only I took care of Mallis. He won't be a problem."

Events began to order themselves in Trini's mind. Despite Merle Woodson's murder playing into Mallis's plans for revenge, the sheriff must have been curious as to the identity of the killer. When he started investigating, talking to Dottie Kerr, interviewing Mr. Henry at the land claims office, he narrowed his suspicions to Daryl Kerr. He'd gone to the bank and found out who owned DOME partnership, then confronted Daryl with the information—a confrontation he paid for with his life.

Trini stole a glance at the frightened girl standing behind Kerr, pinching and pulling her lips, her eyes wide with terror. Trini wanted to keep Daryl talking. Now that she knew she couldn't convince him to let her leave with the children, she was left with one recourse, and she needed Katherine's help to do it. The huge man was simply too powerful for one woman to subdue by herself, but maybe with both of them, they'd stand a chance.

She gently tried to twist her wrist from his grip as she talked. "So let me guess. Your mother and Merle found oil rights while working at the land claims office. They formed DOME to buy the oil and weren't going to share any of it with you."

He sneered. "Stupid people, both of them. Woodson was trying to keep Katherine away from me, and Ma was so stupid, she'd have done anything he told her to. And he told her to get me out of the house. I couldn't believe it. Ma wanted to kick me out of my own home because Merle Woodson told her to. I wasn't having any of that."

"So you killed Woodson first, then your mother. Your own mother. In a fire."

Insight flashed through her. Of course. Right after the fire at the cabin, he'd come by the Woodsons' to deliver wood, like some sort of Good Samaritan. "Just like the fire you used to destroy Parn's cabin when you tried to murder me. You must have been surprised when you saw my truck out front afterwards, when you delivered the wood. You thought I was dead inside Parn's cabin, didn't you?"

He giggled. "You were tougher than I thought. But not tough enough."

"No, not tough enough. And certainly your own mother, a middle-aged woman, wouldn't be tough enough to fight against you."

He wrung her arm with a bear-like grip and roared into her face, a high-pitched hoarse wail, "She had it coming. She was too stupid to do anything right. She let my own father beat me half to death. She never had the guts to stand up to him, not even to save her own kid. I knew she'd do anything Woodson told her." He panted and heaved for a moment. Trini watched him in silence. He loosened the hold on her arm, but didn't relinquish it. "No, this is better this way."

Trini smelled the intensity of his emotion; his hate seeped from him, bitter and sour in his breath that assaulted her face. Daryl Kerr, with his burly body and the woman-voice, was even more formidable than Mallis had been. A feeling of hopelessness weighed on her, and she struggled with a paralyzing inertia. If Daryl hadn't been clasping her arm, she would have sunk to the floor.

"Daryl came to take me, Trini." Katherine's small voice spoke from the parlor threshold behind Daryl. "He came to take me with him." Her voice shook and her eyes reddened with new tears.

Oh, Katherine. Dear innocent child, preyed on by this demon from hell. Trini jerked her arm from Daryl's grasp. She rubbed the bruised skin, and her anger erupted to the surface. "And where, Mr. Daryl Kerr, did you think you could go that someone wouldn't find you? And what did you plan to do with Jake? Kill him, too?"

He threw his head back and laughed, a long, hysterical giggle. "Jake is an idiot boy. Besides, he's gone now." Trini was on the verge of asking what he meant when he squealed with laughter again. "Money can buy a lot, Trini. Including secrecy. Once those oil rights are assigned to me and Katherine, I'll have enough to hide anywhere in the world."

She knew the futility of trying to reason with such a man. It simply didn't fit into his reality that Katherine would not go willingly with him. Trini wanted to ask him questions: How long he'd been molesting Katherine? Had he raped her? What threat did he use to keep her in line? Did Merle find out, and when and what had he planned to do about it? But she knew by probing Kerr, she'd only make him angrier. He'd already murdered twice. She couldn't take the chance he'd fly into a rage, inflate his massive muscles with power and kill again. It was time to bring this meeting to a close. Now is when she'd need Katherine, and she tossed a prayer to heaven for the girl to find the strength to do what needed to be done.

Trini collapsed onto one of the kitchen chairs and stared at the floor. "I suppose you're right. The world is open to a man with money. You'll be able to buy anything you want. A beautiful home. Maybe something in Hollywood even. And you'd have all the comforts you'd ever want. Hot tea, ready whenever you command. Wonderful hot, steaming tea on cold days." She spoke fast and avoided his eyes, trying to keep her momentum going. "That would be so wonderful, to have a cup of hot tea."

Daryl tilted his head in puzzlement, and Trini shifted her eyes to Katherine. She saw her take a step, careful and slow, toward the stove.

"And Katherine," Trini said, "you'll have to be very strong, won't you?"

His eyes locked on Trini, and he stepped toward her. "She don't need your advice," he said.

Trini pushed on. "Katherine will need to be extremely strong," she said. "She'll need to reach down to the place inside where courage lives. To do the right thing."

"Damn it!" His fist thundered on the table. "I'm sick of you and your meddling. Sick of you and—"

The scalding water hit him on the back. He clutched his neck, doubled over and collapsed to the floor, screaming in pain. Katherine stood behind him holding the steaming kettle, her mouth open in stunned surprise. Trini ran to the stove, grasped the handle of the heavy cast-iron skillet hanging from its hook and with the rage of fear and injustice, swung it at his head. The kitchen reverberated with a dull thud, and her arms vibrated with the impact as the skillet hit its mark. The monster slumped to unconsciousness.

CHAPTER TWENTY-ONE

"Tie him up! Quick, Trini, quick!"

Heaving and panting, Trini dropped the skillet to the floor. She glanced at a wild-eyed Katherine who stood by the stove where she'd replaced the steaming kettle. Trini spoke low and calm, "Get something. Get a rope or something." She stared at the unconscious man at her feet.

Katherine turned in a circle, her frantic eyes darting around the kitchen. "I don't know. I don't know."

"A rope or something, Katherine." Trini grabbed her by her shoulders. "Think!"

"A . . . a clothesline?"

"Where?"

"Under the sink."

Trini rushed to the sink, fell to her knees in front of the cabinet, and pushed aside the cloth panel. The clothesline, wrapped into a figure eight, lay at the back behind an enamel tub. Trini grabbed it, stood up and handed the rope to Katherine. "Here," she said. "Undo this while I get his arms."

He lay on his back, so she lifted his bulky shoulder to roll him to his side. His head rolled away from a pool of blood. The gash over his right ear had drained crimson onto the floor staining the side of his face, his neck and his shirt. A slight snore came with his breath as Trini tugged his right arm behind him. She pulled his left arm back to meet it.

"I'll hold his wrists," she said. "You wrap the cord around them."

Katherine stood and stared at the unconscious hulk with her mouth open, holding the clothesline at her side.

"Katherine!" Trini snapped.

The girl shook herself and bent to her task. When Katherine had his wrists bound tightly, Trini released her hold and finished weaving the line around and between the mammoth arms. She stood, and placing her foot on his back for leverage, tugged hard on the end of the rope.

"I hope that holds him," she said.

"Oh God, Trini. Jake. Jake's out in the snow."

"What?"

"He ran out. Daryl bullied him, scared him, and he ran outside."

So that's why the screen door had been open. Trini closed her eyes against the sight: Jake, lost in the blizzard. Just like Lyle—

"Lyle. Lyle Butcher. He's in the meadow. We've got to get there now."

Katherine stood beside her, clutched her arm. "No! We have to find Jake!"

"Try the telephone," Trini said.

Obeying her own command, Trini ran to the telephone on the far wall and grabbed the receiver. She hammered the cradle and cranked several times. Nothing. The line was down. She replaced the receiver. Her stomach heaved, and she wrapped her arms around her middle. She was going to be sick.

"Trini! Trini are you all right?" Katherine was beside her, shaking her shoulder.

Waves of shock thrashed against her psyche, and Trini felt as if every fiber of muscle had been sucked from her body. She bent forward to stop the dizziness. "I don't know what to do. I don't know what to do."

Katherine pulled her to stand and clamped her shoulders in a vice. Like a rag doll, Trini let her. Katherine commanded her, thrusting her face within inches of Trini's. "Yes, you do," she said. "You know exactly what to do, Trinidad Bates. You know exactly how to be strong and do what you need to do to find Jake."

Trini stupidly blinked for a moment. She stared at the red-rimmed eyes of the young woman before her, whispered through her choking tears, "But, Lyle—what about Lyle. How can I live with myself? How can I let a man die? A man who—"

Katherine shook her shoulders. "Stop it. Stop feeling sorry for yourself and do what you have to."

She had to. God in heaven, please help Lyle stay alive, but she had to find Jake. Maybe Butcher would be all right. He was a mountain man, after all, evidently something her own mother had told him long ago. And he was certainly better equipped to deal with the weather than Jake. He'd be fine. He'd be all right. God forgive her for her choice.

Shuddering through a deep breath, Trini ran to the chair where she'd thrown her shawl. She flung it over her head and wound it around her neck. She still wore her coat she'd put on earlier when she'd tried to convince Daryl to let her leave with the children. She buttoned it now, then grabbed Jake's coat from the rack and turned toward the door.

"I'll be back in a minute."

"Oh no, you don't," Katherine said. She dashed to Trini's side and pulled her coat from its hook. "I'm not staying here with him." She sneered through the last word and cut a glance to the unconscious form of Daryl Kerr.

"Katherine, don't be ridiculous," Trini said. "I'll be back. Daryl is tied up." She softened her voice. "He can't hurt you now, sweetheart."

"I'm not staying." Katherine pushed her arms through the coat sleeves and tugged the buttons through the loops. "I don't care what you say."

No sense in arguing now. Trini reached over to Daryl's coat that was lying across the kitchen chair. She dug into the pockets until she felt cold metal, and then dropped his truck key into her own pocket. "Let's get Jake and get out of here," she said. She grasped the door handle and pulled. The snow and wind pummeled them as they crossed the threshold to the outside. Katherine slammed the door closed behind her.

They bent against the force, and Trini narrowed her eyes to peer through the opaque blizzard. How would she see anything? She turned to Katherine who had wrapped a scarf over her scalp and pulled a large round-topped Stetson over that. The brim sat low on her brow, almost covering her eyes. It shielded her bare face from the snow, but her cheeks and chin already burned a vivid red.

Trini yelled over the booming force. "Where do you think he'd go?"

"There's Pa's work shed and a coop and a cellar in back of the house," yelled Katherine. "Maybe he went there. Or maybe he went up to the mine. I don't know."

Trini nodded and they trudged toward the back of the house. The coop and the shed stood yards away, hazy and dreamlike through the veil of snow.

"Do you see any footprints at all?" Katherine asked.

Trini looked to the ground and surveyed the area. She squeezed her eyes closed a few times to clear the white. "No. Nothing. If he came this way, we'd never know it."

They pushed forward several feet into a blast of ice and wind. The Stetson blew from Katherine's head, tumbled to the frozen earth and scampered across the open yard. She gave a startled scream and clawed at the scarf, trying to hold it to her exposed head.

"This will never work," she yelled over the wail. "Dowse, Trini. You have to dowse."

She'd known it had to happen. And she had wanted to, had to, come back to herself, back to her dowsing. She needed to summon the talent. Now. She stared at Katherine, but didn't see her, didn't see the frozen white surrounding them. Instead, she saw inside herself and knew as certain as her heart was beating, the ability was in her. Deep, innate talent housed in her bones and muscles and skin. A part of her hands.

"I've never dowsed with my hands before," she said.

"Then start now," Katherine said. "Just hurry. Do you want something of Jake's? Should I go get a shirt or something from the house?"

Trini shook her head. She pulled off the wool gloves, stuffed them into a pocket and rubbed her hands together. Another gust of icy wind revolved around her and tore the scarf from her head. She let it go. Her black curls billowed behind her. Extending her arms in front of her, the dowser spread her fingers wide then closed her eyes against the storms whirling inside and outside her. She opened her eyes and squinted into the distance.

"Show me the boy," she shouted above the gale. "Show me Jake."

She hadn't really expected anything the first time. It would take a minute to tap into the sleeping giant within her. She rubbed her hands again and rolled her head. Let it come now. She used every force of her concentration to block out the numbing cold and stinging ice that pelted her. Nothing existed but the pull from the earth, the pull that would lead her to Jake.

"Show me the boy," she called again.

She took several steps forward, caught a glimpse of Katherine's red scarf whipping around her, blocked it from her mind. Just the boy. Only Jake, the pull from the earth, the tingle in her hands; let those be the cornerstone of her existence now. She breathed in the frigid air, and at the nape of her neck, felt her senses stirring, as if the power was awakening from a long slumber.

"Show me Jake," she yelled. "Show me the boy now."

A warmth spread across her shoulders, down her spine, and bubbled down the length of her arms to her wrists, almost like the heat of a flame that someone swept along her skin. Now. It would happen now. She wouldn't, couldn't stop it. The familiar sensations suffused her.

She lifted her face to the sky and yelled to the universe, "Show. Me. Jake."

The heat charged through her body, and the whorls in her fingertips swelled and grew tender and painful. She took several steps into the wind, her arms outstretched, waited for the answer to come to her. She turned and started up the hill.

The mine entrance was about a hundred yards ahead of them, but it seemed to be miles. The wind increased, and a low whine sounded in the background as it whipped across the hillside they navigated. Bending their heads to the force, they trudged on.

Trini held her arms in front of her, and her bare face received the full force of the frozen blast. To the left of the shaft opening stood Merle's work shed, a small lean-to. It was open on one side, and Trini could make out a few tools inside: shovels and picks, wheelbarrows and carts. She stopped, panting and gasping in the frozen air, and heard Katherine doing the same beside her. Her dowser's instincts had led her here, and they told her Jake was nearby, either in the mine or the lean-to.

"Where's the boy?" she yelled. "Where's Jake?"

Her hands renewed their swelling and her distended veins swirled up her arms. Her fingers throbbed, sending a message.

"He's there," Trini yelled. "In the shed. Hurry."

They scrambled as fast as the slippery slope would allow and entered the small shed. Bags of seed and fertilizer were stacked in the back corner. An old rusted cart lay facedown on the west wall, and burlap bags were heaped in another corner.

"Jake!" Katherine called. "Jake. It's all right. It's me and Trini."

Trini went to the cart and lifted it. Jake, blinking his eyes wide and curled into a shivering ball, lay underneath. They knelt beside the cart.

"Come on, Jake," Katherine said. "It's all right. It's me and Trini. Daryl's gone."

Trini lifted the cart as Katherine helped her brother to his feet and slipped the coat on him. She buttoned it, then turned to smile at Trini. "Thank you," she said.

"Let's go. We've got to get to Lyle."

They turned from the shed and started their descent, clutching each other for balance as they stumbled down the slope. Thank God, Trini thought, they were going to make it. They were halfway down; Trini was tempted to sit down and slide the rest of the way. Only a little bit more. She reached inside the coat pocket feeling for the frozen comfort of Daryl's truck key. Yes, still there. Hold on, Lyle. Please, oh please, hold on just a little bit more.

A sudden loud crack sounded from the house. The three of them stopped and Trini squinted through the white fury, ducking her head then shading her eyes with her hand. The icy air halted in her throat with her gasp. Daryl Kerr, wild and blood-soaked, roared from the house, his arms spread wide for destruction. Behind her, Jake screamed, and she turned to see that he'd scrambled halfway back to the mine. Shouting his name, Katherine clawed her way up the snow-covered rocks after him. Trini turned to look back at their pursuer. The animal lumbered toward them, bellowing like an injured lion.

Blind and thoughtless panic surged through Trini, and turning to run, stagger, claw, and dig her way up the slope, she followed the Woodson children to the mine. Oh God, Sweet Mary Mother of God, please help us. Please don't let me die.

Chapter Twenty-Two

Trini skidded on an icy rock, collapsing at the mine entrance. Her frozen lungs heaved for air, and her entire body trembled with bitter cold.

"Get in here, quick," Katherine yelled.

Trini lifted her head and squinted at the black hole. Jake, clutching Katherine's coat sleeve, gaped at her. "Come!" he yelled.

Katherine knelt in the rocky entryway. Her scarf was gone and her bare head looked chafed and red. She stretched her hand toward Trini. "Come on. You can make it."

Scrambling to her feet, Trini thrust herself through the opening. The mine yawned before her a solid black, but at least she was out of the blistering wind and ice.

Katherine pulled her inside and the three of them squatted against the rock wall. Katherine's whisper was hoarse and desperate, "He's coming, Trini. He's coming. What should we do? Oh heaven help us, he'll kill us all. What should we do?"

Katherine was right. Daryl Kerr had the capacity, mentally and physically, to kill them one by one. They were trapped. Trini looked out the opening to see their hunter. The stalking giant was halfway up the incline, crawling on his hands and feet, plumes of cold smoke ballooning from his nose and mouth. She heard his deadly panting and his grunts of exertion. He was coming, Lord help us, coming now—Stop it, she told herself. Stop and think.

"Katherine, let's get Jake inside. There's a turnoff to the right, just ahead."

"But what will we do?"

Trini stood and grabbed Katherine's coat sleeve, pulling her up. "Let's just go. I have an idea."

Katherine reached for the lantern and the box of matches that sat on the rock ledge where Trini had left them two days ago when she'd come to see if Mallis had taken the bootleg liquor.

"No," Trini said. "I don't think we should do that. He'll be able to track us when he sees the light."

"But it's pitch black in there," Katherine said.

"I know. That can't be helped. Let's go. Just take Jake's hand and lead the way. Hug the wall. We've got to get inside where he can't see us."

She waited until the children were several feet into the mine, then grasped the lantern handle and swung it against the rock. With a clatter, the chimney shattered and kerosene funneled onto the rock floor. She threw the lantern down and grabbed the box of matches, but the top popped open and several dozen scattered at her feet. She glanced outside and saw Daryl, grinning as he clawed his way up on all fours across icy rocks. He was relentless, and too close for her to stop and pick up the matches. Better to leave them and use the time they had to burrow themselves deep within the mine. She shoved the remaining matches and the demolished box in her coat pocket and hurried to the children.

Katherine grasped her sleeve as she approached. "Trini, what will we do?"

"Quick now," she said. Trini moved in front of Katherine, clutched her hand and told her to hold onto Jake. She led the children into the ebony interior.

The dull light at the mine's opening gave way to a thick void, and Trini fingered her way along the stony walls. How far back was the turn? She tried to remember from her visit two days ago, a lifetime ago, when she'd explored the mine looking for the missing whiskey and Taggert had shown up. She thought she remembered one hundred and fifty-eight steps.

Roy. As her palm traveled over the jagged rock, his image appeared in her mind. Even if he knew where to find her, could he make it through the storm? She doubted it. Lyle Butcher couldn't help her, either. He was huddled near an outcrop of boulders in the middle of a blizzard, and please, God, don't let him die. She was alone. She and Katherine and Jake. Alone. And this abandoned mine, Merle Woodson's cache for his illegal whiskey, could very possibly be their grave.

Her palm never left the cold sharp walls, and she shuffled her way deeper into the tunnel. Could she dowse for the turn? Would her hands show her the way? She might try it—

Her palm hit air. "It's here," she said. "Come on, Katherine. Have you got Jake tight?"

"Yes. I won't let go," the girl whispered.

They stumbled a few steps as they made the turn, and Trini could tell by the change in the echo of their footsteps when they entered the rock room Merle and Parn had used for storing whiskey. The shuffling of the loose gravel under their shoes, the low howling of the wind like a lengthy moan of pain, their own desperate breathing . . . Trini deciphered these sounds as she tried to listen for their stalker. Had Daryl entered the mine? Oh please. Not yet. Just a few minutes more. Where was that fissure? She knew it was here. Should be right about here. She smoothed her hand over the rock waiting for the break in the surface. Here. She found it: the crevice in the wall, barely wide enough for the two children.

"Here. You and Jake go here."

Trini maneuvered Katherine and Jake in front of her and

carefully stuffed them into the wall. Gently, with both hands, patting their coat sleeves, up their arms and necks, to their faces, Trini whispered, "I want you to stay here, both of you, Katherine." She could feel Katherine's face move under her hand, ready to speak. "No, now don't argue with me. I want you to stay right here until you hear me calling you that it's okay to come out. Understand?"

Katherine's desperate whisper sounded in her ear, "No, Trini. What will you do? Let me come with you."

"No, you can't. You have to stay here. I have an idea, and I can't do it if I'm worried about you and Jake."

"But I need to come with you," Katherine said. "I have to." Her words were low and full of rage. "I, of all people, Trini, have a score to settle with Daryl Kerr."

Trini smiled, although she knew Katherine couldn't see her. "I know you do, sweetheart, I know. But you have to stay with Jake, or he'll be confused and afraid. You *have* to stay. Don't you?" She waited. "*Don't you*, Katherine?"

Finally, Katherine answered in a low murmur, "Yes."

"Good. Now I'll be gone for a while, but please, no matter what you hear, don't leave."

"But, Trini," Katherine's voice was pleading. "What if—what if you don't come back?"

Trini drew a shaking sigh. Yes. What if she didn't come back? Because this was real and Daryl was a killer and she might die.

"If you don't hear me after a long time, and you finally hear him leave the mine, then sneak out and make sure. When you're sure he's gone—sure now, Katherine—then you take Jake and leave. Climb up the hill in back of the mine and get to town as fast as you can."

She couldn't think of what else to say. Get to town? Two children alone on the prairie in a blizzard? They'd never survive. She had to save herself. She had to get back to them. She set her jaw to help her grip her terrifying fear. "But I will be back. I will."

She squeezed Katherine's arm and heard her sniffle.

"I'm leaving now." She caressed Katherine's cheek for a second.

There was so much to say. When had the tie been forged between them? She didn't know. All she knew was that the wrenching of her heart for Katherine's safety was every bit as fierce as it was for Parn's. But not now. Time and a rapacious enemy were on her heels.

"Reach into that place where we talked about, Katherine, the place inside you that holds your strength. Be brave." With one final caress, she turned and, holding her hands in front of her, felt for the wall again to start back the way they'd come.

She thought she had walked the length of the off-shoot, almost to the V that divided the two tunnels, when she heard the unmistakable huffing of a man bent on annihilation. Where was he? How close? She took a few more steps and felt the wall come to an end. The divide. By keeping her hand running along the rock, she'd make the natural turn down the other tunnel.

She looked toward the mine opening. A silhouette of a giant was outlined against the white light of the snow. In front of him was a small, floating flame and a surrounding soft glow. He'd lit a match, and in the dense blackness, the tentacles from its flame illuminated far more than she thought it would. She'd have to keep well ahead of the circle of light. Using her hands as a guide, she felt her way around the corner and ducked into the other tunnel. The passage was thick, dark and cold. She knew the sunken shaft was ahead of her, just follow the rock wall. But how far in? Where was that shaft? If she stumbled into it, if she let her foot slip over the edge into the pit, she'd be swallowed forever. But how was she to find it in this inky blanket?

What had she told Katherine? Reach inside of herself and use her strength? She had her own strengths, her own resources. Her dowsing. But what should she ask for? She dared to remove her fingers from the rock wall and held her hands in front of her.

"Show me the center of earth," she whispered. "Show me the center."

Instantly, her fingertips tingled and throbbed, and she knew the veins in her arms had swollen to stretch the skin. The rhythmic pulse of her power moved into her shoulders and hunkered at the nape of her neck, ready to guide her. God help her, save her so she could save the children. She felt hot tears start in her eyes, but blinked them away. No time for self-pity this day. Today was a day for surviving—at any level, at any cost.

She began her dark journey, reciting her litany as she walked, "Show me the center of the earth. Show me the center."

Behind her, Daryl Kerr heaved and panted, and when she turned to look over her shoulder, she saw the yellow circle of the glowing match behind her. Impossible to tell the distance in this blackness. She silently cursed the broken matchbox. He must have picked up a lot of them and was striking them one after another on the rocks. He could go on for miles like that. Trini turned to face into the mine again and called for guidance.

Please, God, let me live.

The toe of her brogan hit a ledge of rock. She remembered the tunnel floor inclined downward near the edge of the shaft, but was this the place? She wished she'd paid more attention when she'd been here the other day. She'd had the lantern to guide her, but of course she'd been unnerved by the scraping she'd heard in the mine, so hadn't thought to count her steps. Had that been Daryl? or Taggert? or her imagination? No matter. Now without sight, every sense throbbed with sensation, trying to hear, smell, feel her way. She brushed the soles of her shoes side to side, feeling for the edge of the shaft. A loose bit of gravel caught under one foot and lightly clattered a few times as she kicked it away, then silence. She stopped and held her breath.

A high-pitched giggle pierced the air, and his eerie voice came to her in the blackness.

"Hello, Trini." Another giggle. "I'm going to get you."

Where was that shaft? Dear God, please. "Show me the center. Show me the center." Her hands throbbed in response and a jolt of energy shot up her arms. It hurt. It hurt so much. She inched her foot forward, stepped up onto another small ledge, and balancing herself while she lifted her other foot, she stood solid.

The reedy squeal carried to her again. "I'm coming, Trini. I'm coming for you." A squealing howl, then a tremor of giggles.

Trini inched her feet forward, and asked again. "Show me," she said. "Show me the center."

She stepped two more steps, and the pounding in her hands and an impression in her mind told her she was there. She was at the shaft. She knelt down on all fours and inched her hands forward. One more time, and her arm dropped into space. There. There was the edge. She glanced over her shoulder. The yellow light shone behind her, small as a star in the night sky. The blackness still cloaked her, but she had to hurry. And she didn't want him turning back into the other tunnel, the tunnel that led to Katherine and Jake. Still on hands and knees, she shouted back over her shoulder.

"You're a murderer and a child molester, Daryl Kerr. You murdered three people and hurt Katherine." She yelled as loud as she could, "You're evil."

The giggle met her again, then stopped. "Why did you have to get in the way? I had it all worked out, Trini. I never did anything to you."

She pulled her coat off and tossed it forward into the shaft. She sat and quickly untied her shoes, threw them over the edge, and pulled off her thick wool socks. She kept her leggings on; all she needed were bare feet. She scooted forward a bit, then slowly, so slowly, swung her feet around and behind her and laid on her stomach.

She let her feet dangle over the abyss and shouted again, "You're evil and horrible, Daryl. You'll burn in hell for what you've done."

Another giggle. "Oh, Trini. You always were such a small thinker."

The knife-edged rock floor tore through her wool leggings into her knees, shins, and palms. As she moved backwards on her belly, her dress hiked up to her hips, and the cold rock scraped her thighs. She wanted to keep him talking, had to keep him talking and coming toward her.

She yelled as she scooted back, "Did you think you could get away with all of this? Did you honestly think you could just commit murder and walk away?"

Her legs dropped fully over the edge now, and her hips jutted into the air. She felt with her toes for a hold, one of the steps she'd seen carved into the wall of the shaft. She found it, and inched her way back a little more. The floating circle of light enlarged as he came toward her, and when he spoke next, she felt like his voice was directly in her ear.

"Don't worry," he said. "Everything will work out just fine. Katherine and I will be rich. We'll live wherever we want to. I have it all worked out."

Her toes searched the rock feeling for the next step down. She caught a ledge and stretched downward, draping her stomach, then her chest over the edge. She took another two steps down to be sure her head would be below the top edge of the shaft. Finally, she stood and put all her weight on a small step. Pressing against the rock, clasping the edge of the shaft with her bloody fingers, she hung on. She balanced herself, double-checked the toehold, then lowered her arms. She didn't want him to see her fingertips grasping the edge. Maybe, maybe he'd stand on the edge, lean into the shaft, so she could reach up and grasp his ankle. If she was quick, very fast, she could pull him off balance and over the edge. Please, God. Let him die.

"It won't work, Daryl," she shouted. "Katherine hates you." She screamed the last sentence. She wanted him angry. Roaring with anger and ready to murder her. "She hates your guts. She could never love a pitiful man like you. You could never be a movie star. Everyone would laugh when you talked. Katherine could never love you, Daryl."

His scream cut through the black cavern, "Stop it! Stop it you whore!"

His footfalls crunched the loose gravel, and she heard his panting breath grow louder, an animal settling in for the kill. He'd be close enough any second. This was her moment, coming to her now, in an instant, but oddly, she felt she had all the time in the universe.

Her mind boiled with images of Roy, Parn, Katherine and the child she had never known, would never know. She thought of her father and mother, and of dear Jim who'd given her exactly the love she needed when she needed it. And as her fingers cramped and her toes tingled with cutting pain and her knees and thighs burned, in one swooping torrent, unspeakable sadness descended upon her. Sadness to never again see her beloved prairie stretching into forever, nor hear the clamoring of the cottonwoods in summer as the wind rattled their leaves, and sadness that she might not be allowed to reconnect to love, reestablish relationships in her life, with Roy and Parn and Katherine and Jake and even Lyle Butcher. She should have let them in. Let them into her heart and her life.

And then, just as overwhelming as the sadness, the soft mantle of forgiveness settled on her. Forgiveness for Mallis and Daryl, for Parn, and most of all for herself. For all her pushing people away, her exaggerated independence, her desire to be alone, it came to her that she was only human after all.

And that was all right. Totally, properly right.

Daryl's soprano singsong lilted over her. "Trini."

An errant stone bounced off her head, and by slightly leaning back and to the side, she saw the match flame hovering above her. One toe of his boot had inched over the edge. *It has to be now.* She'd have to do it. *Do it now.* She unclenched her right hand from the rock and readied herself to grab his ankle when from behind him, a shriek sounded, wild and primitive and from deep inside a woman who'd suffered.

"Push! Push, Jake!"

The ponderous beast screamed as he shot through the air, over her head and then behind her. Jake had pushed hard, and the monster Kerr hurtled headfirst. Trini glimpsed his arms flailing as the match flame went with him, then extinguished. His shrieks faded and she imagined him tumbling and rolling.

She became conscious of her own ragged breathing, then her right knee. She must have cut it deep because it burned and throbbed and she could feel her own warm blood run down her leg and foot. Then she felt a hand on top of hers, gripped warm and firm. A large hand. The hand of an almost-grown man.

"Trini!" Katherine called from above her. "Trini, are you all right?"

She answered, through tears and coughs and gasps of air as the two children helped her climb up to the surface. When she reached the top, they knelt together, clutching, sobbing in the dark until Trini could finally find the strength to stand.

They entwined their arms and shuffled toward the distant white arch of the mine opening.

EPILOGUE

The cottonwoods rattled around her with the new growth of spring leaves, chasing the puffs of clouds across the sky. Trini looked up from her kneeling place in her garden to catch the warm wind on her face. The hum of an engine and the crunch of gravel in her driveway told her Roy was here. Wiping her dirt-smeared hands with the skirt of her gardening apron, she stood as he climbed from the truck and strode toward her. She watched the muscles of his thighs move under the worn denims. He wore a blue work shirt, the sleeves turned up exposing the curves of his forearms. Under the brim of his Stetson, a white grin broke the tan of his face.

"I didn't realize how late it was," she said.

"I'm a little early. Finish what you need to."

He stopped in front of her, close enough to touch, but he didn't. Instead, he shoved his hands into his back pockets and stared at her, still grinning.

"I just finished putting in turnips. Do you like turnips?" She tilted her head and smiled at him, flirting, and he answered her with a look that told her he liked it.

His voice rumbled low and soft when he spoke, "I happen to adore turnips. Especially when they're in a wine stew that I'll be eating with the most beautiful woman in Colorado."

She laughed, her head thrown back to the sky. "You've been talking to Lyle Butcher."

They turned together and strolled around the garden. "I saw

him a couple of days ago," he said. "He was in town buying supplies. Said he was going to try to get as far away from civilization as he could, at least for the summer."

"Yes, he told me when I saw him last week. Did I tell you he came by?"

Roy nodded.

"He looks good, and he's walking very well, despite his poor toes."

Trini had a momentary pang of guilt mixed with still-fresh images of finding Lyle slumped unconscious in the snowy meadow seven months earlier. She and Katherine and Jake had laid him in the bed of Kerr's truck and after an hour of navigating the icy blacktop, had gotten him into Doc Cockrell's. The doctor had been able to set the break in Lyle's ankle, but he'd lost three toes to frostbite.

Trini had never seen one moment of self-pity from him. Quite the opposite. He made it a point to tell her every time he saw her that he owed her his life. He was happy, she thought, happy to have Canary and the mountains and another Colorado summer.

Trini and Roy stopped at the edge of the garden and surveyed the orderly rows.

"Looks good," Roy said. "You about done for now?"

"Yes. I'll finish some weeding when I come back from the Pontos'. Shouldn't take too long for just a simple water dowsing, so there should be part of the afternoon still left. I guess I'd better get my apron off." She reached around in back to untie the strings and felt Roy's strong hands brush her own aside.

He'd stepped behind her and now as he worked the apron ribbons, he brushed his chest to her back and spoke low in her ear, "Let me get that for you, darlin'."

Trini felt the tug at her waist, and closed her eyes to take in his breath on the back of her neck and the faint fresh smell of him that lingered in the air.

His voice was low and intimate, "Now, I know a powerful dowser like you doesn't need much help with anything, but I'd consider it an honor if you'd let the lowly sheriff of Coyote County do this little thing for you."

She laughed softly. "Why, Sheriff, it would be my pleasure. But what would Deputy Taggert have to say about his boss fondling a notorious dowser?"

"Oh, I don't think we have to worry about him. He won't be getting too close to a woman he suspects is a witch."

She laughed again. "Speaking of a witch, I got a letter today from Camille, and Parn, of course. They're settled in Bend, and she said they were enjoying the mild Oregon weather. Parn wrote on the bottom of the page that he's learning all about running the saw mill, and he's enjoying it."

He turned her to face him. The apron hung loose from the one strap around her neck and flapped at her knees in the gust of wind that blew in from the prairie, warm and dry. He set his hands on her shoulders and pulled her close enough so that her breasts brushed his chest. She gazed into the warm gray eyes she'd come to love.

"I told you he'd be fine in Oregon," he said.

"I know, and you're right. I suppose I have to admit that as much as I don't like the woman, Camille LeClair seems to be the best thing for Parn. And Stephanie's good for him, too. I think the responsibility of being a stepfather has made him grow up."

Roy looked beyond her for a moment. "You know I was thinking just this morning about Jefferson being so far away, missing his daughter."

She became aware of the old longing for her own child. Only now instead of battering her heart with pain, the feeling was more of a tiptoe; present, but not overpowering. And Roy understood that. As they'd begun to deepen their attraction for each other over the last few months, Trini had confessed about her illegitimate daughter. He'd been kind and supportive, but he became impatient when she'd talk of her fantasy of finding the child and making a home for her.

She knew he was right to tell her to let it go. But in the deep part of a lonely night, a night when she wished she had Roy's comforting bulk beside her, a night when she wished she'd just go ahead and say yes to his continued marriage proposals—on those nights, the old fantasy about finding her child and running away to some distant life would awaken and lay beside her in her bed.

Even so, she had promised herself she wouldn't again dowse for her Lucinda; she would not succumb to the fantasy to that extent. And she'd kept her promise. But she'd had a bad time or two where she'd found herself climbing the attic steps and sitting at the old pine desk, staring at the drawer that held the maps.

"Well, he's in Paris," said Roy, "and evidently doing well, although I don't like the looks of what's happening in Europe."

"Who?"

"Were you listening to me at all? Jefferson LeClair. Living in Paris away from Stephanie."

"Oh, of course. I just was thinking about something else for a second."

He studied her face, his hands still resting on her shoulders, but didn't question her. He seemed to know when the sudden moods came on her and left her alone, gave her the breathing room to handle it her own way. Now, he pulled her to him and wrapped his strong, capable arms around her, tilting his head up to rest his chin on the top of her head.

"Are Katherine and Jake ready to go?" he asked.

She closed her eyes for a minute, and sighed. Yes, she had

Katherine. And Jake, of course. A small smile curved her mouth, a smile of thanksgiving for blessings that could have been lost.

"I'll get them."

Just then, the back screen door opened and the clattering footsteps of the young people sounded on the porch. The door slammed closed, and Katherine ran down the steps. Jake followed close behind, then jumped from the porch into the grass several feet beyond. He landed in a squat and then ran over to Roy. He stood next to him, shoulder to shoulder, then pulled the Stetson off Roy's head and set it on his own. He grinned and Roy nudged him in the arm.

"I heard your truck," Katherine said. "Are we ready?" She looped a red print scarf over her hair, thin, but now to the tops of her ears. She smiled at the group.

"Yes, we're ready," said Trini. She lifted the apron over her head.

The foursome walked to the truck. Katherine and Jake scrambled into the truck bed, and she climbed in beside Roy.

"Wait," she said. She opened her door again, scooted out and ran to the house. She entered the kitchen, crossed her parlor into the hallway and went to her own bedroom.

Her mother's applewood dowsing rod leaned in the far corner on its two prongs. Trini picked it up and took a moment to run her hands over the worn and stained handles, the smoothness of the wood. As usual, the tactile sensations gave her comfort and definition. She'd use her gift whenever she needed to, to help others to find what they needed. And even though she felt restless still, undecided about the next step of her life, she knew that she'd found the most important things: connections and family and love. She would guard against losing them again.

She carried the rod through the house and outside into the warm day.

ABOUT THE AUTHOR

Rebbie Macintyre spent childhood summers in the area where *Cast the First Stone* is set. She lives in Florida.